CrossTIME Science Fiction Anthology

featuring the winners of the 2001 Paul B.
Duquette Memorial Short Science Fiction Contest

CrossTIME
an imprint of the Crossquarter Publishing Group
PO Box 8756
Santa Fe, NM 87504-8756

CrossTIME Science Fiction Anthology

Printed in the United States of America on recycled paper.

Library of Congress Cataloging-in-Publication Data

CrossTIME science fiction anthology : featuring the winners of the 2001 Paul B. Duquette Memorial Short Science Fiction Contest / edited by Anthony Ravenscroft and Therese Francis.
    p. cm.
Includes bibliographical references.
    ISBN 1-890109-04-5
    1. Science fiction, American. I. Ravenscroft, Anthony, 1958- II. Francis, Therese.
    PS648.S3 C76 2002
        813'.0876208--dc21
                        2002006890

The 2001 Winners

CrossTIME is happy to introduce the winners of the 2001 Paul B. Duquette Memorial Short Science Fiction Contest.

First place – "Mirage" by Barbara Riley
Second place – "Writer's Block" by Craig Clyde
Third place – "Channel Surfing" by Barry Field
Fourth place – "Father to the Man" by Ellen Straw
Honorable mentions to:
"Moonlight" by L.J. Anderson
"Cat and the Yule Fire" by Cat Dubh
"The Follower" by Richard Ferris
"Cat-Skin" by Mary Pat Glynn
"Doctor Courage" by Jean Cottrell Pence
"Asleep at the Wheel" by Tee Morris
"Deviled Eggs" by Tricia Spencer
"The Way Home" by Ellen Straw
"Ezekiel's Wheel" by Adam Byrn Tritt
"Summer Season" by Wolfgang Zeuner
"Superiority" by Sam Zitter

For simplicity, the stories are presented in alphabetical order by the authors' last names.

In Loving Memory

Paul B. Duquette

Paul Duquette and I had been swapping science fiction books for almost two decades when the idea of a science fiction contest came up. Unfortunately the first submission did not arrive until after Paul died of a sudden heart attack. Paul was the author of numerous books on runes and magick, generally taking a historical paradigm as the basis of his work. He was a voracious reader of everything, especially science fiction and alternative history. At the time of his death, he was collaborating on over ten books (some speculative fiction, others nonfiction).

In Paul's memory, we will sponsor an annual contest. If you want to enter the upcoming contest, with possibilities of seeing your story in the next anthology, see the contest description and entry form at the website *www.crossquarter.com* or send a self-addressed stamped envelope to SF Contest, Crossquarter, PO Box 8756, Santa Fe, NM 87504.

Therese Francis, publisher

Moonlight

It was a beautiful winter day in the desert, perfect for a hunt. I loaded my Jeep and headed out to the edge of the valley to see if I could take a cottontail rabbit or two for supper. I had timed my departure so that the westing sun would be above the mountains when I arrived at my favorite place to hunt on the south end of Quail Mesa Ranch.

I pulled my Jeep off the dusty farm road and into the brush. Donning a camouflage vest and hat, I uncased my weapon. It was a classic pre-nineteen sixty-four Winchester. I loaded the rifle with ammo of my own making. The huge 30.06 cartridges were topped with a small .22 caliber slug encased by a plastic sabot to fit the big bore of the rifle. With this round I could shoot five hundred yards with ease.

With my preparations complete I started down the gentle slope towards the dark opening of the tunnel through the brush that had been formed over the years by the passage of wildlife making their way to the Colorado River to drink of its life giving waters.

Thumbing the safety on my weapon, I entered the gloom inside the brushy tunnel. I moved in silence, breathing in the smell of sagebrush, arrow weeds and the other fainter aromas of the wild. I loved to come out here to escape, if only for a while, the stress and pressure of the world in which I am forced to live. A shiver coursed through my body for no apparent reason. I paused listening. Did the light seem to change? My mother used to tell me the shiver meant that somewhere a rabbit had walked across my grave…with a mental shrug I continued onwards.

Unknown to me the game path that I walked upon followed the course of an ancient Indian spirit trail. I am just shy of being a half-breed Indian myself and my mother has the gift or is it curse of second sight. The path knew the tread of my feet and this was a special evening. The planets were aligned and the moon and stars were set just so, giving the trail access to power not normally allowed into this world and so an event took place. I knew this when I reached the far end of the dark passage and stopped dead in my tracks.

The sun was in approximately the same place; the mountains were unchanged, but now there was a forest covering their sides and a shallow river flowed where Tyson Wash, a dry, sandy arroyo had been.

I had read too many science fiction novels not to realize what had taken place. Forget that it was impossible, that it could not be real. I accepted what my eyes and ears told me. Checking the safety on my rifle, I crouched low and sprinted back the way I had come. I was sure that time was of the essence.

Upon reaching my Jeep I grabbed my backpack. I kept it ready on the off chance that I might get away from work on Fridays to do some fishing or camping, along with all the ammo I had for my rifle. Turning, I ran once again for the game trail and the gateway that had opened between two worlds.

Things were changing around me, the set of circumstances that had triggered the event were fading quickly. It felt like I was running through a thick viscous fluid instead of air. With extreme effort I forced my way at last through the still permeable, but solidifying barrier. The sudden lack of resistance almost caused me to pitch headlong into the river. I steadied myself by grabbing an overhanging tree limb and looked around. I recognized the birds flying above as morning dove; I could hear the calls of a covey of quail and there were fresh tracks of deer in the moist sand of the riverbank.

A tremendous bellowing roar shattered the stillness, followed by an eerie warbling sound of something in great pain. As the wall of noise had reached my ears I faded into the underbrush, my camouflage clothing making me all but invisible. Training that had kept me alive in Southeast Asia that I had thought long forgotten snapped back to the fore. My body was singing with fight, flight reflex from the adrenaline being dumped into my bloodstream. Was I the hunter...or the hunted? When nothing attacked I moved off deeper into the bush in the direction from which the noise had come from.

The day was almost done when I found the source of the dissonance that had continued intermittently grating upon my nerves and drawing me onwards. There on a ledge two hundred feet above the river was a sight I thought never to see except in a dream. Crouching low, I hugged the earth and proceeded up the mountain on my side of the river. Tense minutes later I had found a perch where I could see the huge winged lizard clearly.

The ledge upon which the beast lay was a hundred feet below and a good four hundred yards away. Using the Winchester's scope I scanned the opposing riverbank looking up then down stream. About a quarter mile upstream I could see the remains of a bridge, but I saw no sign of its builders.

The magnified view within the scope blurred as I swung the rifle back, returning my attention to the great ledge of stone. A small waterfall splashed down into a shallow pool near the entrance to a large cave. The scope's cross hairs returned to the silver form upon the ledge and I saw what had caused the bellow and subsequent whisperings of pain that had drawn me to this place. It was also evident that it was not an accident that had dislodged the large stone which had fallen from above smashing into and breaking its left wing before pinning the beast in place. I felt uncomfortable, as if I could feel some of the terrible pain the animal must be experiencing beating against my body like a physical force.

As I watched, out of the foliage to one side there stepped a man, a warrior in armor, a Dragon Slayer! He carried death on the end of a long vicious spear and his intent was clear, he would kill the silver beast. My anger now had a focal point; it crystallized into black hatred for what one of my kind was about to do.

Coinciding with the flare of my anger, the dragon raised its great head to scan the far side of the river. It stared intently in my direction before turning to look upon its approaching death.

The warrior struck just behind the foreleg with his spear. Green echor flowed from the wound, accompanied by a high keening wail from the dragon that tore at my very soul. Upon witnessing the dragon slayer's evil deed, my weapon rose smoothly to my shoulder as I powered up the laser range finder and watched the numbers spin out to be displayed in the upper left-hand corner of the reticle. I punched the firing solution into the small onboard computer and the scope adjusted for bullet drop. The weapon would now shoot exactly where I pointed it.

•••

White-hot pain washed over her body as the dragon slayer twisted the spear point deeper into her side. Her suffering was of such magnitude she could not work the magic that she had learned over the years after she had found her way to this place. Pinned by the great stone, her wing broken, she looked forward to death to release her from her torment.

"Beast! Now you will suffer and die as my people have died under the fiery breath of your kind, may your death be slow and painful!" the dragon slayer shouted.

Why did he hate her so? Oh yes, she had taken a cow, a sheep or two, but she had killed no one. Was a beast or three worth her life? The dragon slayer stepped forward to torment her again.

The unnatural thunderclap rolled and echoed off the hillsides. She flinched at the sound; the unintentional movement sending more burning torment through her frame, but the result of the sound when it struck the dragon slayer was profound...and fatal.

•••

From across the river I observed the dragon slayer as he moved towards the prostrate beast intent upon abusing her once more. Holding my breath I peered through the rifle's telescopic sight. I raised my point of hold slightly and the cross hairs settled upon the man's neck just above his armor. I did not trust the small caliber of my weapon to punch through the back plate of the dragon slayer's corset. Gently, but firmly I squeezed the trigger and the rifle spoke with a roar.

A tongue of brilliant yellow-orange flame three feet long erupted from the end of the barrel and the small plants in front of it were stripped of their foliage by the wave of over-pressure from the muzzle blast.

I watched as the man's brain disconnected from his body and it collapsed to the ground as the sound of the shot echoed off of the steep sides of the surrounding hills. The would be killer's head tilted over at an unnatural angle depending from the pulped ruin that short moments ago had been his neck. The body collapsed like a puppet whose strings had been cut, into a widening pool of its own blood. The great spear fell from the now lifeless hands, clattering to the stone ledge and silence returned once more. Even the birds refused to sing, struck dumb by the thunder that had taken the dragon slayer's life.

•••

The dragon looked at the dead man for a moment longer, then gazed out across the river. Something was out there, something with great power, what or who it did not know, but she was certain that she was going to find out. All the silver queen could do was await its coming and see what her fate was to be.

•••

With a practiced motion I worked the rifle's bolt action and returned the bolt to battery, ready to unleash death a second time, but it was unnecessary. "Just one shot."

I whispered softly. Flicking the safety on my weapon, I moved off down the hillside towards the remains of the bridge. The river crossing went without incident and I made my way back down the opposite riverbank then ascended the steep hillside to the ledge on which she lay trapped by the huge stone. I paused, concealed by a screen of underbrush and observed the dragon for a moment while I caught my breath. It had been a long time since I ran through the jungles of Southeast Asia and my body was telling me about it. My heart went out to the beautiful animal before me and I knew that I would do whatever was needed to save it. I stepped out of hiding onto the ledge and into its sight.

The dragon turned its head, fixing its pain filled eyes upon me. *So! You have come to finish what that one started... just take off my head and you will gain all my magic. So strike quickly and be done with it, or are all your kind cruel like this one?"* The words appeared within my thoughts, catching me totally by surprise. Nothing in the books did justice to the reality of telepathic communication. I touched and caressed the thoughts that had invaded my mind; they were cold and hard, tainted by the dragon's hatred and pain, but they had a definite femininity about them.

My right hand was clasped around the pistol grip of the rifle, its barrel rested in the crook of my left arm. With a forefinger I engaged the safety and a hiss escaped from the dragon's gaping maw. The poor beast knew that I carried death in my hands even if she did not recognize its form.

I stepped sideways to the black, basalt rock face into which the cave mouth penetrated, but I never took my eyes off the dragon as I leaned my rifle against the stony wall. Holding my empty hands away from my sides I approached the dragonness until I stood just out of her reach. Searching my memory for words that I had read in a book,

I spoke into the strange heavy silence that had fallen around the dragon and myself. "Draconae, Draconi, Draconis!"

A sound like the rumble of faraway thunder accompanied a surge of feeling the likes of which I had never felt before passed through me, but I guessed what it was and exalted in the fact that it had answered me...dragon magic!

"Draconae I beg you judge not all men by the actions of this one!" The dragon's eyes glanced at the body of her would be slayer then back to me as her thoughts once more invaded my own.

Why should I not? Your kind are violent, hateful and cruel. You would hunt down and kill us all if you could.

"Well isn't that the kettle calling the pot black!" I snapped back. *What?* The dragon queried within my mind for the words I had spoken held no meaning for her.

"I know you are hurting, will you allow me to help you? I would make amends for what one of my kind has done."

The dragon's thoughts were full of bitterness as she cursed the dilemma in which she found herself. Dare she accept help from one of the very creatures that had attempted to kill her? *I do not think I have a choice, do what you will.*

I hope you have good self control." I said, and reached down for the spear. With a hiss of censure at the apparent betrayal, the dragon's head moved towards me with eyes gone red with anger and hate. "Wait! I need it to lever away the stone!" I shouted at the top of my voice. "Lady you better get a hold of yourself, because I guarantee that it's going to get worse before it gets better. Trust me; or eat me…what is it going to be?" The dragon blinked her eyes, watching me closely. "Very well then, I'll get started." I said in a quieter tone of voice. I worked my way around the dragon to where I could get at the stone that held her trapped and helpless. The mythical beast swung her head to the opposite side so as to observe my every movement. It was apparent she did not fully trust me, but I had other things to worry about.

Drawing my large hunting knife from its sheath, I dug away at the underlying earth holding the smaller stone in place. After positioning the butt of the spear behind it, I moved to the opposite end and pressed down on the shaft. The stone did not move and I saw why. The dragon was pushing against the larger boulder wedging everything tight. "Relax, stop pushing against the stone or I will never get it free."

When she did not reply so I took my knife and pricked her with its sharp point.

The dragon shifted her body whimpering at the pain that even so small a movement inflected. I dropped the knife and leaned hard on the spear shaft. The smaller stone popped free and the greater one rolled over the edge to crash into the underbrush along the riverbank far below.

The dragon began to stir. "Hold! Do not move or you could lose any chance of saving your wing." Her yellow eyes regarded me as I moved to where the stone had smashed into the dragon's wing and examined the injury. It was a clean break, the bone had not come through the skin nor had it shattered, but the ends had slipped by each other after breaking. I would have to pull the halves apart to realign them. With some anxiety for my own safety I got to work. It took several quick strokes, but at last the bindings parted and I removed the wicked spear point. Measuring the shaft to its center, I took my knife and began vigorously chopping at it until I had weakened it enough to break it in half. I now had two splints about seven feet long.

Moving to the corpse, I stripped away its accouterments and with a grunt of distaste I heaved it over the edge of the precipice. The body splashed into the river at the base of the cliff and floated grotesquely for a moment before it sank from sight in the muddy water.

I took the dragon slayer's leather undergarment and quickly sliced several strips from it. Returning with them to the dragon's side I turned to face her, "I am going to have to pull on your outer wing to align the break and then I can splint it in place until it heals. It's going to feel like I am trying to rip your wing off! Can you handle the pain without retaliating and biting my head off?"

I hope so, for both our sakes. The dragon mused, steeling herself for the pain that she would have to endure.

That was not the most reassuring thing she could say I thought to myself, but before I had too much time to think upon what I was about to do I reached out and grasped her wing bone firmly with both hands. "Oh, by the way what is your name?" I quipped hoping to distract her as I braced my feet and pulled. The dragon screamed!

The Draconae fought for air, breathing in great panting breaths. Her pain filled response appeared within my thoughts. *Moon...Moonlight!*

Continuing in the futile attempt to keep her distracted, I asked the same question of her again. "I am sorry, but what was your name again?" I twisted the bones in a clockwise motion. *Nicole! MY NAME IS NICOLE!!!* Her powerful mental shout exploded within my mind. The pain was excruciating, greater than the worst migraine headache I have ever had. The dragon screamed aloud once more and passed out from the overload of pain.

I ceased pulling and the ends fit together like two puzzle pieces. I was relieved that she had passed out because of what I must do. Taking my blade I pierced the membrane of her wing just behind the broken bone. I did this three times on either side of the break and threaded the leather thongs through the holes tying the ends loosely together. Retrieving the two halves of the spear shaft, I slipped them through the loops placing one on top and one below. Inserting some cloth, I padded the thongs as best I could and tied them tight before folding the wing against her body.

Her glittering silver airfoils were huge, but they were surprisingly light. I replayed the dragon's names in my thoughts while moving to the opposite side of the huge beast to fold the other wing closed. Moonlight. That fit her perfectly, but Nicole? That was a woman's name for sure...why would a dragon have a human name?

I went to the pool of water below the splashing waterfall and wet a cloth. Returning I stopped to admire this beautiful creature I had befriended. Reaching out I touched the beast, laying the palm of my hand against her neck. Once more I marveled at the feel of her hide. So warm, so soft and supple. It reflected the waning sunlight and was irradiant silver like the glimmer of a full moon reflecting upon still water. Her great heart beat strong under my hand much to my relief. The fingers of my hand stayed in contact with her skin, sliding along her neck as I walked towards her head as if reluctant to break the physical connection between us. I sat down beside the dragon's head and used the wet cloth to wipe away the mud and froth from her jaws. Standing up, I tossed the dirty rag away and looked at the beautiful dragon once more. "I've done what I could, now come back to me sweetheart."

The light was going quickly now as I went about setting up camp for the night. I brought in an excrescent amount of firewood and contrived a ring of stones to contain my fire. After setting some kindling and smaller sticks in the fire-ring I selected a match, closed the plastic vile to keep them dry and returned it to my pack. Reaching out, I struck the match on one of the rocks that made up the ring and was completely unprepared for what happened next. Instead of a yellow flame, the innocuous little stick ignited a two-foot sphere of blue-white actinic star-fire! I stared in confused amazement at this fireball on a stick. With a yell, I tossed it from me and the globe of fire fell into the wood below as I stumbled backwards. With a roar, the wood caught fire and strangely shaped tongues of multicolored flame shot twenty feet into the sky. For a few moments I gazed in disbelief as the flames burned down and began to act like the many other fires I had started. Returning closer, I prodded it with a stick, like a caveman that can't understand the wheel turning before his eyes. Feeding it more wood produced a nice, cheerful and much to my relief, normal fire.

Then it came over me once more. That old feeling I would get when I was alone in the green hell collectively called Southeast Asia and it was centered between my shoulder blades...I was being watched! My weapon was way too far away to make a try for it. "Fool!" I thought to myself. "Charley would eat you alive if he found you today."

Slowly I turned around, keeping my hands in plain sight away from my body and I saw her watching me through half lidded eyes. Eyes that were no longer blinded by pain, the pain was still there yes, but now it was controlled. They were a cold, hard ice diamond blue in color...they were the eyes of a killer and I had no doubt as to who was about to die...

I understood now what a bird must feel when staring at a snake. There was only one way to go and I took it, one entranced step at a time moving slowly towards Moonlight. Her jaws gaped revealing foot long curved fangs; any prey impaled on those deadly spikes had no hope of escape.

Why have you done this? Moonlight's powerful thoughts smashed into my own. I had neither the power nor the skill to keep her out of my mind even if I would have wanted to. *You bound my wing and stanched the flow from the wound in my side. Surely you know I intend to kill you. For not only do you know my name, you know my true and secret name. If you so desired, you could call me by my name and I would be forced to return to be your slave, even in death. I cannot allow you to live!*

"I don't want your servitude, I crave your friendship, but only if it is freely given."

I took a step towards her. "You cannot die, I just found you! And...and dragons can live forever...it says so in the books!" I took another step towards her and stood next to her great head at last. I reached out to her and was heartened when she did not pull away. My hand found the pulse spot behind her massive jaw and felt once again the beating of Moonlight's great heart.

As my hand touched her, Moonlight felt a great shock run through her tormented body. With an effort she twisted her eyes, causing scintillating rainbows of light to flash and flicker within their depths as they refocused. She was stunned by what her sorceress vision revealed to her.

There may be a way...but that which I need must be a gift; it cannot be taken.

"Tell me what I must do and I will do it! If I cannot be with you in life, then I will accompany you in death. I will give my life to you willingly!" I did not mention that she had me dead to rights and what I offered was all ready hers to take.

Your words have been heard and witnessed...human! There was a grim finality in the tone of the dragon's thoughts. Something important had just happened and she could tell I had no idea what it was! Moonlight shifted her focus again and pinpointed not one, but three nodes of power. One in the head, another in the chest and a third lower down. It was the strongest and bound tightly to the power of life itself. She would take that which she needed there, as close to the strongest source as she safely could.

Remove your clothes, the dragon demanded. *There can be nothing between us that is not part of either you or I.*

"What?" I replied in surprise, then moved quickly to do her bidding. Stepping closer to the fire for warmth I stood exposed before her. The dragon approached me with a lithe, sensuous predatory grace and goose bumps arose upon my skin as I watched death incarnate coming for me. She curled her body around the fire and I seated myself next to Moonlight with my back propped against her massive side.

Looking up at her I spoke. "Do what needs to be done whatever it is, but do it now...before I lose my nerve." Her serpentine neck curved in and down. She grasped my left leg within her mouth and I felt her soft tongue caressing my flesh, as Moonlight repositioned my leg to expose the sensitive inner thigh. I was now just an onlooker, but I could see it all happening with a terrifying clarity. I gazed in moribund fascination at her and almost missed the movement between the gaping jaws. Two stiletto thin, needle sharp fangs slid into place beside the massive prey-killing tusks. A drop of crystal clear fluid depended from the points of the smaller fangs and in slow motion the sparkling droplets fell to splash bubbling and hissing across my skin. "Oh gods, it burns Nicole! It's so cold it burns!"

I will be gentle; her thoughts resonated within my own in answer to my cry of pain.

The twin daggers glinted and flashed wickedly in the firelight...then plunged deeply into my flesh, questing, seeking and ultimately finding the magic within. Now it was my turn to scream as her fangs penetrated the femoral artery. My blood rushed up the hollow denticles to enter the dragon's body healing and changing her forever as it scorched its way through Moonlight's veins.

•••

She was hot, oh so hot! Moonlight wanted to rend and tear fragile flesh, to ascend into a bright morning sun and give herself to the paramour of her own choosing! But she held herself with the iron control that only a queen dragon possessed and continued to feed upon the man. Greedily Moonlight drained the vital fluid of life from his body. She gazed at Lyle with her sorceress vision, watching his life fire dim and flicker, wavering like a candle about to go out…

•••

I was moaning and thrashing my head from side to side, delirious as death came for me. I turned my head towards her, my hazel eyes met her blue orbs and I slipped through those great windows into the dragon's soul! Moonlight's defenses could not touch me nor bar my entering her mind and touching her spirit. Thought to thought there could be no lies between us. *Why have you done this?* She called for my answer once more.

Reaching out to her as my heart ceased to beat, I touched the Draconae's thoughts that held and surrounded me. *For the only reason that makes anything or any life worth while…Love…*I slipped out of her mind, my hand falling limply to my side as the blackness took me and I knew no more…

•••

Now Moonlight could see that which had been within the man hovering in the air between their two bodies, free at last released by death from the flesh that had hidden his true self from her sight.

In horror she cried out as the enormity of her mistake struck home. *NOooooo!* She screamed silently in denial of what she had done. *Oh please no!* Wrenching her crimson stained fangs from his leg the silver dragon bit savagely upon her tongue. So great was the queen's distress that she did not even feel the pain, green ichor flowed leaving a coppery taste in her mouth. Moving quickly she allowed drops of her blood to fall into and cover the sightless eyes. Pausing at the slack open mouth she filled it with her essence. Using her tongue the moonlight dragon traced a contorted glowing rune upon Lyle's unmoving chest. Then without hesitation or thought of the consequence of her actions, Moonlight bit the man deeply. The smaller fangs that carried the dragon's bane plunged inwards to find the man's heart; there to inject her deadly venom, which she believed would give not death, but life to the lifeless. For in that brief encounter where they had stood exposed and unguarded Moonlight realized that this one she could not afford to lose. He was not just a man and she was now more than a dragon. They had shared too deeply to be one or the other...each had given, both had taken and neither would ever be whole without the other.

The effect of her bite was immediate and traumatic. That which floated in the air was sucked back within a body that swallowed then took a great gasping breath and howled in torment as the dragon fire burned within his flesh until nothing but the pain remained...

•••

I reveled in the pain as waves of searing agony rolled over me because it meant I was alive! Dead men feel no pain and from the way I felt, I was most definitely alive! Rolling over I proceeded to heave up the contents of my stomach before falling back to lie prostate and exhausted.

Regaining some strength I crawled over to the pool of water that I could not see by following the sound of splashing water from the falls that cascaded into the pool from above. I rinsed the vile taste from my mouth and washed the sticky substance from my eyes. I made my way out of the pool still blinking and rubbing them in an attempt to bring the world back into focus. My left leg refused to obey my commands and I limped back over to the fire.

After I had dried off I donned my clothes wincing from the pain in my leg.

I understood that pain, but why did my chest hurt so? I would have to ask Moonlight just what took place after the lights went out.

Working my way over to Moonlight I collapsed into a sitting position in between her forelegs. "Moon! What did you do to me sweetheart? I hurt everywhere!"

Moonlight's silent voice filled my mind, I could no longer envision a life where her thoughts were not entwined with my own; *I killed you...*

"YOU, DID WHAT!!!" I shouted in total disbelief.

What's wrong, didn't you hear me the first time? I said, I killed you...I took that which you offered and then gave it back with interest when I understood the mistake I had made and the loss I was about to incur.

As a matter of fact I was hearing her quite well. It was like talking to myself, it took place instantly without effort or time lag and now entwined with Moonlight's thoughts her powerful emotions were coming to me also. That was how I knew she was truly concerned and wanted me to live. I reached out to touch her affectionately and somewhat possessively. "Moonlight I must sleep, will you be here when I wake? Or is this truly just a dream?"

Vaguely I heard the dragon thinking about and to me. Moonlight wondered how long it would be before the changes started to manifest themselves and how the one she had chosen would handle them. Would I want to live forever? *Yes, I will be here and no, this is not a dream. Nothing good is a dream; nothing truly beautiful is an illusion.* Moonlight spoke in descant. But I was already drifting off into a deep sleep.

She looked down at me where I lay between her forelegs. *Yes, rider of my soul I will be here now and always for you.* The dragon of my dreams pledged herself to me. *Sleep well, for soon your testing will be upon you. I hope you survive it, because I have grown far too fond of you to lose you now. None of the others possessed that which you take for granted...your humanity.* The last vision I beheld as reality faded away, were Moonlight's phosphorescent blue eyes looking down upon me...

•••

A heavy sigh issued from the dragon as she thought of things and days that might come. Foreknowledge was a gift and a curse that she had learned long ago not to rely upon. The future was far too changeable; a small stone rolling down a hill, a bird flying through the sky could influence seemingly unrelated events half a world away and sometimes separated by vast stretches of time. It was much safer to live in the here and now, but still she kept it in the back of her mind, comparing that which is to that which might be.

The silver dragon curled her long graceful neck around this her chosen one, enclosing him within a protected space surrounded by her silver hide. The transparent nictitating membranes slid across her glittering eyes and she joined her man in his dreams.

•••

Several days later I awoke to find Moonlight sitting back on her haunches close to the edge of the precipice in front of the lair and gazing out over the valley beyond. She turned and moved towards me when she felt my mind awaken and the gaze of my eyes touch her. *Today is the day to remove the splints from my wing!* She felt the unvoiced hesitation in my thoughts. *Yes, we do it today...the time is now!* Moonlight thought impatiently as she turned her head to look at me.

"Moonlight...are you sure about this? It's only been what, a week? Shouldn't we give it a little more time to heal?" I was thinking more along the line of a month; at least that's the way humans healed. Dragons must be different indeed if they healed in just a week. I shrugged my shoulders, who was I to question her judgment. Moonlight knew her body and its limitations, if she said do it today...I shook my head, drew my knife and advanced towards her. I just hoped that Moonlight knew what she was doing. I thought how things had changed between myself and this beautiful creature. If I had attempted to do what I was about to do just a few days ago she would have literally bitten my head off. But now she was calm and relaxed, completely at ease with "her human." I found that Moonlight was much like other females...possessive of things they believed were theirs, quick to anger, slow to forgive and she had a dragon's long memory! With quick strokes the razor sharp edge of my blade cut the bindings on the topside of her wing. The poles I had made from the dragon slayer's spear clattered to the ground.

Stepping under her wing I examined the bindings where they passed through the wing-membrane. The hide that made up the lifting surface of her airfoil had grown around the leather strips. It was yet another example of the amazing recuperative powers of ~my~ dragon.

Moonlight curled her neck around and was watching me out of the great lanterns of her eyes as I reached up to grip the first binding strip firmly in both hands. "Moonlight, this may hurt a little, but nothing like the injury itself." I smiled, caught for a moment by the dragon's beautiful eyes. I gave a quick downward jerk in the same way one would remove a Band-Aid. If you pulled one off slowly it hurt a lot more than if done quickly. Moonlight drew a sharp breath that hissed between her teeth...and I sat down hard. "What was that!" I exclaimed as I rubbed my arm.

The tone of her thoughts was somewhat apologetic. *Sorry...What is mine is now yours. The link between us carries feelings as well as our thoughts. I guess I should have told you about that.*

"Yes...a wee bit of warning would have been nice." I said, with a slight frown upon my face. Hesitating momentarily I yanked the second thong free and grabbed my arm once more. Taking a deep breath I told myself, "this is not my pain!" And pulled the next leather strip through with a snapping motion while reaching for the following one with my other hand. By the time I pulled the last binding strip free I had learned to block Moonlight's sending up to a point, but there was a sheen of sweat upon my brow that had nothing to do with the heat. I took a damp cloth and wiped the small wounds where the strips had passed through her wing.

I raised an eyebrow when I saw the punctures were already sealing over, in a few days there would be no trace of them.

*You could have warned me...*Moonlight threw my own words back to me and I gave her a smile in return.

With the splints removed Moonlight spread her wings wide and flapped them experimentally. Then she began to feed more power into them until a small windstorm raged around her. Twice she broke free of the ground to rise momentarily into the air. Then she settled back to the ground once more, much like the fledgling hawks that I loved to watch back home.

I covered my eyes with a hand trying to keep out the dust that was being blown about as the dragon beat her powerful wings against the air. The wind died down and I opened my eyes to see Moonlight preening her wings. She looked at me and her eyes flashed and sparkled. *Come on my love, what are you waiting for? I'm hungry!*

"Oh! I am sorry Moonlight, how thoughtless of me. I'll go fetch something immediately." I said contritely as I reached for my rifle.

No, not that way...I will hunt for us both this day. Her tone softened to barely a susurration within my mind. *I still do not truly understand why you have done what you have for me. There is a life debt and a bond between us that cannot be sundered now even by death. I have given myself to you for what you have done...and what you will do in the future.*

I came close and laid a hand against her soft hide and a shiver passed through her spreading outwards from my touch. The beautiful silver being crouched down and offered her foreleg to me. I stood unmoving, was she really asking me to do what I thought she was? *Well? Are you coming or not?* She beckoned to me rustling her wings impatiently. Her words broke my immobility and I moved forward to step up onto the proffered foreleg.

With her assistance I found myself perched upon her back. The space between the last neck ridge and her shoulder hump fit me as if Moonlight had been born to be mine...or was it the other way around? In truth I did not care! I was here, she was here and all that mattered was that we were together.

The dragon came back on her haunches, while twisting her sensuous neck around to look at me upon her back. No words passed between us, it just felt right to her for me to be there; as if a piece of her that she had not known was missing had been restored. *Are you ready to ride the wind Lyle?*

My heart skipped a beat and I took a deep breath. *Go for it Nicole, just remember that I have nothing to hang on to.* I spoke silently into her mind.

There was laughter in the thoughts that merged with mine. *When you ride upon Moonlight, you need nothing...I will not let you fall!* Without waiting for my reply Moonlight took three quick steps towards the edge and leaped out into the abyss...

The dragon fell...like a stone!

"Mooonnnn!!! Her name was torn from my lips by the rushing wind. I was terrified! When I flew hangliders in another world I had been in control, but now as we plummeted downwards I was just a passenger, a helpless victim unable to influence my fate. Without thinking, I reached for Moonlight's thoughts. The connection between my soul and that of the dragon strengthened as I fell into full rapport with the beast upon whose back I rode. The line where one spirit ended and the other began became blurred until there was no longer two, but only the one. Time changed or so it seemed until it felt like I had minutes instead of only seconds to make a decision. Her, my, our wings snapped open, the distinction between the two was no longer relevant. I felt the great airfoils catch the air and we were no longer falling, we were flying! I have always loved to fly; but that was suspended beneath an inanimate cloth wing stretched over unmoving aluminum spars. There was no comparison to what I was doing now. This was true flight! I felt more alive than ever before. The wind caressed our bodies, the pressure it exerted against the membranes of our wings manifested itself as a sensual tingling sensation that moved and changed as the air slipped under and around them. I exulted in those feelings as they surged through my body. This was better than coition I thought and another answered back.

Wait until you put the two together. Her thoughts were light and airy, filled with Moonlight's joy to be once more in the air. For the Moonlight Dragon was truly a being of the high deep sky that would come to earth for a short time before returning once more to her true element.

Unconsciously I reached out, gave a command and we dropped several yards towards the river's surface and the act of flying became easier. I felt her surprise at the change and her questions; *I know how to fly Nicole, although never like this!*

I was right! I knew I was right about what is within you! Her bugle of exultation echoed across the valley below, causing the animals to raise their heads and glance quickly around them in fear. Was death coming for them today?

When nothing untoward happened, they lowered their heads once more and returned to grazing on the lush grasses of the fertile valley floor. *Why is it so much easier to fly now? What magic did you cast, I felt nothing? Your touch must be light and sure to work so silently.*

I smiled at the thought of showing her something new about flying. *That is because I used none. It is a law of aerodynamics called ground affect. When you place a wing at a height that is equal to half of its span above the ground the air is compressed...*I trailed off as a feeling of incomprehension came back to me from Moonlight.

But we are above water, came her quick questioning reply.

Makes no difference, I said. *The same laws apply. When an airfoil, your wing, is flying at the correct height above the ground the land below and your wing above trap the air beneath your wing. You can ride the interface using less effort to fly at the same speed.*

The dragon flew on in silence for a moment, musing over what I had told her. *I see there is much I can learn from you.*

And I from you Moon. We complement each other nicely, you know little about physics and I know nothing about magic! I sent the feeling of a smile to her and felt Moonlight's quiet laugh in reply as we continued onwards, the river flashing by beneath us. Moonlight pulled up and away, banking to the right as we climbed. The dragon crossed over the wide sandy spit of land that separated the small tributary stream that flowed by our lair from the main flow of the river. It was not the river that flowed in the world I came from. Instead of the deep blue tamed and controlled stream that had been broken to the will of man by the great dams controlling the flow of its water, here there ran a wild brown current that bowed to no one as it meandered through the valley. It was a powerful beast that would tear down mountains if they dared to stand in its way.

There were many animals on the shore drinking from the river. Moonlight changed direction and began to lose altitude. *What are you doing Moon?* I looked over my shoulder and was momentarily blinded by the rising sun.

Breakfast, came her laconic reply. For she, Moonlight, was the ultimate predator. She had at her command the body strength of a powerful beast bound to and controlled by a keen intellect equal to that of a man. *What would you like for breakfast, beef, pork or mutton?*

The tone of her thoughts told me she was enjoying the hunt immensely.

Beef if you please, I said into her mind.

The animal never had a chance. Coming out of the rising sun, the dragon swooped down upon the herd from behind. The cow continued to take its final drink as its death fell towards it upon silver wings. Moonlight flew onward across the waterway, then turned to follow the river's course upstream, the cow's body clutched in her talons hung limply like a broken toy.

She fluttered down to a landing upon a grassy meadow where a stream flowed forth from the hillside. I brought my leg across and slid down her side to land in the soft grass of the meadow. After dismounting I beheld in her red shot eyes a vestige of the wild dragon I had met that first day. Even the tone of the voice that spoke into my thoughts was different, raw and rough as if there was a deeper meaning to the words she spoke. I hesitated. Moonlight was setting back on her haunches, a forefoot grasping the carcass possessively.

I share my kill with the one I have chosen! As the queen finished speaking she released the dead animal and backed away, but she never took her eyes from me.

What did she want? I could feel that this moment was important to the dragon, charged with subtle meanings that I did not understand. I knew that I must choose my actions carefully. Looking at Moonlight, I spoke to her in that silent form of communication that had felt so strange just a few days ago. *Thank you my queen.* I was unsure why I used the possessive form of address, but it seemed to please the dragon for she began to make a pleasant sound deep in her throat and her eyes changed color to a beautiful cerulean blue.

Moving forward while drawing my knife, I cut a strip of the choice meat along the back strap from the carcass. Glancing at Moonlight, I sliced the bite I had taken free and swallowed. A strange but pleasant sensation passed through me. But was it hers or mine? I could not tell. Walking over to the nearby stream I found a flat rock to sit upon and finish my meal.

Looking over at my friend who was in the act of biting the carcass in two, I watched Moonlight take the front half in her mouth and pause feeling my gaze touch upon her. The forelegs of the luckless animal dangled from her mouth and with a flexing of her powerful jaw muscles the legs were sheared away and fell to the ground to lie grotesquely in the grass. The dining habits of a feeding dragon were not for the faint of heart. With a flick of her head, she transferred it to the back of her mouth and swallowed it whole. After finishing her meal, Moonlight cleaned her muzzle and bloody talons with a flicking tongue, then came over and drank from the stream.

Having finished mine also, I rinsed my hands and face, washed my knife and returned it to its scabbard.

The silver dragon lay her great head down next to me and we enjoyed the sound of the water as it leaped from stone to stone on its way to merge its water with that of the mighty river below. Idly, I reached out and stroked her muzzle. Moonlight's eyelids began to droop and a great sigh of contentment escaped her. Leaves and flower petals were blown twenty feet by the sudden breeze. The intervals between my caresses became longer, until my hand lay still by her muzzle. Vaguely I felt Moonlight lick my hand before she followed me into slumber and into my dreams once more.

I was awakened by the change in temperature of the air as the sun began to set in the west. Rubbing the sleep from my eyes I exclaimed, "Moon, wake up! We slept the whole day away!"

The dragon lazily opened an eyelid revealing the blue colored orb behind it.

So...what is a day to one who will live forever?

I looked at the dragon who had still not moved, but continued to regard me from one shining eye the size of a large saucer. "Easy for you to say oh dragon of the moon, but I have seventy or eighty years of life at most, so every day is precious to me."

The dragon gave a derisive snort that sent leaves once more flying into the stream. I watched them float away down stream. *We will see about that,* came her cryptic retort.

Moonlight rose from where she had been laying and stretched like a cat. The wicked retractable claws on her forefeet, which could almost be, called hands, having four digits and a fifth that was opposable like a man's thumb. Sliced ten groves through the grass of the meadow as she stretched her wings to full extension at the same time. *Come, it is time to fly.* It was not a request; it was a command for me to mount her.

I hit the proffered foreleg at a trot, leaped upward and seated myself upon her back. "Giddey-up horsie!" I exclaimed out of shear delight.

The dragon stood rock still and turned her head to look at me upon her back out of eyes that had an unfriendly color within them. *I...am not, a horse! Further more, I do not even resemble a horse. As a matter of fact...I eat horses for lunch! One more comment like that and you will find yourself walking back to our lair!*

I had to smile to myself. Her words were filled with hostility, but she had said

"our lair" so I was not in too deep a trouble yet. But I thought it would be prudent to say something to cool her temper. She may not be human, but Moonlight was definitely female!

"Nicole," I used her secret name to show my sincerity. "My lovely dragon of the Moon." Her beautiful pixie shaped ears unfolded away from the side of her skull as she listened to my sweet words. "You are more beautiful than any horse borne of this earth, you are more graceful than even Pegasus the great winged steed of the gods! Let every horse be removed from the world so long as you will stay with me!"

She cocked her head as she looked at me, but the ominous color had left her eyes. Then she gave a contemptuous snort and flicked her ears. *Flatterer...smooth tongued ape. I knew your ancestors when they still lived in the trees, fearful of the lions that prowled the savannas.* She looked out across the river valley.

When she turned back to me her thoughts were coy, like those of a young girl that had never heard words of romance or love. Moonlight's eyes sparkled with rainbows as she replied. *But I do so love to hear them.*

Without speaking, she stood up. Balancing on her strong hind legs as she adjusted the angle of attack of her wings. Then taking several quick running steps down the slope of the hillside with her wings spread wide it looked as if she walked into the sky.

Moonlight tucked her legs tight against her body and together we spiraled upward as she caught a weak evening thermal and turned circles into a darkening sky.

The time of my testing was upon me; I just did not know it yet. The silver dragon climbed higher into the sky. Moonlight began to feel the affects of her exertions and the air about us had turned thin and cold, but still she fought her way ever higher trying to give her man as much room as she could for what she was about to do to him. Moonlight did her best to hide her fear from me. She hated to do this, but it was the only way to know for sure that she had chosen correctly, to know if I was to be truly hers as she now realized she so desperately wanted me to be.

Moon...why are we so high? It is so cold here, what are you doing? Moonlight took a deep breath, steeling herself to do the deed. Her body was trembling so badly that I could feel it where I sat upon her back. *Moon...are you all right? You're trembling so...what's wrong?* My words laced with such concern for her well being tore at her resolve.

What if she was wrong? The dragon thought. If I were not her soul mate she would be condemning me to a horrible death. Oh it would be quick yes, but I would know that death was coming long before it reached me and that she, Moonlight, was my executioner. In those last peaceful moments suspended at the top of the sky she reached for my mind and pulled me tightly to her. *Lyle,* her thoughts heavy with emotion touched mine. *Remember...remember this, now and forever I will always be with you.*

And I have fallen for you Nicole. I would rather die than be separated from you.

I spoke softly, tenderly directly to her soul.

With a small anguished cry she rolled over in the sky and shook me from her back! I felt my body slipping away from hers. She heard my scream of surprise and terror and felt my hand slide across her back as I tried to stay with her, but it was to no avail. My life now depended upon me finding my true form that unknown to me lay buried deep within my soul. Unable to hold onto her body, I grabbed Moonlight by her mind. The powerful blast of raw mind-numbing fear that radiated from me tore into her thoughts and froze the dragon in place. *Nicole, why? I don't understand? I have given over my very life into your keeping? I have died for you... What have I done?* She could sense the feeling of betrayal in my thoughts and it wounded her deeply.

Moonlight's lovely mind voice came into my thoughts and I clung to it like a drowning man would cling to a rope. *I have done what I have to set you free! To bring you fully into the world in which I live so that we can be together in body as well as mind. The chains that hold you bound are stretched thin. Exert yourself, break the bindings and be free! Am I not a prize worthy of your best efforts? Come to me my love I am just above you, spread your wings and come to me!* She implored.

Nicole! I have no wings! I shouted my frustration and terror into her thoughts.

Low and calm her unspoken words of entreaty came to me. *Yes, you have...do you not understand? You have wings! Can you not see? The clues are there before you! You have an affinity with fire, you know how to fly...you like raw meat! How many humans do you know that eat their meat raw? Change; change now, we are running out of time!*

I listened to her words again in my mind. She was trying her best to tell me something in a roundabout way that she could not say directly. Again and again I replayed what she had said to me. Fire...flying...raw meat? I paused as the realization of what she might possibly be hinting at suddenly hit me. *Oh, you have GOT...to be kidding!* Moonlight felt the sudden change in my thoughts and hoped it was not to late. Holding my breath, I willed something, anything to take place. Without warning a shiver ran through my body as bones dislocated themselves from their sockets, changing shape; pieces and parts that had not existed at all came into being. There was a moment of blinding white light followed an instant of blackness. I blinked my eyes and my vision cleared, the change to my being had been completed in less than a heartbeat. Great silver wings that were now mine caught the air turning my fall into flight!

I became aware of my close surroundings once more and the beautiful winged being that flew beside me. *Nicole?* I asked, using her secret name once more. *You're, you're beautiful! I have always thought you a lovely creature to look at, but now your beauty is almost blinding. Through my dragon eyes you fairly glow against the black back- drop of the star filled sky above.* Girlish laughter floated in my thoughts as she enjoyed my words of admiration. Moonlight sideslipped through the air passing slowly underneath me, admiring my changed form. I was the only silver male she had ever seen "I must speak to him about choosing a new name," Moonlight thought idly, unaware that I could now hear even her innermost contemplation's and musings. I realized also that I must learn how not to hear them and do so quickly!

On impulse she reached out and touched me with her wingtip as she crossed below me. I stumbled in the air as her touch trailed down my abdomen towards my long tail causing me to lose my concentration momentarily.

My mate pulled alongside me and we flew in silence for a few moments, then together we turned for home and the warmth of our lair. It had been a very long, stressful day.

L. J. Anderson

Born in the Olympic year of nineteen fifty-six, L. J. Anderson was raised on the small eighty acre Anderson family farm in the agricultural community of Blythe, California. After finishing high school, where he acquired a love of reading, he enlisted in the United States Navy and served his country overseas. Upon his discharge, he traveled about the country for several years before returning once more to his home in the Palo Verde Valley. While working as a farm equipment specialist by day, he nurtured his proclivity towards fantasy writing at night as a way to relax after a hard day's work and was soon addicted to expressing his fascination in a fantasy world of his own creation. He lives in Blythe with his wife Kathy; their eight-year-old son Riley and a white honey-dipped Labrador Retriever named Xena.

Writer's Block

"Mr. Stone, this is indeed an honor," the high-pitched reedy voice gushed. "I have experienced all of your tapes. *Orion Beyond* virtually moved me to tears when I achieved the final segment."

Amos Stone turned. The voice came from an equally small, reedy salesman with receding hair and an ingratiating smile. His tiny spider-like hands intertwined as he spoke, forming a little, almost skeletal, cocoon in front of his chest.

Stone turned back and looked at the machine. It gleamed like both moons on a clear night. Genuine wood molding, titanium digitators, fingerprint identification ignition and a silky smooth carmonium shell. The TADLO Series E 6000 glimmered back into his face as he ran his fingers lightly across the shimmering scan-screen.

"You have no idea the effect your work has had on me. Just absolute. That's all I can say, absolute," the man chattered like a small laser-gun as he shoved his hand in Stone's face. "Anatole Gillespie," he said, flashing a crooked grin.

Stone just stared at him, then took his hand. It was one of those limp-fish handshakes. Stone absently wiped his hand on his coverlet. The little man was dead on his heels as Stone walked around the machine.

Enough.

Stone turned and glared at him. "I've seen your ads for the TADLO Series E on my infocube. I thought it might make a good investment for me."

"I've worked with many of the best authors but you are, by far, the most famous. Truly an honor. Truly an honor. I am such a great admirer of your work," he prattled. "And what an absolutely perfect choice for you. The TADLO Series E 6000 is the most advanced thought-transfer servitor for authors introduced in the last two hundred years."

Stone flashed briefly on how authors weren't really writers. They were word processors that people "experienced" rather than read. Nobody could read anyway; at least, only a very few. The art of reading the written word was archaic in the extreme. Using wordwrite processors it was possible now to not only tap the words directly into the mind of the "reader," but also the corresponding picture image of the thought just as the author had conceived it.

Later, Gillespie, still chattering away, processed the credit voucher agreement. As he was handing Stone a copy of the taped transaction, he suddenly stopped talking. He stared searchingly into Stone's eyes. For a long moment Stone didn't know if he should say something or not.

"You are a much better author than you believe, Mr. Stone. Your father was very good, but he never had the word talent you have."

His eyes narrowed strangely. "You could have the power."

"The what?" Stone asked.

"The power of the word, Mr. Stone, the power of the word."

"I'm afraid I don't understand."

"It takes the machine. And it a forbidden machine. But I believe you could do it," he said, rubbing his fingers together nervously, glancing about to see if he was being overheard. They were alone. Abruptly he closed his eyes, then opened them, and said thank you. Before Stone could reply, the little man strode off quickly toward another customer and was gone.

That was one week ago. Now the TADLO Series E 6000 was here in his own envirodome, in his own write-room, beckoning him to try it out.

Amazing what had been done with his craft in the past five centuries. Stone was from a well known and respected line of famous and near-famous authors. His father, A. Llewellyn Stone, was the first chronicler of the Constellation Wars and the first biographer of Hannibal Day, The Conqueror. Authors would always be authors whether they wrote laboriously, as the ancients had done, by hand. Or slipped on the sleek thought transfer helmet and let the Thought-Activated Direct Linguistic Organizer do it. It was the same.

But it was not the same. Amos Stone had been slipping on the sleek thought transfer helmet for two solid weeks and had less than twenty scan-screen chapters to show for it. At first he thought it might have been a malfunction in the TADLO. Though it reproduced his thoughts with perfect accuracy, the thoughts coming out of Stone's mind were dull and unorganized. His mind would wander with the helmet in place. Perhaps because he knew it was there for him to have brilliant flashes of thought and insight. He had to do something. His publisher was expecting the first five hundred chapters on the Ring Shuttle next week. So far he had twenty partially complete, mediocre chapters. And worse, an installment payment of fifteen credits by the first.

He had fought the vacuum for six hours straight this night. Still the same results. Nothing but inconsequential drivel. Blocked. His mind was blocked from producing anything that remotely resembled a best selling author's mind. He knew of the syndrome. He'd experienced the tapes on the early classics. It was a psychological nuisance the ancient masters had encountered. But they had not been bred to authoring as he had. He was genetically perfect. Or as perfect as a Radical Gene Compression Tape would make him. He had literally been sired to particularly fit this one pursuit: authoring. The gift that flowed in his father's brain, and his father's before him, pulsated through Amos Stone's brain. But not when he was using the TADLO Series E 6000. He ripped the helmet from his head and walked onto the Carpetram.

"Shut down TADLO energy inducer. Glow panels too," Stone called to no one.

"Shutting down," the voice came back. It was that unisex voice all Housecomps used. The panels glowed down to a faint blur.

"You are finished for the evening?" the synthesized voice droned.

"That's the word. Finished. Double bourbon, rocks, when I get to the living area." Stone's voice trailed off as he moved farther down the companionway. He thought of the University again. It had been, what, twelve years since he had been a student of literature? Six years of speed-study with the greatest minds of the galaxies, great computer behemoths that stored the vast wealth of information and knowledge from the long millennia preceding modern times. These had given him the tools he would need to author. The bioconcept computer had given him the gift.

He had liked the University in Old New Haven. He had liked the oldness and genuineness of it. The Earth he inhabited was foul and biologically wasted, its considerable natural resources of fossil energy, topsoil, and unpolluted water squandered and used up two thousand years earlier.

The only human beings still inhabiting the planet were merely caretakers for the great repositories within the solitary remaining geodesic dome. Just caretakers and, of course, authors. Still, at the University he discovered that,. though a dead planet in many ways, Earth still remained unparalleled as the birthplace of the greatest race of chroniclers and authors the known universe had seen.

Newton, the autocat, stroked his leg as he stepped off the Carpetram and entered the living area. Stone had acquired a living housecat of the Earth species when he was at the university. He'd ordered the Syndicators to construct one like it for him. Newton. He'd named it after the ancient science author, Sir Isaac Newton. The name seemed to fit. Bending down, he stroked the red tabby-like formfur and the autocat began purring. He liked the touch of it. Having been genetically concocted for a category that necessitated the human touch, he found that living without it was becoming more and more difficult. Authors needed the human touch in order to explain the mysteries of the race. Throughout the seven galaxies, only human beings were authors, and only authors were raised with the human touch. Others did not receive it because it was not deemed necessary by the Triumvirate for sub-mind vocations.

Why couldn't he author? What was the problem.? Was it because that expensive monstrosity had eased the creative pain too much? That was the point, wasn't it? An author has to bleed. Bleed inside as he squeezed all that was in him out — and out — until there was no more. He must feel the pain of reaching for the right word, the right turn of dialogue, the perfect metaphor. Pain, gnawing pain and a hunger from deep within. That was what an author must have.

The TADLO anesthetized the pain into simple boredom. No searching or straining for a thought. The TADLO merely reached into a memory storage lobe of Stone's brain and extracted precisely what he was trying to say before he could crystallize the feeling. And when the TADLO did that, he could not repeat another phrase pattern or creative sentence by himself.

"It's too goddamned easy," he muttered as he stepped back on the Carpetram. Newton scrambled up from primping to follow. "Take me to the parlor," he said softly.

The Carpetram glided forward swiftly and silently while the autocat shared his traveling disk. The parlor was the one thing that was different about his envirodome. It was the best and most expensive, bar none, on Earth. For Amos Stone, the parlor was absolute salvation. The price had been worth it.

The tram slowed indefinably at first, then quickly until the corridor fell silent again. Stone stepped off, clutching his drink and stood before a shining obelisk that guarded entry to the special room.

"Open," he said simply. The obelisk responded to his distinctive voice pattern and dilated soundlessly revealing a glowing energy-paneled chamber. Stone stepped inside and the opening closed, nearly bisecting Newton as it did. The autocat scampered in behind him.

Stone walked to the center of the chamber and looked at the glowing blue-green energy panels. He loved this room. One never needed a vacation with this holoparlor.

A mere thought could whisk the user to wherever, and whenever, he wanted.

"Scan my thoughts," he directed. Instantly, the glowing panels obeyed, showing a blur of random thought patterns, memories and, of all things, music. That was the best thing about this parlor, you could actually re-read your thoughts, hopes, memories, experiences, anything, in three-dimensional authenticity. Cheaper models had only exotic places and prerecords that required the user to merely be part of someone else's memories. The panels hummed for a moment then fell on an Earth scene from Stone's university days. He was standing on the Common of the University, tapetext bag slung carelessly around his young shoulders, a microviewer on his neck. A forgotten Amos Stone perfectly reproduced in three dimensions, standing on Earth as he had stood over a dozen years earlier.

"Amos, you know what I mean," she said, tugging at his arm. "Quit teasing me." The conjured-up memory of her was speaking just as they had spoken years before. His part-time companionmate, Vandra. She was the most important person in his life even today. She'd been long removed from his presence, of course. But that same ache still snaked through his body.

The real Amos Stone and his autocat were standing in the center of the university Common of his memory watching the past unfold before them. A streetskimmer seemed to pass through their bodies as they watched. They were there, but not there — silent observers watching Amos Stone's memory play out in perfect retrospect. Metallic pincer-like headphones emerged from the ceiling and dangled silently above his head. He reached up and adjusted them to his forehead.

"I am not teasing you," the remembered Amos said with feigned innocence. "I can't go to the tape selection ceremonies with you. I'm rearranging my sock drawer. And besides I have to memoryboard tonight."

"Your socks are not the only things that need rearranging. You're always cramming for exams. You wouldn't have to spend half your life with the memoryboard if you studied more," she remonstrated. As the real Stone drank in the scene, a smile slowly creased his face. He glanced down absently at the autocat washing its face with its paws, undisturbed by it all. Stone wondered if cats were washing their faces when they did that, or washing their paws and drying them on their faces.

He looked up. "Scan directly to language communication of time frame." Again the images blurred forward and froze. Stone bent closer to the image of Vandra standing with her hands clasped together. He reached to touch her, and his hand passed through the image cleanly. Just a beautiful memory he could see — not touch. Suddenly, Vandra's perfume washed over him like a tide. Then the music began again. It almost made him faint with longing. He composed himself, looked at her closely again.

"You're sure you can't go?" she asked with mock disappointment.

"You know I can," the young Amos smiled. "I just wanted to see if you would really miss not having me there. You wouldn't."

"Yes I would," she said petulantly, "or I wouldn't have asked." It was true. Vandra never did nor said anything she didn't mean.

"Why don't we skip it altogether and go up to your cube?" He suggested. "We could make our own scan-tape...."

"Because you are supposed to get the award, Mr. Intellectual, and besides it only happens to a very few people." She was smiling but determined, he decided. Newton stretched, as he was programmed to do every day at this time, and yawned luxuriously.

"Scan forward this part," Stone ordered.

As Stone waited for the next phase of his memory to play out its images, he thought of Earth. The living, breathing, sweating, fighting planet that had given rise to humankind in the first place. He was human and that was the problem. This block, "writer's block," it had been dubbed, was of an Earth in the far distant past. It was almost as if he were a genetic throwback of some sort. He needed to write on this Earth the way he would have written on that ancient Earth. A way that did not ease the pain of the creative mind so immediately as the TADLO did. A way that forced the brain to grapple with the context of each phrase, polishing the words until they worked. Suddenly it hit him! He was thunderstruck that he had not remembered before.

"Stop here!" he shouted. The panels slowed immediately and froze on a scene he had not viewed in a long time. Usually, he would scan forward to the late evening in Vandra's cube on her huge sleeping platform, where they had made love until morning. But tonight, for the first time in months, he did not want to view that memory right now. He wanted a different moment. A moment he only vaguely recalled from later in the day.

"Back further!" he snapped. "Maybe two hours."

The panels glowed again, fluttering from the increase of power expended, and resumed backward in memorytime. He began to feel the heat from the main energy sync-generator. "There, stop! That's it! Play at normal sequence." The panel glowed a soft blue-green again, then the colors of the memory leapt before his eyes. The time was late afternoon. He and Vandra were walking alone down a deserted street in the wharf section of the old city. They had walked for hours that day, he remembered, taking in the sights and smells and noises of the time-worn planet. A strong salt-and-sulfur smell permeated the chamber as the real Amos Stone watched with rapt attention.

"I've got something I want you to see in a little shop over here," she said excitedly. "I found it last trimester."

"What kind of shop can be down here?" He was curious. This was seediest part of Old New Haven. Rotting piers from a 90% salted ocean. The air smelling of sulfur and decaying lumber. Scores of junk and curio shops with memorabilia from a thousand different places and a thousand different times.

"Oh, it's just a junk shop," she said, "but I saw something in the display monitor I'd never seen before. It's absolutely perfect for you!" She glowed at the prospect of showing him something he'd not seen nor experienced on a teachtape before.

They rounded the corner to see a small quonset structure built in the old style. It was indistinguishable from the others on the street. A sign in the viewport read "closed." She scurried to the side entrance. Locked. The Keepercomp of the building had the structure in "neutral security drive" until the beginning of the next business day. There was no way in. Vandra was heartsick. He tried to reassure her that they could come. back, but she only shook her head.

"It was old and perfect for you. I wanted you to have it." Her voice dark with disappointment.

The blood-red sun pierced the polluted environment with crimson shards of light that stabbed at Stone's eyes. His countenance shimmered in the halflight as he watched transfixed the image that surrounded him and the sleeping autocat, Stone's eyes masked with a strange and silent look. He savored the long-forgotten recollection. In the afterglow, darting shadows danced on the two figures standing in the middle of the chamber.

"What was perfect for me?" the remembered Amos quizzed.

"The typewriter," she answered.

"Freeze here!" Stone yelled at the main drive compensator. The parlor ground down to a split-frame reproduction of his thoughts. He set his glass on what looked like pavement and strode to the window of the quonset. He peered around the two figures frozen in action to get a better look at the display monitor as he remembered it. Off to the left... there it was... a battered ancient-looking machine with tiny buttons, each indelibly designated by a different character. Old Earth characters representing letters of the Ancients' alphabet. — was what the machine was called.

"Forward!" he commanded, and the walls shuddered slightly before lurching into motion again. Vandra walked closer to the window and pointed to the object.

"A typewriter," she whispered, "it's the only one I have ever seen. That's the instrument that was used to pass on the flow from the creative minds to the masses. I've studied the culture, and though the tapes from the period are sketchy, it seems that this machine was more powerful than even nations' armies."

"That beat-up little piece of junk?" he asked sarcastically.

"I don't know how the power comes out of it, or how the machine was even used. There isn't much informational data on any tapes I've studied. But there was a phrase that seemed to designate its use."

"What?"

"'The power of the word,'" she said simply

After a moment of silence the remembered figures moved off down the street. Stone recalled how he had brushed the incident from his mind at the time. It was just a machine from another time, like the early servitors or wordwrites. Nothing more. He had never returned to the shop with her and, until now, the entire episode had been forgotten.

Suddenly, the panels flared with an intense white flash, then went totally dark. The power of the chamber hummed down to normal non-use levels.

"Up power!" he roared. Stone was angry at being jerked so abruptly from his contemplation. "Take me back to that scene again," he ordered. The panels remained silent and dark. The power drain of that much information and detail had been more than the energy cell could maintain, he realized. That would be all the memory holography for this evening. He glanced down at the autocat sleeping dreamlessly at his feet.

A typewriter. That was what she'd called it. What was it she said? It was the same phrase the TADLO salesman had used. "The power of the word." What power? What word? He didn't know. He had never known anyone who I d ever owned such a device, let alone knew how to use one.

As he reclined in his sleep capsule later, unable to sleep, he thought of the strange machine over and over in his mind. Vandra had seemed so sure that this "typewriter" would be of use to him. Why? Nobody authored with written script anymore. It was all wordwrite processors that translated directly into the brain of the receiver. No. written words down on a... a...? He realized that he didn't even know what you wrote the words onto. He'd go to the infotape repository in Rigel first thing in the morning and research it. He disliked the city but he'd make the two-hour journey to learn what he could. He had to discover the answer. A bio-concept author who couldn't author was of little financial benefit to publishers. Before he fell into a fitful sleep he instructed the Housecomp to prepare his skimmer for the two thousand kilometer flight.

"I'm sorry, that tape is restricted," the nasal tone of the tape custodian droned through the air. She smiled apologetically.

"Restricted? But why?"

"I'm not sure," she snorted. "Just that it is. Has been since I began to work here. The tapes have been sealed for much longer." She pointed to the red warning disk that was lodged in the screen file separator. When she punched the corresponding identification key, the message flashed into Stone's brain: "Tape restricted, not to be experienced. Official ban by the Triumvirate of the Seven Galaxies. Penalties for breach of this order apply under sections 23 and 25 of Thought Code."

Stone glided across the Plaza of the Seven Galaxies wondering why a machine from twentieth century Earth had been closed to all research. Such a restriction didn't make sense. That was nearly fifty centuries ago. What could possibly be threatening about a simple word machine from the dim past? He stayed on the street tram across Hannibal Day Boulevard and into the port of entry zone. Rigel was the only new-city of any consequence on Earth I's western plain. A port zone, it was always bustling with activity. Galactic travelers from as far as the Georgian system would stop here for rest and time off before ferrying their crafts back to the Ring Shuttle for light jumps to other destinations.

Stone looked at the silver needles aimed at the sky awaiting the seven-day return trip to the Shuttle for another cargo. In Rigel every kind of activity catering to the myriad requests and desires of humankind were supplied. Shops bought and sold anything according to caprice. Contraband from every corner of the universe was available to those with the credits to pay. Stone surveyed the different shop monitors.

He stepped off the tram into the mind beam and experienced the name of the establishment. "Gillespie's" was the simple encoded message. He walked through the entry portal and studied the display counters, each filled with rows of unique and strange items. Crystal assassin thought-knives from the Callaban System. Illegal on Earth. A pulsating Decduss, a minute furry creature that lived on blood, captured on the smaller moon of Lazdun. And a dozen or so sets of Copulators, very small human-looking creatures that entertained their owners by mating almost incessantly. Stone didn't expect to learn anything here really. He had been to twenty of these seedy little dens and had found no one who even understood what he was asking.

"Help you?" the voice boomed behind him. Stone wheeled around, startled, to see a huge, ancient-looking man looming over him.

"Yes. I mean I hope so...," he answered hesitantly.

"So do I. That's how I make money." The old man was big, at least twice his size. The hair was snow, the face and hands lined and wrinkled. He was, or had been in his youth, powerfully built. As he spoke, Stone suddenly realized that the man was not as old as he appeared. Premature aging caused by vacuum blood-fever, he guessed. The voice was younger than the body, and the eyes betrayed a youth long since covered over by sagging skin, liver warts, and a yellow pallor.

"The item I am seeking is a device, a machine from the twentieth century. It was called a typewriter. Kind of a manual wordwrite…." Stone's voice trailed off, unsure if he was being understood.

The old man's eyes narrowed. "They're illegal," the owner said quietly.

"So is everything you have here," Stone replied.

"Contraband knick-knacks is one thing. A Thought Code-banned instrument is another." He turned back to his credit counting.

"I can pay your price," Stone said softly. The ancient visage turned back to him.

"You're not one of those freedom fighters, are you?"

"No, I'm an author."

"I can't help you." The big man's face seemed to cloud over and then his eyes went opaque, putting Stone's request out of his mind. For an instant Stone thought he saw a glimmer of recognition flash in the man's eyes before they masked over the emotion.

"You know where one is, don't you?" Stone asked. He could feel something being kept from him. The old man knew and wouldn't say.

"I need that machine," Stone said with quiet pleading.

The man looked at him for a long time before speaking. "I don't need any problems with Galactic Security, and that's exactly what I'd have if someone heard I was selling Thought Code-banned instruments."

"No one will know," Stone stammered. "I can pay your price, and I can keep my mouth shut. Do you have one?"

"I might could get one," he said noncommittally, "but the price would be sixty-one hundred credit tokens. Half in advance. I don't get it, you lose your deposit."

"Done." Stone reached for his credit clip but a huge, gnarled hand stopped him.

"Tomorrow. Come alone. We'll see."

The next day Stone walked from the shop with a small case carrying the machine and a bundle of paper. The paper had cost him another one-hundred credit tokens. That's what the machine required in order to be used to designate the thoughts. Paper. Later he'd experience tapes on language and alphabet to learn what ancient writing meant and how to decipher it. He had his typewriter. He had his machine to break the block.

The next weeks were fevered work. Days and nights blended together as Stone wrestled with mastering the written language, and the manual dexterity required to work the machine. As the days passed the creativity once again began to flow in his mind. Now his fingers encoded the thoughts into language and his eyes learned to decipher and feed the images and emotions back to his brain. In the second month he'd completed fifteen chapters. In three months fifty. In six months two hundred, and still the words flowed.

After completing each chapter on paper he would laboriously feed the text back into the TADLO by voice activation to store the finished work on infotapes to be sent to his publisher. By the beginning of the cold season he was receiving glowing memotapes from his publisher on the excellence of his work. He was being regarded as the new master in authoring throughout the galaxies. His fame was growing to legendary proportions. And still the words flowed.

The typewriter drew him like a magnet again and again to experience the search for excellence, to feel the finished manuscript in his hands, to suffer over dialogue, to draw out the creativity in his brain. His every waking hour was filled with its power. Nothing else in his life seemed to matter except the flowing of the words. Since he'd bought the machine, he had to make two more trips to Rigel for paper and the price had been dear. But then no price was too dear to pay for the creative power he experienced. The typewriter and the words it poured forth supplanted all other facets of Stone's life. The holography parlor sat empty for months. The machine had become the obsession of his life.

In the fourth season after acquiring the machine, Stone was nominated as "Chronicler of the Triumvirate." He was known throughout all of the seven galaxies. People of all vocations made pilgrimages to Earth just to see his envirodome which was now part of a lucrative colonial venture for the arts, tours offered by enterprising agents from Rigel. Every tape he published made his fame grow and with it his power to change minds. Amos Stone was barely forty when his work was canonized by the Triumvirate.

"Mr. Stone, I am Morris, Galactic security. I have been sent from the council to speak with you."

The official flashed his identity disk on the infocube as the Housecomp opened the portal to admit him. Stone barely had time to hide the machine in his sleep capsule before the security officer arrived at his work study.

"Your presence is required," Morris said officiously, "the council wants to 'consider' your work."

The tone was flat and ominous. Morris was a tall angular man, and Stone had the impression that he looked oddly like a tongue depressor from the ancient medicine tapes he'd experienced.

"What is the extent of the consideration the Council wants?" Stone asked.

"That would be security blocked information, sir. The council will advise you. You will be coming."

It wasn't a question. It was a command. The man waited without emotion for a response. Stone nodded slowly.

"That would be a... yes?"

"That would be a 'yes'," Stone heard himself repeat quietly.

The Council probed into his works on the species and his tapes on the preclusion policies of the Triumvirate. The Council was deferential to his status as the only living canonized author, but persistent in its inquiries as to the exact process by which he authored. Stone told them of the TADLO Series E 6000 and lied magnificently about its capabilities of defining the creative.

After two days of close scrutiny on his work, he was allowed to return to begin the commissioned. biography of the three females who comprised the Triumvirate. Stone was not sure if the Council believed him but he knew he must be very careful. He also knew that without the typewriter he was nothing. He worked like a man possessed now. He slept little, barely ate any meals and never left his envirodome. The typewriter was rarely out of his reach anytime day or night. It possessed him, nurtured him, drove him, and finally consumed him.

It was late. He had just finished the biography when the idea struck him. He must give those who experienced him the truths he'd learned from words. He must give them the power to free their minds. That moment, Amos Stone began his final work: The Freedom Tapes.

He worked on the little machine incessantly, resting only when fatigue caused him to literally slump at his writetable exhausted. The pages flowed out of him like an enormous unending stream of water that grew more voluminous by the hour. When his fingers began to cramp from typing, he would go to the TADLO and start the tedious process of feeding the finished manuscript into its memory banks to be compiled and transferred to the Ring Shuttle for delivery to his publisher. Two months after beginning he was finished.

The Housecomp announced that the contingent from Galactic Security was arriving in a few minutes. Stone had expected it to take a little longer, but then he wasn't really surprised that they were here. His publishers would have been in touch with the council as soon as the first chapter had arrived. At least he'd finished. He instructed the Housecomp to drop the skimmer shields and allow the security force in. This time he didn't even bother to hide the manuscripts or the paper he had left. Only the typewriter was secreted away in a hidden vacuum storage unit of his write-room.

"You have transgressed the Thought Code, Mr. Stone," the Lord High Prosecutor intoned precisely into the voice simulator. "The penalties for such a breach of Triumvirate law are well known, I believe?"

The androids sitting in judgment hummed lowly to indicate that they were. Stone glanced, for a moment, at the screen in front of him. The entire population of the Seven Galaxies would be watching this trial. His hands chaffed at the electrocuffs clamped tightly around each of his fingers. He was sitting in a small cubicle in the Galactic security detention fortress of Tritania watching his fate being decided, along with millions of his followers — by proxy.

"In their infinite wisdom, the Master Females of the Triumvirate knew that certain of the machines which the human race had developed would cause general unrest and present a threat to the well-being and general tranquillity of all," the Lord High Prosecutor stated. "This is the most evil and pernicious of all!" The android held up the small dented typewriter.

Stone felt his heart rising to his throat. They had found it! Of course they had. That was their job. It was over.

The Lord High Prosecutor had continued at length on the meaning of the Thought Code and how it was for the good of all, not just the good of a few. At one point, Stone laughed before he could stop himself and an instant painful jolt coursed through his body. His thoughts and actions during the proceedings were being monitored closely by the inquisitor robots. He was not allowed any editorializing.

The outcome was assured. There was merely an ending formality.

Verdict: Guilty

Sentence: Erasure.

Floating weightlessly in the detention capsule, cut off from all contact, Stone thought how he had flowed with the creative gift. He had been able to give words to his very soul with that machine, and therefore had given the souls of all who experienced him a small vision of truth. For this single act he was being totally erased from history. His mind would be wiped clean in one instantaneous flash, erased completely from conscious thought. Amos Stone would be a nonentity from that moment forward.

On the appointed day, at the appointed hour, the inquisitor robots came to take him from his weightless prison. They led him to the cleansing station. Forty other Thought Code violators were to be erased with him. While waiting to fill out and sign complete code-breaking confessions, Stone studied his fellow captives. Some were artists who had painted the truth as they saw it. Some were freedom fighters captured on their missions of unrest throughout the galaxies. Some, just believers in his words. Stone was touched to realize that he had inspired this devotion. These people were actually proud to be erased on the same day as Amos Stone.

"Again I am honored to be in your presence, Mr. Stone," the small voice whispered behind him. Stone turned. It was the TADLO salesman.

"What are you doing here?" Stone asked, startled.

"The same as you, Mr. Stone," the small man replied, "I am to be erased for my Code violations."

"Code violations? What violations could you have committed?"

"The same ones you did," was the soft reply.

"But… you're just a wordwrite salesman, how…?"

"Looks, like thoughts, are deceiving — are they not, Mr. Stone?" He smiled. Suddenly, he wriggled and shook violently. His visage transformed before Stone's eyes. He was the shop owner, where Stone had bought the typewriter! A transmute!

"I knew that you would understand the power and give it to the people who so desperately needed it. You. You were the voice that millions had to experience!" The transmute leaned over conspiratorially. "We had to save the machine, waiting for the day when you would come looking to break the block. You are surprised that I know of the block? I know. Only those who seek to give flow, to the true creative, experience the block. Yes, you were the one. Of course, it had to be a male because all females' thought processes are identical to the Triumvirate."

Inquisitor robots herded them all toward the large cleansing station, and as Stone let himself be carried on by the throng, he thought of what he had accomplished. Perhaps nothing. However, because the galaxies were bound by their own law, his tapes would not be destroyed. He was a canonized author. Only his mind, memory, and personality would be gone. His tapes would be experienced by generations beyond this time, maybe bootlegged into small infocubes to be experienced by lovers of truth and beauty in the far distant future. The millions who would never have a creative thought of their own.

Standing in the cleansing station, head bowed, hands shackled Stone waited for the purification beam to be directed at him. Just before his consciousness melted into the abyss of nothingness, he thought of the small machine that had condemned him to this. Then he thought of his creative flow being stopped forever — but blocked it out.

Craig Clyde

A native of Washington State, Craig Clyde has been in media related ventures during his career. After a stint as a high school English teacher, Clyde began his professional media career in radio and television first in Idaho and then in Utah, where he has resided for the past thirty years. In addition to his media experience, Clyde is an actor who has appeared in over sixty major films and national television programs for all the major networks — as well as numerous stage roles. He is a member of Actor's Equity and the Screen Actor's Guild. He has won numerous awards for his screenwriting and directing (including writing the scripts for the films he directed) as well as over two dozen feature film screenplays and two novels. He is married and lives with his family in Salt Lake City.

Cat and the Yule Fire

In the years long ago, when the world was much younger and things were not so set in their ways, the Lady came to guest at a Yuletide gathering.

Now, this in itself was not so unusual, for she frequently comes to guest in houses where she is welcomed, but this night, a cat, whose name is known only to cats these days, slipped into the house and bespoke her.

"Goddess, I'd have a word with you, if you please." Said the cat.

The Lady nodded, for cats were made clever as well as arrogant, and she was curious to hear what this one might say. Besides, cats and humans didn't live together in those days, and so meeting a cat inside a house was far from unusual. They slipped out of the house, each in their own secret way, and walked under the stars, leaving only one set of prints in the snow.

"Well?" Said the Lady, when she and the cat stood at the distance where the light from the house's windows met the darkness of the cold, clear night.

"Goddess, tonight is the long night, when the humans burn their fires."

"Yes, it's the Yuletide. They burn the fires, so the sun will return and bring the green of spring to keep the world alive."

The cat sat, daintily, and curled her tail around herself. It was a cold night for cats, though it scarcely bothered the Lady, who is cold only if she wishes to be.

"Goddess, what would happen if the humans failed to burn the sun-fires?" said the cat, licking a front paw thoughtfully.

"The sun would dim and fail, and winter would freeze the world, forever. This is no secret, cat. The humans were made to be stewards of the earth; to keep the balances and restore them when the wheel that is the year goes astray. Keeping these fires is part of their purpose, just as keeping the secrets cats hold is part of yours."

The cat's washing had passed, slowly and methodically, to her whiskers, then to her ears.

"Yes," she said, "but humans are forgetful".

"They were made to be what they are, cat. Even we Gods may forget, from time to time, just as cats do. Why should humans be different?"

"Cats never forget the secrets in our charge," said the cat, unruffled. "We cannot. Humans can forget their duties though."

"That's why there're so many of them." Said the Lady, with chuckling softly. "So that, while some may forget, others won't."

"Goddess," said the cat, all pretense of carelessness forgotten, "That isn't right. It isn't right at all."

The Lady gazed reproachfully at the cat. There were limits to what arrogance she'd suffer, even from cats, who were supposed to be that way.

"Lady, listen to me." (Cats can be respectful, you know, especially when they're on thin ice.) "Humans keep the holy days, the balances and the fires and all. Well and well again. But the day will come, someday, when the last of them will forget to do so, and the fires will not burn, and then we will all die."

"So?" Said the Lady, patiently. "All things die, eventually. You know that, cat."

"Goddess, it is wrong that our survival - the survival of cats and everyone else — should depend upon nothing more than the frailty of human memory. The sun is too important a thing to trust them not to forget to call back. This isn't well done, Goddess. It isn't well done at all.

The Lady nodded thoughtfully. "You have a point, cat. Though I think it'll be a long, long time until that day comes, still you have a point."

Then the Lady smiled. "All right cat. I'll put an end to your worries. Come closer."

The cat did, the Lady picked her up, which the cat certainly did not like, and took her back, unseen, into the house to stand before the Yule log burning in the hearth.

"So, you want to keep the fires burning, even though the humans may forget?"

"Yes," said the cat. "Otherwise I wouldn't have bothered you in the first place."

"All right," said the Lady, and with that, she chucked the cat into the Yule fire.

"Owwwwwwwwww!" screeched the cat, who ran smoking, but not quite burned, out of the fireplace. Sparks and cinders flew about the room, as the cat fled through a window left open to let out the extra heat from the fire.

The Lady caught-up with the cat outside, and the cat squared off with her; back arched, spitting, eyes flaming with rage. She picked the cat up by the scruff of its neck to prevent it from scratching her, pulled a leaf out of her bodice with her other hand, then blew on the leaf, causing it to turn into a green mist, which the cat inhaled, sneezing furiously all the time.

Then she dropped the cat, with a flourish, into the snow at her feet.

"Now you have your wish," the Lady said. I've given you, and all cats from this day forward, another secret to keep. I've given you a bit of the Yule fire, and a bit of the springtime green as well. Now if the humans ever forget to light the fires at Yuletide, I'll take them from you again, and together we'll bring the sun back."

The cat managed, at length, to choke out something resembling a thank-you. (Her dignity, after all, had been seriously ruffled, and her coat singed.)

"There's a price to go with it, though. As with all fires, this one must be tended. As it's the fire of the sun, you'll now spend the day soaking-up as much of the sun as you can manage. You'll crave warmth, though you'll still be able to stand the cold. And to keep the green of spring in you alive also, you'll have to eat grass or other green things, now and then."

"I am a cat. I eat grass eaters. I do not eat grass!" spat the cat.

"You do now," observed the Lady with a smile that could've been called smug, were she not a Goddess. Oh, and one other thing."

The cat produced a glare, in reply, which might have been said to be questioning. It certainly wasn't pleasant, in any case.

"As you're now keeping the fires, which is one of the duties given to humans, and since you'll now have special needs, you and the humans will keep company from now on. That will serve to remind you of your new responsibilities, and allow you to keep an eye on them, should they start to get forgetful. It'll also keep you close to their hearth fires, so that the fire I've given you won't perish, even in the cloudiest of winters."

The cat spat, venomously and loudly, at the thought of having to give-up her cherished independence.

"You did ask for this, you know," murmured the Lady. Surely it's better than trusting the sun to something so frail as human memory."

"I am a cat. I am not a servant. I am no-one's servant!"

The Lady shook her head. "Not a servant, no, but an equal. You can work the details of your cohabitation amongst yourselves. That is, once you convince the humans to take you in, of course."

"What?!? Am I to go to them a-begging and pleading for them to please take me in?"

"Well now, your new gift would hardly remain a secret if we told them about it, would it?"

The cat began swearing. The Lady went back to the Yule fire. The cat continued to swear. Swearing, for cats, is an involved and elaborate art form, and it's said this particular cat was at it a week or more. Eventually though, the memories of the warmth and light of the hearth in the house drew her there where, with no little difficulty and a great deal of initial distrust on both sides, she eventually convinced the humans she'd be a fine companion and a useful addition to their household.

And that is why, to this day, the green witch-fires of springtime glow in the eyes of cats. Just in case. And it's also why cats lie in the sun and in the warm places, and why they eat grass, when they think no-one is looking, for they don't want to be embarrassed in front of the other meat eaters, as cats are known to be vain. It's also the story of why, though cats live with humans, they insist upon being treated as equals, and why they frequently look as if they're hiding something.

They are. Cats are full of secrets, but that's another story, one the cats won't tell to anyone.

That is the story of all these things, and it happened just so, many years ago, before anyone now living was born. Oh, and don't ask me how I came to know it.

After all, I promised the cat I wouldn't tell.

Cat Dubh

Born in Michigan, later relocated to the Great Pacific Northwest, Cat Dubh has been an office clerk, computer programmer, technical writer, bureaucrat, and professional layabout. He has had poetry, fiction. and non-fiction published in several publications under various names, including 'The Michigan Voice' and 'Cup of Wonder'. Cat is happily married to an award-winning playwright, and spends his time between Oregon's Willamette valley and its high plains desert. His interests include sagebrush, waterfalls, rock-hounding, photography, and the martial arts, not necessarily in that order.

The Follower

The rain was hard and cold. It was the kind of cold rain that soaked through your cloak, your armor, your skin, and swallowed your soul in its icy grasp. Gavin De Fey was not happy about it at all. He was miserable, utterly miserable. He was going to get soaked and he knew it. His long sword and dagger were probably going to rust right through at this rate. All right, he thought, it was an exaggeration, but there was more than an ounce of truth to it.

Gavin pulled his cloak tighter around himself, as if it would do any good. He had at least another ten miles to the town of Molsher. His horse, however, was already weary from the last three days of riding.

He sighed, resigning himself to dying of a cold. He spurred his horse on. Dying of a cold was not the way for a Temple Knight of Selenati to die. He was supposed to die gloriously in battle. Not from uncontrollable fits of sneezing. With that thought the rain began to fall harder, as if to mock him.

The knight looked up at the cloudy evening sky and started "Selenati, I have served you faithfully. Why is this," he threw up his hands to gesture around him, "happening to me?" Getting no answer, he sighed again and continued riding.

It watched the rider slowly leave the area. It could feel the human's suffering. This was, however, a superficial suffering. It would evaporate as soon as the rider became warm and dry. No, it liked true suffering; but anguish was even tastier to it. There must be a way to make this lone human a tastier meal. There must be some way to increase his torment. As it considered this, its eyes followed the rider.

Gavin stopped his horse and put his hand on the hilt of his sword. He was being watched. He could feel eyes on his back, like pinpricks of ice on his spine. It was a dark, malevolent gaze as if a Tretati demon spawn or an assassin was following him. He slowly, cautiously, turned around, oblivious to the rain. He scanned the open ground behind him. He saw...nothing but his own tracks. His bright green eyes slowly tracked the sky, but nothing flew overhead. Then he stopped and listened. Nothing. There was no noise, except the heavy patter of the cold rain. He looked behind himself again. Again he saw nothing. He spurred the horse on. "Something is not right...or maybe it is just the damnable rain." Gavin De Fey muttered to himself. With that he rode on.

It watched the rider's reaction from the shadows. This was not what it expected. There was defiance and courage in the rider. The human must be a solider of one sort or another. It had not unsettled the human so much as made him more vigilant. This would certainly add flavor to its meal when it did devour the human. Courage and defiance broken by suffering and anguish was a spicy and tasty treat.

The Temple Knight breathed a sigh of relief. Ahead of him was a thick coniferous forest. It was the Silver Forest, if Gavin was not mistaken. The forest took its name from the way the snow and ice glittered off the trees in the winter. Its tall pine trees would provide him at least some cover from the rain. As he slowly entered the forest he looked up into the sky. Between the clouds he could just barely make out the moon hanging low in the sky. He smiled, drew his sword, and saluted her. After all, Selenati was the Goddess of the Moon. He said a small prayer and sheathed his sword. He then continued to ride into the forest. The sound of animals greeted him. Off to his left a squirrel scurried across the trail only taking brief notice of the knight. The soft scent of pine almost enveloped him. Gavin De Fey took comfort in these small things and felt his spirit rise.

Strange, it thought to itself, that the solider stopped and saluted the forest. Was he a ranger? Or a Tretati half-demon perhaps? No, he did not have the Tretati pointed ears, and was not nearly tall or muscular enough. No, he was human.

Obviously, the subtle approach would not work. His thought dripped with malicious intent. Its body coiled up on itself, its eyestalks wavered. Thoughts of pain, agony and terror welled through it. Terror, yes terror, would work on this human soldier. What human could face its creations? It chuckled to himself as a dark plan entered its mind.

Gavin had been riding for an hour and a half and making good time. The canopy of this thick forest was not letting much rain though. The smell of the pine had stayed with him, almost clinging to him like a security blanket. Even his horse's spirits seem to rise. Then the horse started to nicker and stopped unexpectedly. "What's wrong girl?" He asked. Her only response was a shaking of her head. Gavin looked around, but everything seemed normal.

Then the eyes were upon him once more. Gavin drew his sword and swung about in his saddle. But again there was nothing there. He looked around, something was wrong. Someone was following him. There it was again, the complete lack of noise. None, that is, except for his own breathing. The rain had stopped and the animals were not making a sound. It was the quiet of the grave. The calm before a battle, that is what it reminded Gavin of. Taking the reigns by his left hand he kept his sword unsheathed in his right. "Come on girl, lets get moving." he said and urged the horse forward.

Yes, it thought to itself as it floated through the woods, this would work well. It would be wonderfully delicious. It smiled at its own cunning.

Up ahead Gavin could see a small house, a large hut or cottage really. Its thatched roof had not been repaired recently, but looked serviceable not the less. The walls looked to be made of oak and well constructed. The rock slab chimney, at the back center of the cottage, had obviously seen better days. There looked to be some sort of garden behind it, but Gavin could not make it out from where he was. There was a scent emanating from the house as he drew closer, it smelled like apple fritters. Gavin smiled, he loved those as a child.

Gavin sheathed his sword as he approached the cottage. It would not be proper for a knight to ask for aid from a family while carrying naked steel. Gavin swung off his horse and walked to the cottage. He could see a light in the main room. Through the windows were curtained he could hear movement inside.

Gavin stepped up to the old pine door and knocked. He heard shuffling from inside the house. He threw back the hook of his soaked cloak. As he did so the door creaked open. Standing there was a man and a woman both looked to be old, close to his grandparents' age. As he smiled at them he noticed their smiles had fangs and the old woman's hands had claw that she was drawing up to rake him with. The old man made a hissing noise and jumped at him his claws bared

Gavin dropped to his right and rolled. He sprang to his feet drew his sword and slashed. The blade connected and dug deep into the old man's chest sending him reeling back. Gavin followed through, then reversed his swing aiming higher and decapitating the old man. The feigns body fell to the floor and ruptured into flames. The Knight flinched from the brightness, and momentarily dropped his guard.

The old woman rushed at him and slashed at his chest, ripping his cloak. Her claws did little damage against his breastplate. Gavin retreated back a few steps and she rushed again.

She clawed at him again. His sword came up and awkwardly parried the blow. With his left hand he grabbed his dagger and stuck into the old woman's chest. She stumbled back a foot or two. It was enough; Gavin brought the sword up and completely through the woman's chest from the bottom left pelvic up to her right shoulder. She staggered back a little further. He brought the sword back around and cut clean through her neck. Blood spurted from the wound. Gavin jumped back as the body hit the ground and burst into flames.

The cottage was on fire; the ghouls it had created from the human couple were dead. However, it was all for not. The human soldier was fortified; his courage shinned light a beacon. He was weary, yes. He was tired, yes. But he was not in terror.

Then a thought struck it. The soldier's sword had caused the ghouls to bust into flames through out the fight. Only a consecrated sword, a holy sword, would do that. He was a Temple Knight, not an ordinary soldier. Temple Knights were trained to fight creatures of darkness, like those ghouls. Its fangs slavered as he thought. There was one way to make a Temple Knight feel terror. It had not done this in a long time; perhaps this would be fun, even exciting.

Gavin De Fey sat on the ground catching his breath. He was tired, his arms and legs seemed to be barely responding to him. He slowly felt his chest heave for air. It was not so much physical exhaustion as mental fatigue. He had never faced ghouls before and the suddenness of the fight had surprised him. That on top of his four-day journey had wiped him out. His fingers began toying with his crest moon medallion, the holy symbol of his order.

He looked up in time to see his horse fall to the ground in heap. Gavin sat there in studded amazement. What was going on, he wondered. Then, his fatigue seemingly forgotten, he jumped up his sword at the ready.

At first it was a whisper, then it grew louder, it sounded like rushing air, a strong breeze. Then turned into a roar, by then the sound was all but on top of him. There, emerging from invisibility was a creature with a huge fanged mouth and five eyes stalks bobbing from its head. Its head sat on a serpent-like body from which seven tentacles slithered and prepared to strike. The foul creature dripped with a blue, gelatinous slime.

It sprang on him and its teeth connected with his left shoulder, tearing through his armor, ripping apart his flesh and muscle. Gavin screamed in agony as the pain shot through his body like hot iron.

The creature whipped two of it tentacles at Gavin. By reflex, and nothing more, his sword came up and parried. In doing so he severed one of the tentacles. The scream the monster let out sounded like the roaring fires of a furnace, and felt like such. The creature struck again this time the Knight was ready and severed both tentacles. The creature's agonizing scream almost overwhelmed him. Gavin could feel the terror in that scream; it made him shudder in fright. But it also emboldened him, this creature bleed and it knew pain, he could kill it.

Gavin dropped to the ground as the creature dove at him, then thrust his sword upward into the creature's body. Another scream, more agony for both the creature and him. For as the sword tore through the creatures flesh it's blood poured out on to him. The creature's blood burned into him, as acid would have. He screamed in pain and dropped his sword. He rolled up to his knees. He watched the creature turn and stare at him; he stared back at it. Silence hung in the air. The moment hung for an eternity. Neither flinched, neither moved, they simply stared at each other.

Slowly Gavin grabbed his sword and stood up. He was a Temple Knight, sworn to protect the weak and defend the world against such foul creatures. He was a Temple Knight; he would not give in to fear or terror. He couldn't, Gavin would not allow himself to. With a war cry he charged the creature. The creature let loose a blood curdling scream and charged him. Gavin's sword met the creature's flesh. The creature's head connected with Gavin's chest.

It slowly limped through the forest, bleeding. Being half-blind it was not very aware of where it was going. It did not matter, it just need to escape. It looked back only once on the figure of the Temple Knight, kneeling there wounded, but alive. Yes, the Temple Knight would live, it was sure of that. The knight was an exceptional human. He could turn his fear into courage, his weakness into strength. That was to be respected, that was to be feared.

Richard Ferris

Richard Ferris is a "Navy Brat" raised on both the east and west coast. He graduated from San Diego State University, with a BA in Political Science. Not long after this, through a strange tale, he ended up in St. Paul, Minnesota where he lives with his wife, Christina. The story was inspired when the author got caught in sudden down pour while going to school in San Diego.

Channel Surfing

Rebecca Kaufman, disciple of the New Age, believer in astrology, reader of Tarot, and frequent patron of The Ark metaphysical shop, waited impatiently for Stephan to show up. She felt so spooked she'd turned all the lights on and the TV off, and was pacing between her tiny kitchen — plates and pans waited to be loaded into the dishwasher — and dining room. She held the remote control in one hand, and every now and again her free hand automatically shoveled imitation butter flavored microwaved popcorn from a clear glass bowl into her mouth. With her preoccupation she barely tasted it.

She couldn't get Aphrodite out of her mind. The woman had appeared without warning, and now Rebecca had no way to get rid of her. Who was she? A messenger from God? It didn't seem likely, in spite of her angelic beauty. The blond whose image and voice were transmitted from…somewhere could be a goddess. Yet even with her angelic beauty, she seemed too sensual, too casual to be speaking for the One Source of Everything. She might be a being from another star system, or a spirit from the Other Side.

Rebecca had read Ruth Montgomery on walk-ins, the messages of the Pleiadian emissaries, and the entity Bashar's optimistic forecast of earth's future. All their lofty words and predictions, replete with the mysteries of multidimensional knowledge, had been directed towards the human race in general, and discussed larger, cosmic issues. But Aphrodite almost seemed to address Rebecca directly, and dealt with practical, even mundane, questions of relationships, as though she were part evangelist and part pop psychologist.

Rebecca recalled her pilgrimage from Santa Fe to Seattle for a Seth intensive a few years before Jane Roberts died. She'd sat in a large hall where rapt followers listened as Seth replaced Roberts' own personality. He'd talked about human reality as camouflage for the many spheres of nonphysical reality those inhabiting a body couldn't fathom. People had difficulties with overdeveloped egos that kept them bound in their illusory physical perceptions. He'd used the same words over and over, speaking repeatedly about alternate systems of reality, of consciousness as the force behind matter, and of the necessity for compassion in transforming the earth.

Rebecca — forty-three, blond hair permed into curls, a chunky 175 pounds at five three, blue eyes intensified by tinted contacts — failed to recognize that what she took away from the channelings above all else were envy and resentment. She envied Roberts because Seth chose her and not Rebecca as his earthly contact, and she resented Seth's assumption that she couldn't understand. She prided herself on her humility as an actualized individual. She delivered her favorite saying, "I have to live in my truth," with a hint of superiority, and her self-understanding was remarkable for its almost complete absence.

Stephan knocked on her door. Stephan because he never used the doorbell, and because she expected no one else at this hour. She opened it.

"What took you so long? I am totally freaking out."

He towered over her by a foot. "Long? You woke me up, for Christ sake. I have to go to work in the morning."

"Hmm. Your aura's kind of muddy. A lot of brown." She rarely thought of apologizing. When someone's point of view differed from hers, she chalked it up to short-sightedness.

She shut and locked the door. "It's that satellite thing they set up this afternoon. It's creepy."

"If it isn't working right I can take care of it another time." Stephan, who programmed classified computer simulations having to do with nuclear waste disposal at Los Alamos National Laboratory, served as both her boyfriend and handyman. "It's working fine. Sort of. I just want you to see what's on. Then tell me I'm not going crazy. It's the strangest thing." Sometimes Stephan, like most people, responded best to being told what to do. "Don't be irritated until you see what it is. Come and sit on the sofa."

She pulled out a of couple of diet Cokes from the fridge, set the bowl of popcorn on the coffee table, and sat next to him. "Are you ready?"

As the top salesperson of the year at Western Natural Botanicals, Rebecca had won the system: thirty-two inch flat screen TV, four head super VHS VCR, DirectTV hardware, and a year of the full HBO and Showtime package She'd forged new territory with the young company, bullying regional buyers of Whole Foods and Wild Oats, along with lesser chains, into buying the entire line of shampoos, skin cleansers, creams, and rinses. "I'm not selling you the Antioxidant Skin Purifier unless you take the new White Sage Hair Treatment Program. Shampoo, Conditioner, and Restorer....Start with three dozen cases of each for a few stores and I'll call you in a month....No, a dozen cases isn't enough." The attractively packaged products usually sold well and her bravado paid off.

Stephan washed some popcorn down with a swig of cola. "I'm ready. This better be good."

She pointed the remote in the direction of the new hardware and pressed System On. "Look. Channel One."

The digital picture resolved into a woman's image from the shoulders up. She wore no jewelry and a simple white pullover blouse that covered her shoulders. She seemed to be in the middle of speaking, yet they tuned in at a good starting point. "I have only one message, and I will explain it to you as many times and in as many ways as you need to hear it. What you are lacking in life is the knowledge of how to love. What you need to learn first is the difference between love and attachment, so that is where we'll begin. Your fear of loving another, you believe, protects you from pain. In reality, it's your fear of losing something you possess which generates pain."

She stopped for effect, giving her words time to sink in.

"Her name's Aphrodite," Rebecca said. "Like the ancient Greek goddess of love."

The figure on the screen continued. "When you say, 'I love you,' what do you really mean? You tend to equate love with a strong bond of connection, or a desire 'to have and to hold' as marriage vows declare, or perhaps an intense feeling of wanting to be with the other person. You may say you're in love when your world becomes colored by overwhelming warm and tender feelings, or when the image of the other person so dominates your inner life you can't escape it."

"She's beautiful, isn't she?" Rebecca asked. She was, in fact, the most flawless blond Rebecca had seen. Rebecca wished she looked like that.

"Angelic," Stephan said.

Aphrodite resumed her monologue. "Love is none of these things. The bonds you associate with love, however natural they seem, contradict the basic liberty love requires. To have and hold indicates possession, and love's house has no room for acquisition. When you truly love someone, you support that person's highest good. Freedom and possession cannot exist together. Love is not attachment."

Rebecca pushed the mute button and watched the silent lips continue moving.

"So what's the problem?" Stephan asked.

"First, it's on Channel One. There's not supposed to be anything on Channel One. There's never anything on Channel One. I called DirectTV and they said there's no programming on Channel One." She pressed Guide and the channel menu came up, starting with Channel Two.

"You're getting an extra channel for free, then."

She handed him the remote and told him to go to any other station. He switched to the movie menu and pressed *The Way We Were*. A Central Park scene came on.

"OK. Now turn it off." He found the power button, pressed it, and the set went blank. "If you turn it back on, what should happen?"

"We get to see how Barbra Streisand and Robert Redford looked when they were young."

"Go ahead."

He pressed the button and Aphrodite's perfect features filled the screen. "When you fall in love, the other becomes the epicenter of your universe. It feels wonderful, but it isn't love, since it occurs before you really know the person. You see only the positive parts of the other, or project what you want to see based on your own needs."

Stephan pressed the mute button. "That's odd."

"Try to delete it," Rebecca commanded.

Stephan read in the instruction manual how to remove unwanted channels. He eliminated a Spanish network, which Rebecca couldn't understand, and an evangelical Christian one, in some ways even less comprehensible to her. But Channel One wouldn't obey, and the talking head with the mellifluous voice reappeared every time he tried.

"I thought at first maybe it was me. You know, maybe I was losing it. But it's really happening, isn't it?"

"You have an oddly behaving channel," scientifically-minded Stephan concurred.

"It's more than odd. I feel like my home has been invaded." She turned off the television. "Stay with me tonight. I don't want to be alone."

"It's still just a TV, and I have to be at the office early."

"Then let me stay with you. That's even better. I don't want to spend the night here."

"Not tonight, honey. Just keep the tube off."

Rebecca slept well that night in Stephan's queen sized bed, although she kept him awake by rolling several times onto his side of it, then pulling the light cotton blankets off him when he pushed her away. The following afternoon he complained about having ticked off his supervisor by missing an early meeting.

Her sales calls she drove south to Albuquerque for small accounts that placed reliable but unspectacular orders went well that day. She returned home with some trepidation and hesitated at the front door, fearing more than expecting to see her casita rearranged, hit by a poltergeist, or blond Aphrodite relaxing in a chair casually sipping a lemonade.

She'd decorated her little adobe house, originally guest quarters set behind a larger home, in Southwest style: Taos sofa and chairs, brightly colored Talavera vases, a rustic armoire and Mexican chest and banco. A few blocks west of Sanbusco on a quiet cul-de-sac, it was only a ten minute stroll to Santa Fe's historic plaza, a walk she always eschewed in favor of her car.

She let herself in. It was just as she had left it the night before, including the partially full soda cans and glass bowl with a few unpopped kernels. She picked up the remote and turned on the television.

"Giving yourself fully and completely to love is the most difficult task you will ever face." The blond paused. Rebecca shrugged. What was so difficult about it?

Light suffused around Aphrodite like a halo, she smiled delicately, and spoke in the comforting tones of a loving mother. "You naturally fear death, annihilation. Unconsciously, you equate this with the disappearance of the ego, the swallowing up of the self that comes from deep union with another. 'But I want intimacy,' you say. Then what prevents you from staying close?"

Rebecca had an answer for that one. Men. How many times had they rebuffed her efforts at intimacy, telling her they needed space?

"When you look for an explanation outside yourself, when you blame someone else, you lose the opportunity to know your own heart and to open yourself to love."

This Aphrodite could get tedious. Finger hesitating on the power button, Rebecca continued listening.

Aphrodite went on, "Closeness itself produces the anxiety that you'll be engulfed, demolished. The easy solution is to back off, and that's exactly what you do. Yet you're afraid to stray too far because you'll lose the connection altogether. So your fears, of closeness on the one hand and of distance on the other, keep you oscillating back and forth."

Who did this woman think she was, teaching Relationships 101 as though lecturing a freshman college course? What qualifications could she claim? Rebecca, who would have denied her anger had anyone been there to point it out, took satisfaction in turning off the screen. She cleaned up the kitchen and ran the dishwasher, then returned to the living room, drawn to the couch with no intention of watching the blond bimbo. She fiddled idly with the remote, and, unaware of conscious intention, lightly depressed the switch.

"You move emotionally closer, wanting the blissful union love will bring. But before you get it, or perhaps *because* you get it, you are suddenly too near. You fear, most likely unconsciously, that your individuality will be swallowed up. Your ego will dissolve. In panic you back away, farther and farther."

Okay, she'd just heard this drivel. Yet she let the voice drone on.

"You're comfortable now, at a safe remove. You won't be assimilated. But soon you get the sense that things aren't going well. You're so emotionally unavailable that your loved one seems to be at too great a distance. Maybe you notice he needs more than you're giving. Or, after a while, you need more than he wants to give. You begin to fear losing him."

Why all this talk of a "he," as though the disembodied image on the screen knew a woman was watching?

"Acting from fear of loss, you allow the feelings of caring, those nice warm fuzzies, to come up again, and you feel closer. So your life goes on like a yo-yo, back and forth endlessly. Everyone has a string of a different length, maybe a different color. Some of you spend more time in closeness, holding the yo-yo in your hand, and some spend more time out at the furthest length, circling your loved one at a distance, going around the world. But you're all attached to the end of the string."

Rebecca couldn't stand other people thinking they knew more about her than she knew about herself. And Aphrodite might not even be a person. She muted the TV and walked away.

As much as the pseudo-Greek got on her nerves, Rebecca acknowledged her speaking abilities, her consistency of thought. Which gave her an idea. People like Jane Roberts made good livings from channeling enlightened beings, angels, or spirits from the Other Side. But no one had ever seen such an entity. Until now. Anyone could see and hear Rebecca's TV without having to rely on a medium, whom some skeptics dismissed as fakes.

She began thinking fast and grabbed a bar of Godiva chocolate from the pantry. Her minuscule casita — she'd seen kitchens bigger than her living room — couldn't accommodate more than a few people, so she'd have to rent a hall. Santa Fe had so many people tuned into the New Age that she'd need the biggest and best, probably the Lensic. She'd advertise in *The Reporter* and *Pasa Tiempo* and put up posters around town. She'd charge ten, no, fifteen dollars for a two hour viewing, with several TV's and the Lensic's state of the art sound system.

She pulled out her calculator. An audience of five hundred at fifteen a head equaled...seven thousand five hundred dollars. Each hundred people would add another $1500 with no additional expense. For one show. After her first success, she could sell discounts for a series. Aphrodite might be pompous, but she was still a technical anomaly, perhaps more, and a lot of people would relate to her message of true love and all that. Rebecca might take the show on the road. Audiences would grow, fame and fortune following.

After work the following day, Rebecca attended the Circle of Healing Life Energy, a network of women dedicated to hands on balancing or regeneration of the essential life force. She'd started participating six weeks earlier and held to the assembly's basic tenet that a person could be healed of an illness through transmission of God's dynamic love focused by pure intention. The Circle referred to the sick people as receivers, since like electronic receivers they soaked up healing energy and transformed it. The week before no change had occurred in the receiver, a middle aged woman with Multiple Sclerosis. Rebecca thought that on a metaphysical level the receiver had blocked the energy transmissions.

This week eight of them showed up at the home of Celeste, whose mansion off Gonzales had a tennis court and guest house. Views looked down on Santa Fe, east to the close Sangre de Cristos, and west to the Jemez beyond Los Alamos. They gathered in a large, magnificent living room: hand-troweled plaster walls, saltillo tiles, thick vigas, Indian Market prize-winning pottery on display, two original Fritz Scholder oil paintings.

Rebecca, who intended to invite them for a private viewing before going public with Aphrodite, could barely contain her excitement. She liked these women, sister soul mates dedicated to alternative healing, working together — no payments allowed — for the benefit of others.

Mary, the founder, began. "The first item of business, today…this is hard…but we have to talk about Becky."

"Me?" Initially astonished, Rebecca wondered if Mary wanted to acknowledge her leading role the Wednesday before.

"I'll be honest with you," Mary said. "We've all talked since last week's transmission." Mary looked around the room and the others nodded. "We've reached the conclusion that you don't really fit in with the group."

"What do you mean? I think I fit in great."

Mary appeared uncomfortable and Celeste picked up the thread. "Mary started the Circle in 1994. I became part of it two years later. It's grown and changed, but we've been blessed by the ability of our unique human endowments to work in concert as a conduit for the therapeutic love of the universe. Do you follow me?"

"Of course. That's the purpose of the group."

"When you approached us several weeks ago you said you wanted to learn about energetic healing. I'm sorry for this, I don't want to come across as attacking you, but from the beginning you acted like you already knew everything. It seemed like you thought you were the teacher who was supposed to show us how to do it right."

"I don't feel that way at all."

Jamie, who had been silent so far, tended to mix metaphors. "I can't read your mind, but your energy has been kind of like a bulldozer that doesn't pay attention to anything in its way. Honestly, I feel my own battery being drained instead of being charged when you attend the Circle. It doesn't feel good."

By now Mary had regained her composure. "Last week was a disaster. You worked in the Circle with a recipient for the first time, but you took charge of the whole thing. I felt the clash of energies, too. It's not surprising that the recipient got nothing out of it."

Rebecca could see Mary struggling with more to say. She also concluded that to remain part of the group she'd better show contrition.

Celeste spoke again. "The worst part of it was when you told her it was her fault. Do you have any idea how that made her feel? She's been living with her condition for more than a decade. Mary worked with her for months until she felt safe enough to come to us for a transmission."

"I didn't exactly blame her."

"She thought you did," Celeste continued. "She felt so hopeless that she made a suicide attempt when she got home. Mary spent two days with her in Saint Vincent's critical care unit."

"Not because of what I said."

Mary's frustration showed in her speech. "Yes, Becky, exactly because of what you said."

Rebecca looked around the room at sad, disapproving faces. "I'm sorry. I won't do it again."

"You're not going to get the chance to go it again," Celeste said.

"I can change." Rebecca tried not to sound defensive. "Maybe I've been too enthusiastic. I get that way sometimes. But I can listen to feedback."

"We've been trying to tell you for weeks but it's been like speaking to a foreign soldier who doesn't understand the language and who wants to shoot first and ask questions later." It was Jamie.

"Well, I'm listening now."

Back to Mary. "I'm sorry, Becky. It isn't going to work."

A long silence followed. Rebecca noticed an antique Indian basket on display, probably from the nineteenth century, that hadn't been there the week before. The lights of downtown Santa Fe had come on, white and yellow, some twinkling. The sun had set but the sky behind the Jemez Mountains retained a bluish tint that allowed her to make out the silhouette of peaks, ridges, and valleys.

"We have a recipient coming soon," Celeste explained. "You need to go."

"Right now?"

Despondent and rejected, Rebecca left a message for Stephan, but recalled something about a series of briefings with the number two man from the Department of Energy in Washington. She listened as Aphrodite went over the same points about love: what it wasn't, the issue of love and possession, the polar fears of annihilation and loss.

All right, I heard that already, Rebecca thought restlessly. Then she recalled the Circle accusing her of not listening and paid closer attention.

"If love represents a natural flowering of our deepest nature, what makes it so difficult? You've already experienced the reasons in your own life. Even though the core of love is freedom, you mix up attachment with your love, and there is no attachment without loss." Rebecca, whose father often left home for days and sometimes weeks at a time, and whose mother died before Rebecca finished college, knew what Aphrodite meant.

"Attachment is not love, and love in its purest form can exist without attachment. Yet many people think they love because they are attached. A common example is the attachment of a child to an abusive parent. You become attached to your parents because you're as hard wired for it as the ducks and monkeys scientists have studied. And you're built that way to survive."

Aphrodite, she admitted, had something important to say, and the image's quiet, soothing gentle tones penetrated Rebecca's outer layers of resistance to experiencing her own inner world. Not everyone is like me, Rebecca reflected, apprehending the accuracy of the assertion. I need to let people do things in their own way.

Had it been able to percolate through further layers of her being, had it touched her visceral core, that realization might have changed her to avoid the coming devastation in her life. However, after holding the thought for a few minutes, Rebecca isolated it with her intellect, forgot it, and moved on to the more important matter of marketing Channel One.

She and Stephan walked to Pranzo the following night for dinner. He wore the button down short sleeve shirt, light chinos, and sandals he preferred when not working. She wore a turquoise and silver necklace with one of her many loose-fitting dresses that draped shapelessly over her. With town packed with summer tourists, they had to wait a half hour for a table, then they sat in the large windowless main dining room — a great place for being seen — and spoke loudly to hear each other over the noise. She knew she shouldn't carbo load, but her palpable excitement overrode dietary moderation, and the pasta dishes had the virtues of good value, quantity, and flavor. So did the excellent tiramisu.

She dominated the conversation, passing briefly over her disappointment with the Circle the day before, then turning to the future of her satellite show. "Aphrodite's going to be a star. Maybe eventually I can get a contract with one of the networks for an hour-long weekly show. We could do it every night, but I don't want her novelty to wear off. It's a whole new form of reality TV. Virtual reality TV. She's so beautiful it would be a great venue for Western Natural Botanicals to advertise."

She spoke rapidly, jumping from one topic to another rather tangentially. "We take love for granted, but we don't even know what it is. I'm not so egotistical that I think Aphrodite is here just for me. I believe she came to teach the world. I'll need at least a half-page ad each in *The Reporter* and *Pasa Tiempo*. Oh, I've got it. I'll get a reporter from *The New Mexican* to come to my place to see Aphrodite for himself. An article in the paper is worth a lot more than an ad. But I'll still have to advertise."

She failed to notice Stephan's flagging interest, and it never occurred to her to ask about his meetings with the Assistant Secretary of the Department of Energy.

"I'm going to need your help," she said. "All the equipment has to be transported from my place to the theater and set up. We need to rent a bunch of televisions so everyone can see. Get tickets printed. Let's make a list." She pulled a pad and pen from her purse. "Okay, we start by calling the Lensic. I wonder what it costs. What next?"

Stephan took a sip of Chianti.

"Come on, I need your input here."

"Becky, do you know you've done nothing but talk about yourself since we got together?"

"I'm talking about Aphrodite. The future."

"To me it feels like you're talking about your Aphrodite, your future, your needs. The only place I fit in is to run errands."

"I admit I'm excited. I can hardly think of anything else."

"But that's how you always are."

"No I'm not."

Stephan sipped the wine again and Rebecca nervously did the same. It was starting to sound like Mary and Celeste.

"We've been dating…" When he paused to calculate she looked at the concave curve of his face where his wisdom teeth must have been pulled, a detail she'd never noticed before. "Almost a year. And instead of feeling closer to you, I feel more pushed away. It's as if you don't care about what I do, what I think, what matters to me. You're the one in the spotlight and I have to pay attention to you, but it doesn't work the other way around. I'm out of patience."

She felt panicky inside and grasped at a way to hold onto him. "Should we go to couples counseling?"

Their eyes met as he seemed to consider the proposal. At length he answered. "I don't have the energy for it. Every time I'm with you I feel like I'm having to fight just to be listened to. I don't want to pay someone for the privilege."

She'd been running under full sail with a billowing spinnaker, but she ran out of gas, as Jamie might have put it, becalmed in dead winds for a couple of days after the breakup. She liked Stephan: his intelligence, his availability to her, his wide range of interests, his kindness. He helped cook and clean up, enjoyed dancing at salsa parties, listened to Cheryl Crow and Beethoven. He was pretty good in bed, too.

She missed him, but had too much to do to allow herself to sink into depression. "I must live in my truth," she reminded herself, and continued working on a contract with Neiman Marcus she thought she could close in a few weeks. Of course, once Aphrodite took off, she would quit her job and devote herself full time to promoting the show.

"Love takes courage," Aphrodite said. "It's not for the faint of heart. Yet one of the miracles of love is the expansion of your own capacity to live fully through the act of loving another."

Rebecca had other challenges on her mind. Ramon Martinez, a reporter from *The New Mexican*, almost hung up on her.

"All I'm asking you to do is to take fifteen minutes out of your schedule. If you still think it's a hoax or something, fine. I won't bother you again. But if there's something to it, you have an incredible story."

He asked for her address and said he'd be there in five minutes. She called the Lensic Theater downtown on San Francisco Street. The cost for a night —not much more than $1000 for

833 seats — seemed like a bargain, especially since it included tickets, box office sales, and listings in the Lensic's flyers. She was trying to get through to the James A. Little Theater for a comparison quote when the doorbell rang.

She let in a Hispanic man dressed in dark blue khaki pants and a short sleeve pullover collared shirt. His average height made him a few inches taller than she, and he moved with an unhurried pace she didn't expect in a reporter. She liked the unusual intensity of his aura, a shading of red into peridot green with touches of a darker green, like tourmaline. She didn't know what it meant and held her tongue.

She repeated the history of the woman on her living room screen, and let him run through the same procedures she and Stephan had. She liked Ramon: handsome, polite, nicer than on the phone. They talked pleasantly while he took notes, accepting her offer of lemonade.

"She always wears the same blouse," Rebecca said as the figure appeared again.

"Love exists only with commitment. Any instant that commitment ceases to be, so does love. As soon as that covenant comes into being again, so does love. You can't will yourself, wish yourself, or think yourself into loving. The way to love yourself and others is to remain in touch with the wisdom of your own body."

"The wisdom of your body," Rebecca mused. "I wonder what she means by that."

Ramon asked several questions about the wiring, hidden Tivos or CD players. "Unless you're trying to pull a fast one for some reason, you've found the most angelic Latina with the sweetest voice I ever heard. I could listen to her all day."

"Latina? She's blond."

He grabbed the remote device and the digital image appeared.

"Jennifer Lopez times five," he said.

"Golden blond. Skin so white it's almost pink," she said.

Ramon Martinez returned an hour later with a photographer, an electrician, and a DirectTV technician. The next day he showed up with a priest and a former CIA electronic surveillance professional. Rebecca couldn't believe her good fortune when the article appeared on the front page of Sunday's paper.

UNEXPLAINED APPARITION BAFFLES EXPERTS

Imagine you turned on your television one day and a program appeared on a nonexistent channel. The program never changed, and you couldn't make it go away. Whenever you turned on your TV set, the program came up automatically like an Internet home page. The company providing your service knew nothing about it.

That is exactly what happened to Rebecca Kaufman two weeks ago when her new satellite equipment was installed.

Rebecca scanned the summary of Aphrodite and her message of love and relationships. The article continued:

George Broom, a licensed electrician, examined all wiring and remote devices. "Everything's in order," he said. "Whatever's causing this phenomenon, the wiring in Kaufman's house and television is normal."

Mark Griego, who installed Kaufman's Direct TV system, determined that nothing was unusual. "Everything's working just the way it should," he said. "I've never seen anything like it."

Thomas Lerner, Vice President of Public Relations for DirectTV nationwide, had this to say in a telephone interview. "The particular signal in question does not originate in the DirectTV system. Our satellites broadcast only to our equipment, and our equipment in the home only picks up signals originating from DirectTV. So what's happening, in theory, is impossible."

Father Jimmy Jimenez is Bishop of Saint Francis Cathedral. He emphasized that he was speaking for himself rather than the Catholic Church. "It is unlikely that the Church would investigate this matter," he said, "even though it is quite intriguing. Miss Kaufman isn't Catholic, and there is nothing about the situation that indicates a true miracle." In spite of Bishop Jimenez' doubts, there are several unexplained aspects of the appearance of the figure, who calls herself Aphrodite. Extensive testing has failed to detect any origin for the signal Kaufman's set is picking up.

The most remarkable phenomenon, however is Aphrodite's appearance. A group of people looking at the television image was asked to describe her on a piece of paper without discussing it ahead of time. The descriptions varied widely and no two were the same. Her hair was alternatively seen as blond, brunette, black, red, or silver. An Afroamerican wrote that her skin color was similar to actress Thandie Newton's, whose Zimbabwe mother was black. Hispanics tended to see her as Hispanic, and so forth. Everyone agreed that she wore a white blouse without jewelry.

Just as inexplicable was the impossibility of taking a photograph of the image. A *New Mexican* staff photographer was able to take pictures of other channels of Kaufman's television. The screen for Channel One, so-called Aphrodite's channel, appeared blank on the film. The television and other items in the room were visible.

"I want to share Aphrodite with the world," Kaufman said. "I believe that her presence here is to teach human beings to love each other." Kaufman plans on renting out the Lensic Theater October 12 for a two hour viewing of Aphrodite. Tickets will be $15.

Rebecca shifted into overdrive. She began work earlier in the morning to make time for telephone calls and meetings to set up *An Evening With Aphrodite*, as she decided to call it. She signed a contract with the Lensic and wrote out a nonrefundable check for the full amount of $1,150. She met with the theater's technicians, whose work would be an extra charge. She contacted Santa Fe Audio-Visual to project the TV image onto a large screen and provide a dozen extra sets. They accepted a nonrefundable deposit of $500, over half the total price.

At times the mounting costs made her nervous, but she pushed aside momentary weaknesses with her MasterCard. At first DirectTV quoted an approximate price of $300 for moving her system downtown and back, but it turned out that the dish would need to be mounted on the Lensic's roof, another $200. A full page advertisement — Rebecca now considered nothing smaller — in the weekly *Santa Fe Reporter* cost almost $1500, and she would need to run it at least twice, and maybe in the equally expensive *Pasa Tiempo* as well.

As the big day got closer, phone calls — from friends, reporters, strangers as far away as Boston who wanted tickets — became so numerous that her voice mailbox was overflowing at the end of each day. She hired a secretary to return calls and correspondence, and the Lensic reported brisk sales.

All this activity helped keep her mind off Stephan. She tried denigrating him to herself, emphasizing his faults, telling herself she was lucky to be rid of him. But her demeaning thoughts rang false. She had liked him when they first met, had appreciated his lack of pressuring her for sex, and had enjoyed his company. Had she exploited his giving nature?

She had no time to consider that possibility now. At night, she would collapse on the sofa with her microwaved popcorn and watch Aphrodite. Sometimes, exhausted, she would close her eyes and just listen.

As she absorbed Aphrodite's main points, Rebecca became convinced that she kept people at a distance. Now she wondered, more with curiosity than with a compelling need for an answer, if she had done that with Stephan, as he had claimed. And if so, was it to protect herself from being hurt? To remain in control?

"When you are in love, you tend to become attached to outcomes: how your lover will treat you, whether he'll be faithful, whether he'll leave. So you live in fear of being hurt. It would be nice if this anxiety were all in your imagination, but the truth is, if you are attached, you will without doubt experience loss. People move away. Their affections change. People die. No matter how the leaving happens, you experience withdrawal of love as painful. Say you are feeling frightened and need to be held, but your partner, who has had a difficult day, needs some time alone. You experience the unwillingness to give you affection as painful lack of caring, while your loved one experiences your need as an intrusive demand. Such events happen in countless ways in the course of a relationship."

She thought of calling Stephan, but nothing would be different from before, and she had no desire to intrude. She didn't realize it, but that internal act of taking into account his need, the boundaries of which she had heard Aphrodite speak, represented her first major change in approaching others.

She had scheduled *An Evening With Aphrodite* for a Saturday night. On Wednesday, her sister flew in from Connecticut and by Thursday the show was sold out. Over $12,000 in sales. *Sixty Minutes* called wanting to cover the setup, the event, and the mystery itself, and the Lensic staff told Rebecca to expect reporters from the Associated Press, *The New York Times*, and *Time*, among others.

Cameramen, photographers, and reporters descended onto her little house Saturday morning. They created confusion by shouting to each other as they crowded the small living space. Even with furniture pushed to the side, the installer from DirectTV and the technicians from the Lensic — she wanted every piece of hardware in her home including the television moved to the theater — barely had room to work. A convoy snaked the few blocks from her home out to Agua Fria, onto Guadalupe, and created such a traffic jam on San Francisco that the police had to close off the street and redirect traffic.

Inside the brightly lit Lensic (she had only been there for performances and had no idea of the wattage it could put out) the surprisingly competent technical help began to set up. The satellite installer ran cable from the roof down the rear of the building through a back door. Santa Fe Audio and Visual employees connected their projector to her television and ran more cables to ancillary monitors in the rear and up in the balcony. Lensic techies tested the sound system. Reporters crowded around her, asking as many questions as the set up crew, and CNN already had a segment on the day's news.

"Do you believe in spiritual entities from other dimensions?" a reporter asked.

"Yes."

"Have they ever been in touch with you?"

"No, except for Aphrodite. But she doesn't seem to have an existence outside my TV. And she talks, she doesn't respond to questions."

Finally, with everything wired, she succumbed to pleas from the cadre of reporters to give them a preview two hours before the show. She turned on the system exactly as she did at home, aiming the remote control and pressing the power button. Onto the television and projected onto the big stage screen, larger than life, came *Gilligan's Island*.

All day Sunday she shut out the world completely: told her sister to go home, turned the ringer off her phone, refused to answer a knock at the door, wouldn't turn on the radio and certainly not the TV, and stayed in bed eating Ben and Jerry's. Ever since the chatterbox had appeared, speaking lofty words of love, Rebecca's life had gotten progressively worse. She'd been rejected by the Circle and her boyfriend, and betrayed by Aphrodite herself. She had lost over $7000 in Saturday night's fiasco and had earned a reputation as a charlatan.

Images of the Captain, Gilligan, Mary Ann, and the Powells ran repeatedly in her mind as though mocking her. Even Cherry Garcia couldn't block out the endless replays of the frantic efforts of the installer and technicians, the laughter of the reporters, and her own helpless rage as she checked every channel one by one. She had reported to the box office and left the Lensic before the first ticket holders arrived.

She called in sick to Western Natural Botanicals Monday. Promising herself that after today she would get back on her feet, go to work, and put the whole thing behind her, she decided to watch a morning movie and switched on her set.

Aphrodite smiled. "It's time to put your knowledge of love into action."

Rebecca stood. "You bitch," she shouted. "You ruined me."

Then Rebecca had a new idea. She put a tape into her VCR and recorded about fifteen seconds, something about love as a creative endeavor. Then she rewound the tape and played it back. Visual and audio static. She checked the connections and taped something from Fox, rewound, and it played perfectly. She tried recording Aphrodite again as unsuccessfully as the first time.

If nothing else, she could record the voice with an independent unit, market the tapes, or transcribe them for books. She watched the meter on the cassette recorder as Aphrodite spoke, the motionless needle indicating that the machine was picking up nothing.

Rebecca took a sixteen ounce hammer from the tool kit in the pantry and stood menacingly in front of the white-clad entity. She liked the feel of it in her hand. "Shut up or I'll smash your face in," she threatened. She raised the hammer.

Aphrodite continued speaking, but Rebecca resisted the urge to trash the top of the line Sony. She placed the hammer gently on the floor. Then something inside her gave way and she burst into tears.

What broke was not some wild spirit, as when a horse is trained and tamed. Instead, the armor which had been protecting her cracked, and self-accusations took over. Rebecca looked back on her life as hopelessly without direction, filled with recurrent floundering. She saw herself as a failure. After a while she looked in the freezer but she had eaten all the ice cream, and her self-pity passed beyond crying.

At the time, her life looked so bleak that she could not see the episode as the breakthrough it was. She wallowed for hours in cataloging her mistakes, criticizing every major decision she could think of in the past twenty years, hating her own ego-driven need to achieve. She became so exhausted that she finally felt nothing but a vague emotional numbness and a throbbing in her head. She took ibuprofen, curled into a fetal position on her bed, and waited for night.

She must have drifted into sleep, because when she awakened the sun had just set. She went outside. Over the flat rooftops of pueblo style houses, she saw a horizontal strip of blue, and above it a mass of clouds reflecting warm reds and purples. Her headache was gone, the fissure in her protective shield had widened, and self-pity gave way to a more dispassionate assessment of the past, tinged with regret at all the time she had wasted. Over the years she had imposed her will on others, seeing situations as contests in which she could prevail through persistence. The result: few if any real friends, grandiose plans that often failed, years of short term romantic involvements.

Many of her difficulties, she thought, originated in her inability to open herself to the miracle of love, as her nemesis would put it. No, nemesis was wrong. She decided not to blame Aphrodite and to accept responsibility for creating her own problems. From now on she would treat the virtual female as a friend rather than as a presence to exploit. Perhaps the avatar was a gift to Rebecca rather than the larger world after all.

She turned on the television, and suddenly, unexpectedly, the gentle voice filled her with hope. The message of love she'd been hearing for so many days was taking a new shape, developing fuller meaning. Rebecca took her seat on the sofa — minus popcorn, chocolate, ice cream, or chips — and listened.

Aphrodite seemed to talk more slowly, with pauses that allowed her words to sink in. "What you understand depends on how you look at things. Maybe at this point in your life, you have experienced that your way of attacking the world no longer works. Judging yourself as bad isn't the solution, since it perpetuates your attachments and negativity. Let's look at why."

It seemed absurd that the woman, who had no reality beyond scanned electrons, could address Rebecca directly. Yet the image spoke to the heart of her concerns, and she listened until late into the night, as Aphrodite recast the same material in different words, with barely a break. Sometimes the beautiful figure would pause to drink water, just like a real person.

This time Rebecca got it. She went through the motions of work the next day, made arrangements to meet with the Neiman Marcus buyer in Dallas, and couldn't wait to get home. She microwaved an organic brown rice dish from Whole Foods and ate it before watching Aphrodite.

"Another manifestation of attachment is the exercise of power. You try to *make* him give you more, give you less, give you something different. You try to *make* him pay more attention to you or to see your point of view. The variations are endless. In all these patterns one constant remains: controlling your partner completely obliterates love."

Rebecca had done those things. How could she not have seen it? She kept the program on until late at night again, until she had the strength to listen to her telephone messages. One was from Stephan. "I hope you're okay. I came over yesterday but you didn't answer the door. Call if you need to talk." Another was from Ramon Martinez *The New Mexican* reporter. "What happened when your system was hooked up at your place? Did she come back?"

She did need to talk. She looked at her watch. Almost midnight. That had never stopped her before, but she knew that Stephan generally went to bed before eleven. She would wait.

The next day she left a voice mail message for Ramon that she'd lost Aphrodite permanently. She also spoke to Stephan's secretary, who said that Stephan was leaving for a conference in Los Angeles. He would be delivering a paper and visiting relatives and would not come home for a week. When she returned home from work she gathered up all the foods on which she binged, the comfort foods that helped her keep the weight that formed part of her protective gear, into a white plastic trash bag. She walked onto Manhattan Street and threw it in a dumpster on the other side of the train tracks, near the Santa Fe Southern Railway tourist train. She enjoyed the walk.

Rebecca thought Stephan might be more comfortable meeting on neutral ground, so she suggested Downtown Subscription, a coffee shop with its own parking lot. They sat on the rear patio under an umbrella. She had given up coffee a few days earlier and drank herbal tea. He ordered a decaf latte.

"I'm sorry for how I treated you," she said. "I don't know how you put up with me for so long."

"I like you," he replied. "You're bright, dynamic. You're interesting. I've gone out with women who got boring after a while." He smiled. "You always had ideas, I could talk to you."

"But I was so selfish. That's what gets me. It's like all I could see was what I needed. Everything had to be done my way." The tea tasted a little flat without a dose of sugar, but she wanted neither empty calories nor the chemicals of artificial sweetener.

"That was the problem," he agreed. "I felt like I was drowning in your needs."

She said goodbye knowing it was too soon to request a second chance, and understanding she had too long a journey ahead of her to ask him to wait. She joined a gym and began a morning aerobics class before work each day. Aphrodite had never said anything about body types or slimming down. In a flash of insight, Rebecca recalled that she had begun putting on weight in college after her mother died, during her first serious relationship. She grasped the aptness of relevant metaphors. She learned to throw her weight around. She wasn't someone to take lightly. What she wanted carried weight. The time had come in her life to change her self-image, to relate to her own body in a new way, as Aphrodite had been discussing in the past several days.

"The real key to making your life work, to loving with minimal interference from your attachments, is learning how to tune in to your own body. It's not about finding something wrong with yourself and fixing it. You must learn how to check in with yourself, to allow your inner being to be your pilot."

She took on a softer approach to sales. In the hours of Neiman Marcus negotiations over a two day period, Rebecca checked in periodically with how the interaction felt in her chest and gut. Believing in the products she sold, she responded based on what felt right. She no longer had the heart to harass a retailer into buying products, and sensed that such an approach would have gotten her nowhere in Dallas. As it turned out, the Neiman Marcus contract almost doubled the company's sales, and her commissions, overnight.

"As your understanding increases, you never lose the need to listen to the intelligence of your body." Aphrodite placed her hand on her chest. "The knowledge in here is far greater than you realize. Don't be afraid to be guided by it."

As Rebecca learned to check in with her feelings, at least several times a day, her presence became quieter. By midwinter, she'd lost over twenty pounds. She put most of her clothes on consignment at Act 2 and began shopping for outfits at J. Crew and Eddie Bauer, and for the first time bought elegant designs at downtown boutiques like Origins, Laura Sheppherd, and, in honor of Aphrodite, The White House. Men liked her slender figure, the stylish haircut by a gay genius named Ralph, and her new empathy that made them feel that they counted. Women befriended her, and she was accepted into a healing circle at the Unity Church, where she felt no urge to lead the team. She gradually slowed down, contented, and each night she wrote in her journal at least three events for which she felt gratitude that day.

When Stephan found a girlfriend, a physicist at another department of LANL, Rebecca bought a pint of Ben and Jerry's and a whole cake from Chocolate Maven after work. She had maintained the hope that they would get back together, and she tried to obliterate her disappointment by eating so much food she had no room inside for anything else. But all she felt was uncomfortably stuffed and disgusted with herself for resorting to old habits. So she went into the bathroom and did something she'd only read about: stuck her finger inside her mouth several times until, gagging and choking, she made herself vomit.

"Remember," Aphrodite said gently, "love comes into being when you support the greatest good of another, in a way consistent with your own heart. When you have that commitment, you consider what best allows a person to fulfill his or her own uniqueness. Not on your terms, but in the framework of the loved one's universe." She gave several examples, then summarized, "What works for you isn't what works for the one you're with. Your attachments, not love, determine what you want for the other. Love means you accept who is there."

For the next two weeks, Rebecca went through the motions of working as she nursed the pain of losing Stephan and attacked herself for still feeling so attached.

Her constant companion asked, "What role does trust have in loving another?"

Rebecca let her bitterness out. "Only fools trust."

Aphrodite said, "If you insist you cannot love unless your partner guarantees he or she will never hurt you, then you are doomed to a lonely life, because your partner *will* hurt you, assuming you remain attached. All you can trust in is your own capacity to re-create love once you have let it go. You must have faith in your own ability to open your heart again after you've closed it, however long it takes."

Which, after a while, Rebecca did. She turned inward, focusing her attention again on her sensations and emotions, and found that holding onto her expectation that she and Stephan would be reunited had caused her downward spiral. Attachment, as Aphrodite had warned over and over, led to her suffering. Without trying to change anything, she slowly let go of Stephan, although she never stopped loving him.

By the time Rebecca and Ramon Martinez bumped into each other at an early summer party, ten months after they had initially met, her appearance — including naturally straight hair, hazel irises — and demeanor had changed so much he failed to recognize her at first. She listened to his stories about life as a news reporter, and he asked about her. He invited her to go out to dinner, and on another date after that.

When she turned on the television Monday night, Aphrodite was drinking from a glass of water. "Well," Rebecca said, as though speaking to a real person, "I met this guy I really like. It feels good just to let things take their course and not act like I'm in charge of it all. But it scares me, too. What do you think?"

Aphrodite put down her glass, smiled, and disappeared for the second and final time, replaced by Ally McBeal complaining that her relationships with men never worked out.

Barry Fields

Although raised in New Jersey, I have spent most of my life in the West. I earned a Ph.D. in clinical psychology in California, then moved to Aspen, Colorado. I spent most of my spare time in outdoor activities such as skiing and mountain bicycling. After a long career as a psychologist, I moved to Santa Fe, New Mexico for my own personal growth, and to pursue writing. For the past few years, I have been involved with the spiritual community of The Celebration in Santa Fe. My food and travel articles have appeared in the Los Angeles *Times* Sunday Travel Section, the Chicago *Tribune*, New Jersey *Monthly*, and *la cocinita* (no caps). "Channel Surfing" is my first fiction piece accepted for publication.

Cat-Skin

Hey, diddle, diddle, the cat and the fiddle, it's time to spin out a tale. Gabriella's over by the hearth, flicking away the ashes with her white tail. Now she's made a jump and landed in my lap, her claws piercing the green satin of my gown. Careful, my pet, after all we've been through, haven't your learned prudence yet? Ah, it's the tale you're wanting, as long and as lush as your own. You know it's about you and I, my pet, you know it's about spinning and the fate we ourselves create.

Very well, shut those sapphire eyes of yours, and purr between my thighs. The cauldron is simmering, and does not need stirring yet.

I shall begin my tale when the action starts to boil. There I am, standing before him, the king, as he sits stuffed into his throne, beard like a bristly porcupine, grease on his purple robe. Beside him hovers Avernus — his name like *avarice* — the king's chief councilor, whispering like a weasel in the king's ear. Ah, they're a fine pair, one a veteran to the gluttonies of the banqueting hall, the other spending his days in the treasury room, lapping up gold coins like milk. It is regrettable that the first of these is my father.

"Well?" I say, like ice. My left foot is tapping, like a branch against a window. Around my right foot you curl, Gabriella, like white smoke. "You call me here for good purpose, father? I leave important work for you."

"Daughter," he frowns, "you prove an embarrassment to the kingdom. Out of my fifty knights I have questioned, thirteen have admitted they have enjoyed your bed."

I glance at Avernus, and he puts a lace handkerchief to his sharp nose, and sniffs. Well aware am I of my informer. I've seen him quivering about keyholes, and the curves of my body. He would bed me himself, if he could. Gladly would I scratch out those spying eyes — I am not called Cat for sheer idleness. But your own sapphire eyes counsel caution.

"I have introduced you to great kings and noblemen, and you scorned to give your hand to all of them," my father continues. "Not only do you choose to remain unmarried, which in a woman is a most unnatural state, but you seduce my knights, a situation I will not tolerate. Daughter, I have no recourse but to banish you from this kingdom. And may you hopefully find a husband in your sorrowing exile, though of that I doubt."

I laugh then, for this is a rich turn of affairs, rich as cream, and not unexpected. My father has been attempting to pass me off on fops and fools for the past three years. I laugh at their pale, prissy faces, the garish jewels set in their scented hair, and that sets them clattering away on their high heels. I shall marry whomever I please or not, and everyone, especially my father, knows that.

Hypocrite! That he should say such a thing to me about knights, when I have heard of him tumbling three wenches in one evening, calling for more wine, then tumbling one more. No, this business with the knights is a ruse. It is what I do in the tower room that really unsettles him.

He invaded it once when I was thirteen, and threatened to break my spinning- wheel, which had been bequeathed to me by my mother. I, in turn, threatened to break his bones, and staring at the smoldering twigs I had snatched from under my bubbling cauldron, he knew if I broke them, his bones would indeed snap, as easily as he snaps the bones of fowls during his gluttonous meals. After he hastily left, I set a blocking spell at the door, if he should be so foolhardy to return. He never did.

Yes, I was thirteen then, but already grim. Hadn't I watched my mother as she lay gasping out her last, with her porcelain face and hair spread like golden wheat upon white satin pillows, while my father made the first bloody kill of the season, a huge stage whose antlers adorn the banqueting hall?

I have the same face, the same hair and the same gift as my mother, but the difference is I refuse to be cowed. This, then, is the real meat of the matter, why I am to be banished. Men smell the pulse of power on a woman like blood, and it terrifies them, like stallions that spook at thunder.

"So be it, then," I say, and it startles them, this demureness of mine. But wait, I am not finished with those wicked conspirators.

"Yet every bride needs a trousseau, father, and I shall prove no exception. Before I go, I require three things: a dress as golden as the sun, one as silvery as the moon, and one as bright as the stars. These must be so fine as to be packed away in a single walnut shell.

"Furthermore, I require a hood and cloak to be made of a thousand types of fur, one from each animal of your kingdom. Only then will I go, and not before."

Avernus drops his handkerchief, and my father turns as red as the plums that in summer hang ripe in the palace orchards. "Witch!" he finally roars out.

I make him my most elegant curtsey. "Correct, most noble sire. And if you would rid yourself of a witch, you must perform witchery to do so."

In the end it is I who perform the witchery. For thirteen days and thirteen nights, I watch while feverish seamstresses, lashed on by the whip of my father's tongue, prick fingers on spindles and needles, attempting to create what ordinary fingers cannot, for what ungifted maiden can spin, weave and sew dresses made of the sun, moon and the stars? Sweaty huntsmen return from the hunt, their bags bursting with game, but again, what unblessed man can seek and find all the animals in the wide, wide woods?

On the thirteenth night, therefore, the night of the first full golden moon, I take pity. Remember, Gabriella, how, with a bag in your teeth, you crept over the window-sill and down the tower wall, while I set the cauldron boiling with herbs, and crooned melodies, as I spun my spinning-wheel? Behold, I soon made me three shimmering dresses, which I slip into the shell of a walnut. Behold, my clever white huntress, you return with a bulging bag. I take up knife, needle and thread, and soon I have me a many-furred hood and cloak.

Several last deeds before we depart. I remove the golden ring from my finger, the one that belonged to my mother, and pop it into the walnut shell. I take a spoonful from my cauldron, and cast it over my spinning-wheel and reel, which turn golden, then shrink to the size of my smallest fingernail. Into my walnut shell they also go.

Ring, reel, wheel.
Such tiny things
will be my bait
wherein I shall create
my lucky fate
with ring, reel, wheel.

Ah, Catherine, my feisty Cat, you are truly a cat-skin now. You have bound back your golden hair, you have blackened your face and hands with cinders, as well as that of yourself, my beloved cat, you have covered your body in a strange-smelling cloak, with a hood to cover your face. Will we prowl and howl together under the mother moon, my Gabriella? Help me, my familiar, for I am none too familiar now.

We awaken to the sound of hunting horns and hounds. We are hidden in the hollow of a grandmother tree whose voice, as we fled through the forest by the help of

mother moon, called out: welcome, daughters! Two weary beasts, we crept within her womb and slept. But it is dawn, now and we are trapped. The baying of the hounds as they encircle us make my head ache. You spit, and your eyes shine like small, blue moons of hate.

But there is no time to spin a guarding spell, which I neglected to do the night before, since weariness claimed me as soon as we had crawled into our tree. There is the tread of footsteps and shouts, and we are hauled out, and birthed into the cold dawn.

"It's not a beast, it's a woman!" cries one hunter, his mouth agape.

"A woman with her face begrimed, and wearing the cloak of different beasts!" cries the second.

"And to think we were afraid of capturing this — this catskin and her cat!" cries the third. They laugh and jostle us about.

"I'll show you that both these cats have claws!" I hiss, as do you.

And then he appears. Dressed in blue velvet and sapphires, and astride a great, black stallion, he comes galloping up to us. His retinue trail him, a colorful blur, for I'm not noticing them, I'm taking in his hair, as black as his steed, and his eyes. When I come to those eyes, I am transfixed, for they are as blue and as burning as your own, Gabriella. Then I am as undone as a witch can be.

"What the hell's going on here?" says the man. "Where's that beast our hounds have been following for the past hour? If you've lost it, I'll flog you all for your incompetence."

The three huntsmen bow. "Begging your highness's pardon," says the first, "but this *is* the beast." He thrusts me in front of the man who's apparently a king.

The king's blue eyes widen. "What, this woebegone girl, dressed in this fantastic garment, with a black cat? Why do you dress like that, girl?"

I make him a clumsy curtsey. "Since I live among the beasts with my cat, this is the only way I know how to dress." The noblemen and huntsmen snicker.

"What a smell!" says a nobleman, and raises a handkerchief to his face, like simpering Avernus. I have all I can do not to spring at him. Instead, I bow my head.

Another nobleman sidles up to the king. "What say you, your highness, to bringing this smelly, ignorant wench back to the palace kitchen with us? She'd make a perfect kitchen-maid. She's so very dirty."

"What say you, beast-girl?" the king asks me.

"I would like that very much, your worthiness."

"Don't call me that!" he snaps.

"But I must call you what you are. Unlike my poor, humble self."

"Well, what do they call *you*, beast-girl?"

"I am a motherless girl, with neither kith, kin nor name, so I shall take the name your huntsmen have given me, that of Cat-Skin."

The company laughs again, and the king gives a derisive smile. "Very well, Cat-Skin, my huntsmen will take you and your cat to the palace kitchen." He wheels his black steed about and disappears, his retinue following.

With much jeering, we are hoisted onto the back of a saddle. My mind is boiling. Damn him, my handsome, haughty king, he *will* see me! I have had kings, dukes and princes transfixed by my beauty. This, too, shall happen to him, by my power as a witch.

I begin weaving plots. Clasped to my breast, you give a weary purr, for you have been through this many times before. But this is different, my pet, this is for keeps. His eyes are twin sapphires burning into my heart. I plot bewitchery, but it is I who am bewitched. I am as undone as a witch can be.

"Cat-Skin here! Cat-Skin there! Fetch wood! Carry water! Peel vegetables, pluck fowls, and sweep the cinders from the hearth!

"Ugly, black Cat-Skin and her black cat! The cinders are where you belong! Look at your face! Look at your hands! Why do you wear that smelly, mangy cloak?"

So laugh the kitchen-maids and scullery-boys, as they pile dirty tasks upon me. Those that attempt to kick you out of the way soon learn respect. They bear your scratches for many a month.

"Get that damn cat away from my soup!" That's Helcar, isn't it, the chief cook, a scrawny chicken of a man, with a scar running from his left eye down to his chin, a scar that he received, the gossips whisper, in a fight with another cook who put too much pepper in his soup. They also whisper the other cook fared far worse. Yes, Helcar is most particular about his soup.

We aren't deceived by him, though. Haven't I often seen him sneak you a choice bit of fish or meat? And doesn't he often catch me by the arm and mutter, "Rest a moment, lass, you must be weary." If kings would only act like cooks, or if cooks could be kings.

Speaking of kings, I haven't seen mine for three weeks now — why should I, an ugly kitchen-maid such as myself? — but I get myself a glimpse of the splendid ballroom sprawled in the middle of the palace, and I begin to spin out a plan.

On the night of the first full moon when it gleams like a gold coin, you creep, my white ghost, into his room and you sit upon his broad chest, and as you knead his flesh under your claws, you send him dreams of gold: golden dresses, golden hair, a huge, golden ring which encircles him like a hoop. He awakes, all feverish and cries out for a ball.

A ball! A ball! Such a scrubbing and a polishing, and a cooking and a baking as have not been seen for these three ages! Finally, the night is upon us: the chandeliers gleam, the smell of flowers and the sound of violins make everyone giddy.

We are alone in the kitchen, you, me and Helcar. The others are crowded onto the servants' gallery, as they stare at the festive scene beneath before they rush back to begin serving the feast. But Helcar is sleeping. You jumped upon his lap, and as he stared into your blue moon eyes, he fell into a slumber thirty men could not awaken him from.

Then it's quick! quick! quick! into our little chamber under the stairs, where no light comes in, and it's off with our cinders, and off with my cloak. Then out comes the golden dress from the walnut shell, and down comes my golden hair. Look how we have changed night to light, and how the light shines all around.

"Who are you?" the king hoarsely demands, as we whirl about in the glittering ballroom. But now is not the time for revelations, now is the time for you, my white wonder, to streak amongst the painted ladies and gentlemen, which causes them to shriek, and the king to drop my hand.

Then it's quick! quick! quick! back to our room, where again we are changed to lowly beasts. Once more you become a midnight cat, and I become Cat-Skin of the cinders. Into the walnut shell I pop my golden dress, and out comes the golden ring. Now for the spell.

I make a good soup, a thick soup and when the cauldron begins to bubble, I pop in my ring.

> *Hold, ring, hold.*
> *Encircle him with gold.*
> *Ring him round*
> *bring him bound*
> *but willingly*
> . *to me, to me.*
> *Hold, ring, hold.*

So I sing as you jump upon Helcar's lap, making him wake and curse himself for a thrice-born fool for sleeping, when the king's soup still needed to be made.

"Peace, Helcar, I have made the soup."

He stops, tastes and stares at me in wonderment. When the servant has borne it away in a soup tureen, he watches me as I peel a bowl of potatoes in my lap. "Lass, wherever did you learn to make soup like that?"

But his wonder changes to fear when he is summoned by the king. "You have let some of your strange hairs fall into the soup!"

The king, on the other hand, accuses me quietly, for I am summoned soon after Helcar, as I knew I would. Hooded and cloaked, I face him as he sits upon his throne, his thumb and forefinger clasping my ring. To one side is a table with the empty bowl and spoon, in front of which stands a miserable Helcar.

"My chief cook tells me that you have made this excellent soup, since he was so derelict in his duty as to actually fall asleep," says the king. "Is this true, beast-girl?"

I drop him a curtsey. "It is, your worthiness."

"Then why did you put this golden ring into my soup?"

"I know nothing of golden rings, your worthiness. I only know of fetching wood, carrying water, peeling vegetables and sweeping cinders from the hearth, for I am the kitchen-maid, Cat-Skin of the cinders."

"And the best kitchen-maid in the palace!" This from Helcar, for which I throw him a grateful look.

"I've been having...dreams," whispers the king, but not to me, but to the ring. "Tell me, beast-girl, have you seen a golden girl about the palace?"

"And what would I, a beast-girl, be knowing about golden girls?"

He sighs, and looks haggard. "Then, Cat-Skin, since you make such wonderful soup with — unbeknownst to you — such wonderful surprises in it, you shall make all my soup, after every ball."

"And are there to be many more balls?" I ask, and Helcar gasps at my audacity.

"Yes, until I find out..."

"Find out what, your worthiness?"

"Nothing," he mutters, and returns to his absorbing task of rolling my ring around and around. See how already it encircles him.

The next dream you send him, when the moon sails like a silver pearl upon her midnight waters, is of silver: trees wreathed in silvery ice, a huge, golden spinning-wheel spinning the moonbeams into a spider-web dress, all silvery and rustling of secrets.

I am in that dress, dancing with him, or is it you, Gabriella, lifting your delicate, white paws? He awakes and — so I hear from his gossipy valet — knocks over his cup of morning chocolate, and orders the second ball.

"Tell me, my lovely one," he asks, as we dance, "do you bring my dreams, or do my dreams bring you?"

"So we're to discuss the nature of things?" I reply. "I can discourse quite well upon this weighty matter, your worthiness."

I break apart to twirl, but he grabs my hand, even though the dance does not call for it yet. "What did you call me?"

A slip of the too happy tongue! I must chaperon my own words. "I called you your highness, which is what we must all call you."

"You did not. You called me that which no one calls me, except a scrap of a smelly kitchen-maid. Who are you, lady? Your face and voice seem familiar to me, though you spring up like smoke in my ballroom." His hand tightens over mine. "You will tell me your name."

"My cat!" I cry, for you've arrived again, my white darling, leaping among the glittering silks and satins, while servants try to chase you down.

"The cat!" the king exclaims, and that's enough for me to pick up my silver skirts, and for the both of us to dash to the kitchen, where once again, we undergo our bestial transformations.

To the accompaniment of Helcar's snores, I now make my second pot of soup, and pop in my tiny, golden spinning-wheel.

> *Spin, wheel, spin.*
> *Envelop him in*
> *a web he will willingly*
> *stay forever in*
> *with me, with me.*
> *Spin, wheel, spin.*

"And now I find in my delicious soup *this,*" says the king, holding out my spinning-wheel, when I stand before him for the second time. Behind me I have left a bemused Helcar, muttering of strange sleeps that suddenly come over him at every ball, and of stranger kitchen-maids, who drop golden ornaments into kings's soups.

"Well, can you explain this, beast-girl?" says the king.

"Alas, your worthiness, I still cannot."

"No one calls me that, but you and..." His blue eyes burn into me. "You are as black as the cinders, Cat-Skin, as your cat I saw that morning in the forest. Bring me your cat!" he cries, leaping up.

But you are already there, Gabriella, dancing between my feet and prancing up to him. "Black, by God," he says, slumping down upon his throne. "Black and never white."

"Your worthiness?" I ask, but he waves me away, and buries his head in his hand. Ah, a fair web for him I am spinning.

Then it's time for the third and final dream, the third and final drama. The diamond moon gleams as you sit upon his heaving chest, and bring him a dream of a huge, golden reel reeling in the stars. He awakes, sweating — again, my source, his valet, is most graphic — but quite calm, and orders the third ball.

"I swear I'll not fall asleep again tonight," scowls Helcar. But when you jump upon his lap and knead your midnight paws into his thin thighs, he's no match for your magic, and soon is snoring beneath you.

When I appear in the ballroom in my dress bright as the stars, the king is waiting for me. He's looking grim, as if he's about to behead someone. "If you won't tell me your name, lovely lady, will you at least accept this ring from me?" He slips my own ring upon my own finger. "Does it have the ring of familiarity to it?"

"Why should it?" I laugh and look around for you, for it's time for me to vanish and make my soup. Finally, you appear, but the king will not let me go, until you leap up and scratch his hand. Then he releases me with a curse, and we are able to hasten back to our room. And though there would be time to coat my white skin and your white fur with cinders, I do not, but instead, I fling my cloak around my bright dress, crack open my walnut shell, and pluck forth my final golden treasure, my tiny, golden reel.

And now for the final spell. I sing it softly, as I throw my reel into my cauldron of soup.

> *Turn, reel, turn.*
> *Make him not only*
> *burn for me*
> *but also make him*
> *see me*
> *as I really am.*
> *Turn, reel, turn.*

So for the final time I stand before the king as he holds out my reel. "Three dreams, three balls, three dresses, three golden ornaments that are far from ornamental. But, I think, one woman and one cat. Or, if you prefer, two cats."

"Of what do you speak, your worthiness?"

Then he points to you, sly puss, who have appeared in your true, white fur, and it is time I do the same, strip myself down to the essentials. No more bewitchment, for he is truly reeled in, or it is I who have been reeled in by him? He takes my hand, and the whiteness of my skin and the goldenness of my ring shine forth. You tug at my cloak, revealing a gleam of my bright dress, and he pulls off my cloak and hood, and the brilliance of my dress and my hair shine all around. "Hello, my golden girl, my Cat-Skin of the cinders," he says, and we embrace.

And you, my beloved familiar, purring by my feet, you dance along with me at my wedding feast.

Mary Pat Glynn

"Cat-Skin" is based on the Grimms' tale, "Allerleirauh" (meaning "of many different kinds of fur") and a children's version, "Princess Cat-Skin" by Shirley Goulden, illustrated by Nardini.

When it came to my own re-telling, "Cat-Skin," I wanted to keep the rich details of the many-furred cloak, the three dresses, the three spinning talismans and the three balls, but I wanted to make the princess more empowered. A witch, in fact, called Catherine or Cat with her own cat, Gabriella, as her familiar. Through my poetry and the three dreams foreshadowing the three balls, I wanted to create a colorful, hypnotic effect for the enchanted king and the reader.

I write fantasy and poetry for both children and adults. My poetry has been published in such journals as *Anthology of New England Writers 2002*, *New England Writer's Network*, etc. Currently I am working on a young adult fantasy novel about the tarot.

Asleep at the Wheel

Tonight's traffic was, for a delightful change, light. Usually the infamous Beltway was nothing more than a perpetual backup of every make and model of car from the Virginia-Maryland-D.C. metro area, tags of all kinds either designating diplomats from foreign countries, nicknames, or quick little messages to other commuters who could make the long trip home a deciphering game. The rules of the "license plate game" were simple. First, successfully crack the plate's code. (For example, if a tag reads "CMORFIT," was it "Seymour Fitt" or "See more of it"?) Once the message is translated, figure out why the driver put that on their license plates. (See more of what?)

Tonight there was no such game. It was just a long drive home. Tom had been asking himself for the past month exactly why he was still working out with this acrobatic team. It was his *ex*-girlfriend's idea to work out with them, so why was he following this routine?

The past two years had been one big joke. Meghan had sold him on the idea of performing a dead art form from Renaissance Festival to Renaissance Festival. *All right,* he begrudgingly thought to himself, *maybe not dead but definitely in a deep coma.* Their workouts with the gymnasts were limited due to Meghan's "chronic motion sickness." That should have been his first warning. When had he stopped being honest with her? Tom thought back over the relationship. They started off great. The sex was amazing! When she left for the conservatory, the distance was manageable. It probably started when he actually met the staff of her "conservatory" and saw the footage of what the students had spent a good part of the year developing...

"One step above Children's Theatre," he muttered aloud.

Maybe it was the whole issue of seeing her there, but Tom could deal with it. The exercise routines kept him busy, fit, and out of Meghan's way when she did show up to "work out" with the team. He was no acrobat, but he did learn how to do a killer cartwheel and enjoyed the results of these aerobic workouts, far superior to any gym or weight room. It was nice to be in better shape now than in high school or college. Now he had graduated to another routine — cardio-kickboxing — courtesy of the gymnast's next-door neighbor. It was a "user-friendly" approach to martial arts and a satisfying workout, especially when turned loose on a punching bag.

He turned the music up a hint louder. The down side to all this physical conditioning was the long drive. The routine began with finding a seat (hopefully) on the metro by eight, catching a return metro train by half past four, out to the gym for martial arts and acrobatics, then home sometime after ten. Eat a late dinner (usually his own "Burrito Supreme" creation), try and wind down, fall asleep by midnight, and begin this cycle again at the sound of his clock-radio alarm. Following one of his workdays in Virginia, the last thing Tom relished was a trip deep into Maryland, but the return trip home guaranteed down time. During the drive, he silently assessed how much his consulting firm wanted him involved in the day-to-day operations and how this commitment would affect his acting career currently in a "rebuilding" phase after Meghan's influence.

Suddenly, Tom remembered his checkbook was in desperate need of balancing.

His mind was much like his lifestyle, working in several directions simultaneously and he liked it that way. He took after his dad in this multi-tasking approach to life. Tom loved being an actor, but he also took great satisfaction in teaching computer applications. Now he could feel a martial arts bug gnawing at him. Then there was his personal website. His first design. It was still a hobby, but he could easily see it becoming a nice little side business. *Yeah, that me,* Tom thought to himself. *Jack of All Trades, Master of None.*

He blinked his eyes a couple of times, turning up the music. Or was it talk radio? It was a surreal feeling. Tom could not ascertain what he was listening to. It could have been classic rock. It could have been a late night shock jock. The sounds of the radio, the wind, and the hum of the Ford all coagulated into a dreamlike static.

How loud was the radio?

How far was the window down?

He *was* aware of being in his own lane.

His last conscious thought was that he had just passed the Georgia Avenue exit. *Not much longer. I'm halfway home ...*

•••

The plexi-glass slid away as he felt a wave of consciousness come over him. The taste in his mouth was horrific and his biggest annoyance with the whole hyper-sleep process. He could deal with the muscle stiffness, waking up with five to ten minutes of disorientation (but he actually got it down to three with a couple of yoga exercises he pulled from a CentralNet site), and removing the intravenous feeds of chemicals and nutrients attached to his body. Tom let out a loud yelp as his feet touched the cold floor of the *Walter Raleigh*. *Okay,* he thought hazily, *maybe the taste in the mouth is a close second to the cold floor.* Close by the sleep chamber was the mouthwash he swirled around in his mouth and forced down like cheap gin. It was considered hazardous to swallow the company's mouthwash, but it was the closest thing to alcohol on the ship.

Tom's feet instinctively slipped his feet into the 'bear-foot slippers,' a late twentieth century novelty that never wandered far from his chamber. He constantly got ribbed from other pilots about these ridiculous slippers. They were obnoxiously huge and faux-fuzzy with farcical claws protruding from the front. Tom could care less what they had to say about his slippers. They were his and they were warm. He had found them on a CentralNet "Antiques & Heirlooms" site where collectors were placing bids on them, probably for some collector who would have taken these mint-condition slippers and put them in a glass case for display. It cost him a good chunk of his savings from his last few hauls, but with the chill of the ship's metal floor the cost was justified.

Worth every credit, Tom thought pleasantly as he wiggled his toes inside the slippers.

The cockpit appeared exactly as he last left it before going into hyper-sleep. The comm-set was attached to the headrest of his pilot's chair and the checklist panel was in its pocket next to the armrest. The computer displays indicated the artificial gravity had been active for the past hour. *Ah, I see. You activated the artificial gravity but didn't bother to warm up the floor. Thanks, Cujo. I'll remember that.*

"What time is it, Cujo?" Tom yawned.

"Ship's chronometer reads that it is 0321 hours," the ship responded. The computer's voice was a disturbingly calm, female voice, void of emotion. No mistaking that it came from a computer. "Thirty-seven years, two months, two days, and seventeen hours since leaving Jupiter's orbit. Nine years, one month, six days, and eleven hours since passing through the Alpha Centauri checkpoint."

"I just wanted the time, Cujo. I just wanted the time."

Tom stared at the display for a moment, knowing full well that the computer could not see the frustration in his face. He laughed in spite of himself. At least he always got the last word with this computer every time he addressed the interface. In the fleet of colony ships, every central computer was called "Watchdog" as it protected the ship from space debris, changed course to avoid any ship-to-ship collisions, or activated its defense grid when threatened. Tom's sense of humor and love of classic literature could not stop him from calling the ship's computer "Cujo." While his fellow students bought "Cliffe Disks" that poorly summarized and analyzed the Academy's required reading, Tom actually read this author's works in school. This one book, *Cujo,* was his favorite. Reprogramming "Watchdog" to respond to this new name was just a start. Tom went so far as to change the alert signal to bark as a wild, rabid dog in case of virus infestation or operating system errors.

Tom glanced at the navi-grid to the right of him, a dotted line deviating from a solid line that stretched across a star map. Currently, according to stellar charts as drafted by Earth Central, they were traveling through the IR24 system, about ten years clear of the Alpha Centauri colonies. *Those checkpoint hotshots probably did their fly-by's so close they knocked an antennae out of whack,* Tom thought bitterly, *and its taken this long for Cujo to pick it up.*

To reach a colony's destination, computers and company navigators plotted extremely precise courses, the computers for accuracy and the company navigators to pinch pennies where they could. Be it an asteroid or a star, if it had any kind of gravity, the company men would make it part of the slingshot formula. Any deviation from that course and Watchdog would correct. If it failed, essential crew would be awakened from hyper-sleep.

Tom was the pilot and therefore the essential personnel.

"So is this the problem, Cujo? Course deviation?"

"Yes, sir."

"I see." Tom cracked his knuckles and flipped a couple of switches on the controller stick in the right armrest. "Starboard thrusters at twenty percent."

There was a flash from the right side of the ship. Tom watched the field of stars slowly move. The computer was supposedly a "state-of-the-art" product of Artificial Intelligence, but Tom was essential in performing a function any "shake-and-bake" of five could perform. The genetic "shake-and-bake" prodigies programmed for flight are considered "too valuable" to risk on deep space exploration, and now "homegrowns" are back in demand. Humans created "the old fashioned way" were needed to do the dirty work. He sighed and ran his fingers through close-cropped hair now turning gray at the temples. *I'm not even thirty,* Tom thought grumpily, *and my hair is turning gray.* One of the lovely side effects to repeated hyper-sleep. He could not help but wonder when he became so jaded on the job. When space flight become so...isolated. That was probably what made him so grumpy. Not the hyper-sleep, but an overwhelming sense of loneliness. He could not remember ever feeling this lonely. He should have felt this after his first haul.

Tom enrolled in the Mars Academy Pilot's Program. It was a better alternative than spending the rest of his life on a planet of rust or returning to a dying planet. He was six when the *Unity* Incident of 2103 occurred. The station's orbit began its decay, and projections indicated it would splash harmlessly in the Pacific Ocean. The computers, however, were pulling information from the station's original schematics, not from its upgrades between 2014 and its decommission. When it impacted the Earth, the nuclear reactor upgrades on board exploded with such force that it was similar to the "Asteroid Calamity" scientists had been continuously droning about for centuries. Hawaii, Japan, and half of Australia were buried while the San Andreas Fault in North America gave way. The debris kicked up in the air reeked havoc with the environment. Orbital way stations and resorts on the Moon and Mars quickly became science experiments as to the potential of life on other worlds. Colonization programs were accelerated.

So for Tom, there were very few options.

The Academy emphasized from Day One the majority of a pilot's life is spent in hyper-sleep. Outside of other pilots, family, friends, and intimate relationships were impossible. Tom recalled his first assignment. It would take him on a fifty-year orbit. He said goodbye to his mother and father for what would be the last time. The pay was fantastic. He felt no regret. No loneliness. It was something he had to do to survive.

So is it finally catching up with me? Am I finally suffering from Hyper-Sleep Isolation Disorder? His mind wandered back to a time far gone when it was a different kind of ocean pilots like him navigated. He read all about it on CentralNet. The oceans were not a void of black but a vast uncharted region of the deepest blue, sometimes calm and inviting and other times turbulent and rebellious. There were no sleep chambers or slipspace propulsion drives. Only the wind carried ships from port to port. It was a far simpler time.

A far simpler time, Tom thought languidly as he stared across the stars stretching out to infinity before the *Walter Raleigh*.

Some people called him a "romantic" and fellow pilots took great delight in reminding him of problems in ancient history, right up to the twentieth century. No, the first millennium was a far-from-perfect age. Still, there was something far superior to that ancient method of travel. What a time that was. No artificial air. The warmth of true sunlight. Tom could hear the sounds of the ocean lapping against the sides of the vessel. The sunlight baking his skin to a golden brown. He could feel the wind on his face, cool, refreshing, full of the scent of life. Turning up the volume of the radio, enjoying the sound of classic rock. He could feel his grip tighten light on the steering wheel...

Tom paused. *Steering wheel,* Tom asked himself. *Where the hell did that come from?*

"Cujo, perform a diagnostic on my sleep chamber." Tom returned the comm-set to its headrest and slowly made his way back to the cylindrical bed, "Was I programmed for REM sleep?"

"No, sir. Sleep chamber is operating within normal parameters." The computer's voice continued as Tom took a seat on the bed of his sleep chamber , "Article 24, Section 3 of your contract states that you are not to be subjected to Rapid Eye Movement. Your chamber is regulated to keep you in a state above REM, its benefits synthetically replaced during your hyper-sleep."

This was a constant clause in his contracts: REM sleep was prevented by the ship's medi-computer. If Tom did happen to slip into this state, his dreams were monitored and recorded by Watchdog. The company kept careful documentation of his dreams to assure he was not slipping into deep space dementia. Cujo would not have hesitated to mention a faulty sleep chamber or if his supply of the synthetic adrenaline, Stimuline, failed to keep him out of REM as it was supposed to do, was low or empty.

"Report the last dream I had since departing the *Galileo* Way Station."

"No dreams have been documented on this journey."

"When was my last attempt at REM?"

"Last dosage of Stimuline administered in 2353, thirty-one years, six days, 3 hours, and 24 minutes from this present awakening. I would comment the yoga exercises downloaded from CentralNet have proven quite beneficial in regulating your sleep."

No, Tom thought anxiously, *I was dreaming. I wasn't here. It was vivid. It was real. I remember turning up the radio and hearing the Classical music station. The song was "Love in an Elevator" by Areosmith...whoever they are. I was driving a car...*

Tom only knew of cars from his history disks and CentralNet. The author of Watchdog's namesake wrote about a car once...

"Captain Martin," the ship's computer chimed, interrupting his thoughts. "I cannot return you to hyper-sleep unless you fully recline."

"Cujo...access Mainframe." Dreams were still believed to be the first symptom of deep space dementia, but there were other studies and theories. He wasn't cracking. This dream was so clear, like a memory. "Tell me about Lucid Dreaming."

"Mainframe accessed. **Lucid Dreaming** — the term was coined by Frederik van Eeden in 1896 when he used the word 'lucid' in the sense of mental clarity..."

Tom sighed heavily, "I don't want the details, Cujo, just the general idea. Simply put, what is Lucid Dreaming? How does it occur?"

The computer's voice hesitated as if editing its search results, then continued with its findings. "Lucid dreaming is a dream within a dream. Dreamers will dream within their dreams and become aware of a second dream when noticing impossible or unlikely happenings, such as encountering deceased loved ones, walking through walls, or obtaining flight without mechanical assistance. Lucid dreaming is achieving awareness in a dream that one is dreaming."

Would that explain how real it all was? I could feel the grip on the steering wheel. I saw the exit signs. Georgia Avenue — that was the last one I passed. Could I have confused the medi-computer in dreaming within a milder dream? Or could I have slipped into a deeper REM the computer couldn't recognize?

"The quality of lucidity in a dream varies from subject to subject," the computer continued. "Lucidity at a high level is an awareness of everything experienced is a dream. There is no threat. The dream subject is fully aware of being asleep in bed and will awaken shortly."

"Is it the same as dream control?" Tom asked. He had never heard this tone in his voice before. It reminded him of his mother trying to convince him not to become a colony ship pilot. It was imploring, desperate.

"No, sir, but it is possible to control dream parameters without being aware of the initial dream. Lucidity in a dream increases the extent of the dream subject's influence of both the initial dream and the second dream. Dream subjects can resume the second dream with full knowledge of existing in a dream and maintain the ability to redesign their dream parameters."

"Is it possible to be in a state of lucid dreaming and accept the dream reality as present reality, thereby obtaining a higher level of lucidity within a dream?"

Tom thought about what he just said. *Maybe I am losing it ...*

"Insufficient data to comply to query."

He hated it when a computer said that. Was that supposed to be a more intelligent way of saying *I don't know*? It made sense to him. Achieving a state of consciousness within a dream. If it were possible then maybe his idea would work.

"Thank you, Cujo, that will be all."

A far simpler time.

Tom knelt by the sleep chamber and pried open the control panel. The multi-colored wires extended back to the motherboard. *I can do this. I can. This will work!* His hands shook lightly as he checked each wire, tracing where it led. The green-white wire controlled the medi-computer. This was what prevented him from dreaming. With a quick jerk and a shower of tiny sparks, the medi-computer was taken offline for his sleep chamber.

"Captain Martin, I detect an error in —"

"Thank you, Cujo, that will be all."

"Captain Martin, I am programmed to inform you of —"

"Thank you, Cujo," Tom snapped. "That — will — be — ALL!"

Tom searched for the red wire, the last and most crucial in the array. This was the connection to all environmental controls such as oxygen, temperature, and other critical systems. It was this wire that was the only flaw in his plan. Disconnecting this would keep him asleep. Disconnecting this could kill him.

If he could return to his dream, why would he want to wake up? He could see his parents waving goodbye to him. He could see out of his transport's window a dying Earth. As it was on Mars many decades ago, there were few options for him. It was a far simpler time waiting for him. A better time.

A far simpler time…

Tom climbed back into the sleep chamber and reinserted the intravenous feed to make certain nothing appeared to be wrong to the others when or if they awakened. The cover slipped over him as he began his breathing exercises.

I am asleep at the wheel … I am asleep at the wheel …

He closed his eyes and breathed deeply, each muscle in his body easing into a more relaxed state.

I am asleep at the wheel …

•••

Holy —

The median wall was close enough to catch serial numbers off each individual segment. It was close. Far too close. He didn't know how fast he was going but it was too fast.

Across four lanes…

Across two lanes…

I'm losing control of the car. Please God…

The wheel began to steady.

I'm awake! I'm awake!

The car was back in its original lane. Tom was wide awake. The most wide awake he had ever been in his life.

He glanced in the rear view mirror. The closest car was a half-mile to a mile away. There was no one in front of him. *Talk about riding with the angels.* He looked up and saw the exit for Rockville. The window was opened a crack, and the winter air rushing in hit the newly formed sweat on the back of his neck, sending chills down his back. The music deafening. A talk radio show host was playing Aerosmith. *Is that what woke me?* He turned down the volume, but there was still the bass track reverberating in his ears.

Tom then realized the "bass track" was his own heartbeat reverberating in his temples.

He was now aware of every detail, signaling turns well in advance. His speedometer never challenged the limit. Tom refused to relax, even when he turned right to go into his apartment complex.

He sat in the car for a moment, the only light coming from the street lamps in the parking lot. He hated this car. It was such a lemon he was convinced a mechanic could make lemonade from it during an oil change. A piece of crap. If he were to describe it in a single word — *unreliable.*

Tonight, he wanted to give its bug-encrusted grill a big sloppy kiss.

Get out, Tom told himself. He got out, his legs unsteady. *You're okay and you're home.* He was still taking deep breaths. *Not until I walk through the door.* The keys were shaking but they found their way into the lock of Apartment 301. When the door shut behind him, he let out a heavy sigh.

He was home. He was okay.

Tom remembered passing Georgia Avenue. Then he saw the median wall. *Did I really nod off?* He couldn't recall what had happened in the long stretch between Georgia Avenue and Rockville Pike.

He set his gym bag by the couch, thanking whatever it had been — God, a guardian angel, or just plain Fate — that woke him. He walked over to the mail awaiting him by the answering machine; and in an instant, it all came back. The damage control on his acting career, the upcoming bills, dealing with this computer training firm, and balancing his checkbook. The fear now yielded to the reality of what was. The bills were arriving. *Life goes on*, Tom sighed *Thank God*.

Tom's eyes happened to land on his tiny library in the entertainment center just underneath the television. It was a modest collection of books in his entertainment center, a varied collection of different science fiction authors. Bradbury. Roddenberry. Bauchman. He thought with a wry grin, *Wouldn't it be nice just to get away for a while?* Far off worlds where computers took care of mundane responsibilities like bills, cooking, and programming the VCR. One hour car trips were a mere blink of an eye and other worlds were only a short space cruise from Earth. He smiled at what fantastic place he wanted to visit from his flights of fancy.

If only I could see that time, *thought Tom*, a far simpler time...

Tee Morris

"Asleep at the Wheel" is science fiction based on true events. The idea for this story came to Tee the night he avoided a horrific accident on the Washington D.C. Beltway after falling asleep at the wheel. Losing control of his car (as depicted briefly in this story) actually occurred on a February night in 1997 somewhere around 10:30 p.m. Miraculously there was no one around him in the *four* lanes surrounding him.

"Asleep at the Wheel" is his debut short story, and one of three premieres for him as a writer in 2002. You can also find Tee in the computer section of your local bookstore with *Adobe Premiere Power!*, a "how-to" approach in working with digital video. In the fantasy section he is there opposite Miss Lisa Lee with *MOREVI: The Chronicles of Rafe & Askana*. (For more on this historical-fantasy epic, visit www.morevi.com.

Doctor Courage

Doug lay back in the laboratory's look-alike dental chair, a padded leather recliner, his fingers gripping the edges of the arm-rests.

"Are you sure you want to go through with this?" the young Dr. Courage asked for the tenth time.

"Adam, it's ok. You have to try this on a human being. I'm it. This is my contribution to science. You're the nervous one. I'm calm as a cat!"

That was a long-standing joke between these two childhood friends. There had been a lazy feline who canvassed their neighborhood for handouts and wouldn't move swiftly if a tree branch plopped down almost on top of its head or a mouse ran between its front paws. The little boys watching the animal's reaction to those incidents had doubled up with hilarity until they were spent, sides sore from laughing.

"You won't be unhappy if this doesn't work?"

"Aw, what am I now? I'm 26 years old and didn't get out of grade school, that's what. I can't be any more messed up than that. I'm serious, Adam, I don't want to live life with a mind that can't learn anything but stuff any 8 year old can do. I want to be like you. Get on with it."

With the elder Dr. Courage and Dr. Nels Bruder, anesthesiologist, prepared to assist, Adam motioned to Cam, acting as nurse, and the experiment authorized on a human began.

"First, drink this to bypass the BBB."

"I remember. That's blood brain barrier!" the patient gloated. "It's working already, and I only took a swallow!" He sat forward on the chair now, kicking the footrest with his heels, and looking as though he might jump off at any moment.

"Now we need to make the dendrites in the brain receptive to the insert. That's what will tell us if we've succeeded. Just calm down and let it work."

"I know that, too, Adam! What you said, dend, dend,—"

"Dendrites."

"Yeah, I know what you said! That's a bump thing that'll catch the learning and put it into my brain. Oh, Adam, I'm better already!"

Doug Willinbe suddenly slumped back, head slack.

"He's under, I think," Cam said to Adam, checking blood pressure and heart monitor as the anesthetist supervised.

"Watch him carefully," the young doctor cautioned. "His vital signs have to be very stable or we have to abort the project."

Though at an age when most fellows were still racing cars, loving and leaving girlfriends and evidencing other hormonal outlets, Adam was already making a name in the field of neurophysiology for his treatises on brain research. The impetus for the young doctor who had already spent years of concentrated work in the neuroscientific field was knowing Doug and understanding how crushed that young man was when he could not cope mentally with his peers Now that that the young surgeon was preparing to upgrade his childhood chum's mental capacity, he fervently prayed his knowledge was adequate.

As the junior Dr. Courage waited for the patient to stabilize so the probes to freeze the spots he would work on could be inserted, his own mind flashed back to how his life had reached this point.

Adam remembered how he lay on the lower tier of his new bunk, patting the oak side rail and wondering why his mother had not come home. Martine had helped her two-year-old son pick out his new furniture, assuring him that he was now big enough to leave the crib for a real bed. After the delivery men rode away in the biggest truck that had ever come to their house, Father pulled the new sheets and a tan blanket with its bucking bronco design onto the mattress so the boy could lie down. His drawn and tired-looking Mother sat in the rocker, telling Father, "I want to see him enjoy it before I go."

The child did not know where she went, but before Martine left him to his nap yesterday afternoon, she kissed him and told him, "Remember this. I will always be with you." He heard her on the telephone telling someone she was leaving for the "horsepital." That sounded exciting and he wished he could go, too, but fell asleep before he could ask his parents if they'd take him along..

Father had gone with her, and he wasn't working today, either, but he was not home. Sarah, the babysitter that read horse stories to the boy, had come over to stay with him.

The telephone rang, and Sarah's voice said, "Oh, no!" very loudly. Then she came into his room, and he could see the old lady was very sad.

"You poor baby!" she said, bursting into tears.

"I'm not a baby! I'm a big boy now. Mama said so." He thought that news might make Sarah feel better.

He got up and had breakfast, but it was a very dull day. Sarah was not in the mood to read to him, and he soon tired of playing with his toys. He asked his sitter if he could go play with Doug next door, a child just a little older than he, but she told him that he had to stay home and wait for his father to come back.

When he returned, it had already turned dark outside. Father took Adam on his lap, and in a very shaky voice, said, "We have to be brave, you and I. God needs your mother in heaven now, and she has gone there to help Him. We'll have to get along by ourselves until some day when it's ok to see her again."

"She can't go, Daddy. She promised me she would always be with me. She has to come back right away." The toddler cried and called for his mother until he fell asleep from exhaustion.

Doctor Matt Courage had a decision to make about Adam's future in the next few days. He was a molecular physicist, head of the University's research team studying crystals and the new technology of nanowires, a very busy man. Yet even in the depth of his own grief, he knew he could not abandon Adam, who was aching desperately because of Martine's abrupt death. In the child's mind, it was nothing less than a betrayal by the mother he adored.

The doctor felt instinctively that to avoid emotional problems that would continue throughout his son's life, he had to show the boy that his other parent would not disappear.

Matt was very persuasive as he assured the dean that the well-behaved youngster would not be disruptive to his own work or to students who researched with him, and received permission to bring the boy with him to his lab each day. Dr. Courage's cohorts helped him set up "Adam's Corner," in sight of his father's desk, but safely away from the working area. It held a small replica of his father's desk and a child-sized chair, a brightly painted playbox, a bookcase, and the upper half of that new bunk bed set, resting at floor level and providing napping space for the little boy.

Adam loved going to "work in my lab." Sarah still babysat for the Courage family when the boy's father had to attend an important meeting, or for a playtime session with the next-door neighbor, but Matt had his son with him most of the time. As the child became more comfortable with the students and professors, he began to watch the progress of the research, and listening to what his elders were saying.

"I can't send him off to elementary school, not to be among all the children who have mothers to care for them, and besides, he's already getting an education just paying attention to what's happening at the university. Why, his vocabulary contains 50- dollar words like "permeable" and "kilobit." He couldn't get better schooling than he's having now, being in contact with these terrific teachers," Matt confided to the university president when it was time to register his son to attend school. He made arrangements to "home school" the boy, though some of it would have to be done during the father's idle moments at the lab.

Adam was an inquisitive child fascinated by the work of the lab, and absorbed the lingo and procedures of the various experiments as they were carried out. He thrived on the type of schooling he was getting. When state tests were given, he consistently scored higher than his grade level, and astonishingly high in math and physics. At times, scholars would come unobtrusively into the lab and observe the boy, quietly remarking many times that here was a full-blown genius in the making.

His father worried that his son would become a one-dimensional person, and encouraged his friendship with the neighbor. Doug had a number of friends, but enjoyed being with Adam, whose lifestyle gave no opportunity to have any other buddies. The two boys got along famously together, even though Adam's pursuits were mostly intellectual, and Doug was a natural sportsman. Their friendship continued as they entered adolescence and adulthood.

Whenever the boys had free time, it was common to hear either calling to the other, and cries of "Oh, Doug! Get your bike," or "C'mon, Ad, let's kick the football around" were frequently heard. Doug taught Adam how to play football and soccer, but when Adam tried to reciprocate by helping his friend with his studies, he found it difficult. Doug had adequate language skills, but seemed to have virtually no long-term memory. Except for sports activities, if he was taught something one day, he forgot it the next.

"Time for a reality check, Adam. I'm just not as smart as you," Doug complained one day after working for several hours trying to learn the concept of algebra.

"No, it's not that. Your mind absorbs sport information like it's already in your head, where I have to concentrate hard to remember it. There ought to be some way to get knowledge into a brain besides someone reading it or being told."

"Yeah, computers ought to get into people's heads, huh, Adam."

"Hey, there's an idea. Computers transfer data all the time. Scientists need to get brains to do that."

"You invent the way. You're the big intelligence around here."

The boys laughed, and punched one another's shoulders, are boys are wont to do. Doug promptly forgot the conversation, but Adam began to dwell on the problem. What was the sense of pushing knowledge into a kid's head, one tiny element at a time, when an entire program might be acquired all at once as a transmittal between minds? He started to pay intense attention to every embryology, neuroscience and gene study lectures he could find, and take part in conversations in the lab, debating with knowledgeable scientists in his effort to find out all he could about the human brain and how it learns.

Dr. Matt and his associates were assisting in the study of atomic pixie dust, the process patented by HP Labs. The thought of chips the size of bacterium fascinated the youth and he tried to fit that concept into his search on a new system for educating the human brain. Putting knowledge on a chip was relatively easy; inserting it to be picked up and used by the brain's neuron system was not.

He talked to his father about the passion he felt to overhaul the way human knowledge is obtained. The young man envisioned setting up a system of transferring learning directly into each person rather than spending precious years cajoling or threatening students reluctant or not quick enough to learn. Or worse, ignoring people's need to know when they themselves did not have ambition or insight enough to see the necessity of comprehending vast amounts of instruction to understand our own ever more complex world and the others being discovered in the universe.

"Look at Doug, for example," Adam said. "He's a great guy, willing, strong, honest, a generous soul. But it's a terrible struggle for him to keep up with his classes. No matter how hard he tries, a lot of the work is beyond him, and he's already 2 or 3 years behind where he should be. It's making a really grand person think he's a failure, when he should be seen as a model for mankind."

Mark nodded in agreement.

"And, Dad, maybe there's a spot in the brain just waiting for this kind of development. You know how if someone stares at you behind your back, eventually you know it, and turn around? That shows there is a weak system already installed that can pick up perceptions by means other than sight, touch or hearing. Vision and the other senses have progressed, perhaps at the expense of this extrasensory awareness. Maybe the cortical region has lagged behind in growth of this area but could be connected up, if I can find the right synaptic terminal to go into. Then all I'd have to do is turn on the program once it's loaded in, and I'd have it made."

"I don't know how successful you'll be at your project. It may be hundreds of years, even more, before mankind reaches the goal you suggest. I'm not even sure anyone has ever thought of the way of educating the brain that you suggest. But you'll learn a lot yourself, and can leave good research for those who follow you. Go for it. I'll back you any way I can."

The pair now set up "Adam's Corner," as a research center of its own, with reference books, one of the new super speed computers, enclosures for flies, snails and mice, and multiple file cabinets separating the corner from the rest of the lab.

Mark worked late hours at the lab, and did not question his son's willingness to work on his own project the same hours. He only insisted the boy eat properly, get some exercise each day, and keep up the more conventional studies.

Shortly before Adam's 13th birthday, University President Travis Linkbine approached the young man's father.

"You have an exceptional boy, there, Mark. Looks to be an authentic genius, based not only on his IQ, but on academic tests he's taken and close observation by a number of your colleagues. They're all talking about him. If he were tutored in the few disciplines in which he's only a few years ahead of his peers," the president grinned at the absurd statement he'd made, " the board and I would like to see him enter the university as a freshman this next semester."

"I don't know what to say."

"This is a marvelous opportunity. Don't pass it up. We're prepared to waive tuition for the coming year to have him join our student body, or maybe on a longer basis if he's as brilliant as we think he is."

Adam didn't have as much enthusiasm as his parent or Dr. Linkbine for starting university work because he felt his research might suffer. Above all, he did not want to lose sight of his goal to help Doug, who in spite of his handicap, had been the one to suggest the possibility of Adam doing investigative brain exploration. Because Father assured him he wasn't to feel pressured, and if the planned curriculum didn't work out, he could always go back to his former studies, the youngster did agree to enter the program designed for him

At the tender age of 13, he became a university freshman, but tried to follow his father's advice. "Now, remember, you've got to live a little, too. Don't neglect normal fun or give up a social life for a dream, no matter how desirable."

Months passed into a year, then more, as Adam whirled through course after required course. His thesis finished, he only lacked a few credits now for a master's in neuroscience. Though the title was premature, students and some faculty had taken to calling him, "Dr. Courage." His proud father was immensely amused, though sharing a name led to a few complications. Adam was mistakenly notified to suggest changes in university policy several times, and on one occasion, Mark was telephoned by a very young lady trying to make a date for a dance. Father and son chuckled over the confusion that resulted from the assumption there could not be two men called "Dr. Courage."

"One of us may have to go to a different university," the accredited Dr. Courage

laughingly suggested.

"Guess it'll have to be you, Dad. I like my life here," Adam jokingly responded. Their lives continued as before, both content to endure the minor glitches.

"Oh, Ad!" the familiar cry came before his alarm went off one Friday morning.

"Shh! What do you want, Doug?"

"Want a date tonight? My girl's got a cousin in town, and we could go to see 'Destruction of Planet Terrus.' It's playing at the Citadel and it's supposed to be terrific. We could take the girls out for pizza afterwards."

"Gosh, I don't know. I'm piled up with homework that I think will take me all weekend to do."

"Aw, c'mon. You work twice as fast as anybody else, and you'll have it done before the evening news on Sunday. You know you will."

Allowing his persuasive friend to win, Adam joined the others for an evening's entertainment. He thought his date, Cam, was a super girl, but knew his reputation among his peers as the head nerd would keep her from seriously considering going out with him. Adam thought of Doug as something of a man of the world because he had managed to take out girls several times; Adam seldom had done so.

Knowing little about women, even young ones, he did not realize that a

broad-shouldered, 6' tall, blue-eyed blond such as he was, was prime dating material. Cam explored the near future with remarks like, "I'm going to school here the rest of the year," and "I just love going to movies, don't you?"

"Sure, but I don't get to do it much. I'm pretty busy," was his diffident reply.

He noticed Cam rolling her eyes. Girls did that when with him; he was beginning to think most females were myopic, having as much trouble controlling their eye movements as they did.

The next time the boys got together, Doug said, "I got a surprise for you!"

"What's that?"

"What'll you give me to I tell you?"

"I won't play football with you if you don't!" The two grinned at each other.

"Ok, I'll say the secret. Cam likes you."

"I don't know about that."

"Yes, Tina said so, and she's her cousin. Cam wants you to ask her out."

That was the beginning of their relationship, and it was a given that instead of

returning to her home town, Cam would continue her education nearby so that she and Adam could see each other frequently.

Adam's interest in the brain's functions initiated Cam's interest in becoming a nurse, and then to form her decision to specialize in neurology, which she was able to do at the university hospital. Time was limited for both of them, but the two took an hour or so for a drive as often as they could. One particularly impressive moonlit night prompted Adam to say, "I can't imagine life without you, Cam. I love you very much. But it's going to be a long time before I can support a wife. If you'll wait, I want to marry you." They agreed "to be engaged to be engaged," until the future was more secure.

The young man was too excited to sleep after they reached that decision. He stood for a long time at his window, dreaming of their lives ahead.

Looking out, he saw a figure sitting on a bench in the Willinbe yard. He recognized Doug, and was about to call out a good night to him when he realized his friend's shoulders were shaking. Running outside, he could hear stifled sobs as he drew near the bench.

"Hey, what's the matter? Can I help?"

"No, nobody can. Oh, Adam, Tina won't go out with me any more. It's because I'm so dumb."

"Did she say that?"

"No, but that's it, I can tell. Everybody calls me a blockhead, and you know what? It's true. It feels like there's a cement block inside my head and what I'm supposed to learn hits it

and disappears. She's ashamed of me, and she said don't call her any more. She's dating some wonderful guy that's going to be a lawyer, and I can't even
get out of grade school. I love her but she doesn't want somebody stupid like me. I wish I was dead!"

"It's not the end of world. There are other girls. You're a great guy and you'll find somebody."

"I don't want somebody. I want Tina. Nothing's any good without her."

Adam could not tell his friend that it would be all right. Unless there was a breakthrough in memory research, it would never be right for Doug and others like him. Silent, they sat on the bench for a long time, until the sad young man's racking sobs stopped and Adam told him to go get some sleep. He was unable to get any himself that night, and lay there pondering how life for him was so bright, and so depressing for his unlucky best friend.

He determined to work harder to find some breakthrough that would help the fellow. He'd started slowly, researching flies, duplicating what had been done by others, following how the axons in the brain connect to the cells they control, then moved on to snails and the study of blocking their memory.

Moving up to mice, he invited Doug to the lab to watch the work.

Doug was very impressed. He walked around, touching cages and letting the mice nuzzle his finger.

"Hey, this one's a good guy."

"Yes, he is. I work with him a lot so I gave him a name. I call him 'Teeka' after our old teacher. Remember the teacher with the whiskers whose name was that?"

"Yeah, sure. That's a good one, all right. A teacher mouse."

Adam could tell that Doug did not remember their former instructor at all, and recognized for the first time that his friend had become adept at covering up his memory deficiencies. Doug was bright enough to know his mind wasn't up to scale. That thought depressed the budding doctor more than his friend's defect.

The mouse learned to find food by running a very complicated maze Adam had built; then using what he had learned with snails, he shut down what he believed to be the rodent's long term memory. That done, the little animal was so confused next time it entered the maze, it did not know which path to take, and thus took none. Then came the important part of the experiment. Adam now implanted the blocking molecule, and after a moment of indecision, the mouse raced down the path to the previously forgotten food dish.

With similar trials using a large number of other mice, Adam built up a large volume of evidence to back his theories on just where the connections that governed long term memory could be accessed.

Cam had finished her courses and was determined to work right along with Adam on his lab tests. He was delighted at her decision, but she wouldn't have been chosen except for his continual prodding of the powers that be to hire her.

He was past mice and into primates when Cam joined forces

"Good," she'd said. "I don't like mice, but I think monkeys are cute."

"Wait until we educate them how to play music and plant gardens. They'll be adorable"

"Can I take this one home once in a while?"

"No, their environment has to be controlled in order for the evidence I present to be accepted. But you can name them if you like."

The one she called "Valiant" was their most promising subject.

"Val can grow axons better than any other animal I've worked with, and look at the PET scan! It's almost as though it's showing off to me so I'll know how it's done."

"I think that's because I hug <u>him</u> a lot," the smug nurse replied. "And don't say 'its'. That's demeaning for such a smart animal. Say 'him'."

"Yes, love. I bow to your wisdom. You know, you may not just be joking about the hugging. He's at an age where the density of synapses is highest, and every experience adds to his brain function. Unfortunately, that quick grasping of information slows down as an animal, or human being, passes the early years of life. It will be a lot harder with an adult like Doug."

"Are you always thinking of him?"

"He's why I went into this field."

"And you're why I got into the field."

If doctors aren't supposed to kiss their nurses, they both failed that rule.

"See, we both owe whatever success we attain to Doug."

With the willing Valiant, Adam learned to manipulate the gene amplifier to expand the monkey's long-term memory capabilities. The animal could recall complex instructions for getting around in the laboratory building, locating a designated lab assistant it was directed to find, and driving a child-size electric car on the roadway system they'd built for that purpose on an unused piece of university land.

But this was only repetitious memory. It merely proved there were certain tasks the animal was capable of learning. The doctor felt he was now ready to insert instructions to cause the animal to do something it was incapable of doing itself.

He invited the head of the university cooking school to provide instructions for

selecting, preparing and actually cooking Val's favorite foods on a conventional stove that was fitted with buttons a primate could use.

Adam spoke the instructions on a disk in simple words familiar to the monkey, then transferred the information to a miniscule chip. Sedating the animal, Adam inserted the chip into its brain, following the intricate plan he'd concocted from his knowledge of cortical regions and midbrain connections. Cam and the elder Dr. Courage assisted.

No human had better care than Val as he recovered. At first, his eyes were frightened, and he moaned a great deal, but Adam and Cam were tireless, taking turns staying by the animal's side. After a few days, the monkey started playing peek-a-boo and simple games with them, and Dr. Adam pronounced Val well enough for trials to begin.

Activating the implanted device was accomplished by using the handheld switch the junior Dr. Courage had devised. When he clicked it, the monkey's eyes flashed wide in surprise, and he turned in search of Cam, as though for reassurance from her that the odd feeling he experienced was not anything sinister.

Adam's theory was that slow manipulation of the head, similar to what is done to treat positional vertigo, would now start the CREB amplifier which governs memory and learning in adult animals.

When the exercises were complete, Val started sniffing the air, as he normally did when his food was being prepared.

"I believe we've succeeded! Now, let's shut down so as not to overstimulate Val, and go ahead and feed him the meal he's anticipating."

The following day President Linkbine, board members, and nearly every professor and student in the neurology section that could crowd in, stood behind the one-way viewing glass into the laboratory to watch the experiment continue.

On a table lay an assortment of food. Fresh and flabby carrots lay side by side, ripe apples and newly picked yams alongside shriveled tomatoes, sprouted potatoes and rotted rutabaga. All of these were favorites of Val's, no matter their condition. He preferred his rutabaga and yams cooked, and would pout if given these vegetables raw.

Adam followed the procedure of the previous day, and led the monkey to the table when the head exercises were completed.

The animal observed the food for a few moments. Slowly, as though reading out the instructions, he proceeded to pick out a good carrot and apple and thrust them into his mouth. Fingering the bad tomatoes and potatoes, he hesitated, but left them in their places. He gathered the two perfect yams in his arms, and picked up the rutabaga, held it close with the other vegetables, and looking sad, set it down again.

Then he walked over to the stove, an appliance he had shown great curiosity for, clambering all over it for several days. Then very deliberately Val placed the yams, covering them with water from the sink faucet, into a pan which he placed on a burner. This step he had seen people do, but in the kitchen, not in the lab.

Hands on hips, he contemplated the situation for a moment, then hopped up onto the stove top, pushed the button that was colored red as the instruction chip directed, and bounded down again, clapping his hands and looking for approval.

Cam ran over to him, hugged him and told him he was a very good boy. After he disentangled himself from her embrace, he strode over to Adam and solemnly held out his hand to be shaken. This was the last instruction on the chip.

The experiment was repeated almost daily, giving all the university students a chance to observe the phenomenon through the window. After a few weeks had gone by, the monkey would rush through his duties, so that hug, approval and handshake would arrive more quickly.

Then he began to act "smart-alecky," as Cam called it. He would throw the bad fruit and vegetables into the pot, with a mischievous and sometimes a defiant look.

One day, shortly before the time for the experiment to start, he started to throw the soft, overripe tomatoes around the room, clapping his hands at the fun. When Adam scolded him, he took the two eggs which were a treat he usually received after his "show", pitched them at Adam, and when they fell to the floor, stamped on them.

His increasing rebellion made the crew realize that Valiant had grown too large to be manageable any longer. Cam joked that the rapid growth was the result of eating all his favorite foods. But it was not humorous when he started biting and pushing his handlers around and a decision had to be made.

"I've tried manipulating his behavior, but I don't have the formula for that," Adam admitted. "That's a different neurological problem altogether."

Valiant retired to a private zoo where he could hide in large, comfortable quarters, coming out occasionally to make menacing motions to any audience that was ready to watch him. Behind his unbreakable enclosure, he could harm no one. Understanding keepers kept his no longer inquisitive mind moderately active.

Other apes followed, though none was as pliable as Val had been when that animal was first learning. Chip implantation worked every time and could be demonstrated, though in creatures with less dexterity and comprehension, it did not function as well.

Still tinkering with his undertaking, Adam learned that temporarily freezing cells in the regions that implement long-term memory, made the exchanges between medial temporal lobe, cortices, and midbrain quicker and more reliable. He refined the chip he used to withstand such temperature changes, and found his animals responding better to the surgically induced learning process.

Authorization for human research was maddeningly slow, but was finally granted.

Doug insisted he wanted to have the process done on him.

"I got nothing to lose. You put all you know into my head, so I'll be smart like you. You hafta do this for me, if you're my friend," he constantly begged.

Adam wrote up intensive lessons on math processes, neurophysiology and computer science, then condensed the data, putting it first on disks and then converting to his bacterium-sized specialized chip as he'd learned to do.

"Actually," he reflected, "I am putting a lot of what it took me years to learn onto this molecular speck. I've got to make it work so Doug will finally be 'smart'. Then we can go on to help others like him, and eventually to revolutionize the education process. Maybe instead of registering a child for school, a chip can be inserted instead to give the youngster the knowledge needed to live in the modern world. Children would continue in school until they'd matured in body and mind, but would use that time learning how to get along with others, to respect the diversity of mankind, to employ statesmen and not political hacks to manage countries, that the purpose of history is to teach mankind that if we don't learn from it, we are required to repeat its mistakes. Their early years would be spent becoming wise enough to be invulnerable to insincere promises from those with their own agendas, astute enough to be able to resist tyrants, the power-mad, those bent on brutality or villainy, any who prey on their fellow men."

He had told his father that day before the procedure began, "There's only one possible downside I see. The unscrupulous might seize the technology if they could get it and use it for mind control of the world's populations. There'll have to be world-wide legislation to prevent misuse and abuse."

The elder Dr. Courage concurred. "I think it will be easy to get unanimous agreement on that because it would affect every person and every nation alike. We can't stop progress. Once something can be done, it will be done. If not by you, then by others You'll see quick action before the process is universally used, I'm sure."

Staff and students had been gathering in the hall outside of the lab to watch the delicate operation. That qualified people would be observing was carefully kept from the patient so that he would remain calm and unafraid throughout the procedure.

The history-making process began. Adam removed the probes in his friend's head, inserted the microscopic chip, counted down the wait time, and then rapidly brought the brain temperature back to normal. Gently awakening Doug, who seemed surprised to find the operation was over, the inventive doctor used a much improved switch he'd designed and clicked the chip on and to the "use" position.. Each switch was unique and worked only with the chip designed for the individual patient.

At the moment the chip activated, the previously noted reaction of the subject's eyes flashing was again observed.

"Now I have to move your head around to different positions, Doug. You must let me do it for you. Don't fight me, just hang loose, old buddy."

The patient obeyed, and then sat up and looked around the room. "I don't feel any different. Though I do have one question. Do you think the hemispheric specialization of the brain will have any effect on how I react to this technique?"

Cries of "wow!" and "hurrah!" and "it worked!" could be heard in the lab and in the hall on the other side of the one-way glass. Adam, Cam, the elder Dr. Courage, and Dr. Bruder gave each other quick high-fives and turned to include Doug, who had not yet realized what had happened. The viewers from beyond the lab burst into the room, congratulating the doctors and the patient.

As the congratulatory and ever growing crowd remained well into the evening hours to talk excitedly about the breakthrough in memory research, the last time Adam noticed his friend among the admiring throng of people was when he overheard a snatch of conversation Doug asked a visiting neurologist, "Do you consider the neural activity of the axons crucial in .....?"

"C'mon, Cam," the younger Dr. Courage urged. "I'm bushed. Let's go over to my house, put our feet up, have something to eat, and watch some show with no redeeming value. Dad, do you mind driving Doug home when he's finished overwhelming his audience?"

In the days to come, the university faculty members were so impressed with Doug's ability, they insisted he be given lab privileges and arranged a grant for him to study the effect of enhancement surgery on the brain.

Adam's greatest reward was Doug's colossal grin as he strode into the lab, slapped Adam on the back, and said, "You did it, man! I owe you my life, and I'll never be able to thank you enough. I always knew you could do it, though. That's what kept me going. AND, guess what? Tina called me and congratulated me on my turnaround and my new life and said she wants to go out with me again!"

Cam's dreams were realized as Adam became free and certainly eager to set a date for marriage, their honeymoon to be combined with the forthcoming trip to Europe to receive the Nobel Prize he'd won.

The elder Dr. Courage's compensation was the conviction that in spite of his own bereavement and uncertainties, he'd provided the right kind of life for his talented son so Adam could reach the full range of his potential.

"I've lived up to the family name," he told himself. He knew that a long ago king had awarded the unusual name to Mark's ancestor who by his bravery saved the king and his court from certain death. "I had difficult decisions to make along the way. Courage doesn't mean ploughing on in the face of certain disaster; it means recognizing problems, assessing consequences and forging ahead with plans to solve them. I'm satisfied I've taught my boy that philosophy, also."

Jean Cottrell Pence

Mrs. Pence and her retired husband live on a bird-attracting pond in balmy Florida. The business "up nawth" is sold, the children are grown, the garden is doing well by itself, thank you, and the genealogy written for descendants about ancestors is as complete as years of research can currently make it. Thus Mrs. Pence now has time to return to her first consuming avocation, narrating stories.

Her fiction has won several awards, and one piece was published in the last issue of *The Storyteller* with an additional tale accepted for September, 2002. A story of hers is to be printed in the next edition of *Beginnings* magazine and a narrative will be included in a forthcoming anthology of the *God Allows U-Turns* series

Mirage

When he reached down, Martin did not expect to find the floor wet. His glasses were where he had left them, but water dripped down his cheeks as he pushed them on his nose. His room looked the same except for the five inches of water soaking the bottom drawer of his storage locker. Since he never closed that drawer, he could see his treasured antique paperbacks, now sodden, soaking water up to his only other pair of clean pants.

He closed his eyes tightly and then opened them. Wiping away drops of water that ran down the side of his neck from his glasses, he looked around in disbelief. There was no water on this rock pile. Whatever water they had was precious after being hauled in from the other side of the known universe. It didn't soak shoes on the floor. It didn't drip off his nose from clammy glasses.

Martin Roundacre had been on this nameless planetoid for almost a year. Go West, young man. He had. To the westernmost mining camp of the Saurenean system on PL18-629. Roundacre had placed well on the PrelimVoc Instrument. Preliminary Vocational Instrument scores were mandatory for all graduate students to help the government find suitable voluntary space recruits. Involuntary recruits took the same tests after having qualified for them with unsuccessful but ingenious crime. Roundacre didn't place well enough to command, instead he was identified as ideal to work alone in advance of less disciplined teams who would eventually run the systems he set up.

Roundacre had already earned several commendations from the All-Planet Board of Review. He was precise. He was relentlessly self-motivated. His reports were intelligible. He had no discernable sense of humor. He appeared to function well alone. At this rate, slow and steady, he was sure to make all of his promotions in the order they were offered by Mining Personnel. Someday, he would retire to Earth and have real dirt to garden.

Roundacre knew all this. He reviewed it occasionally when a landscape seemed particularly bleak. Mining required him to know the vital statistics of asteroids and meteor showers only as ore-provident sources. For a long time now, he hadn't been on a planet big enough to remember what a sunset on a flat horizon was like. Sunrise over an ocean was a childhood memory. One he could hardly wait to escape, actually. He'd worked hard and never looked back. All that was behind him.

He stuck one foot in the water by his bed. It was really cold. It was water. WATER? There wasn't any water on this damned planet. There wasn't a rock formation any place he'd tested which could support water. The whole place was too cold, too hot, and too rocky for water to hang around. Only he had a roomful of it. He put his other foot on the floor. Wet to his ankles, he sloshed to the door. Water eddied gently around desk and chair legs. Goose bumps hardened on his legs and he shivered involuntarily.

"Wilson," he roared. "Wilson!"

Wilson's door was open. No one was there. Roundacre looked down at his feet. They were dry. He looked back into his room. The dusty plastic mat by his bed was smudged with months of his footprints. He took off his glasses. They were dry.

Roundacre hadn't wanted to train anyone. Without asking him anything, he'd received a **Top Priority/Scan Now** transmission saying Blake Wilson was being dispatched to the site to be trained to take over. He, Martin Roundacre, was needed at the Fentriblian Cluster for possible titanium reclamation. ASAP.

"Received?" Click.

"Yes," he received the message. And then he stewed about sharing his small, barely adequate quarters with some unknown rookie. Then the All-Planet landing craft turned up with the most misshapen, disfigured human being he had ever seen. Wearing a giant cowboy hat. Roundacre panicked.

Blake Wilson spoke through a computer in a whirring drawl. His throat was scored with a cross-hatching of thin scars.

"Martin Roundacre?"

Roundacre nodded, speechless. The man's body was compressed into a vehicle that allowed him to roll across the landing strip. Evidently, there was volume control to his voice mechanism because he could shout easily over the departing landing craft.

"Can you give me a hand with this gear?"

Roundacre started. He must have been staring.

"Yeah, sure. I'll go get a U-truk. Unimaginatively named and abbreviated like 1950's advertising, the equipment and buildings kept their "U" designator even after being uncrated and in use. "Utility" meant non-perishable and needs assembly rather than eat with gravy. Good distinction for the supply people to bear in mind.

Taking advantage of the privacy of the U-shed, Roundacre wiped his hands on his legs. Since he was in a Single Piece Breathing Apparatus, wiping his hands had absolutely no effect on the damp queasiness he felt, except to force sweat to the backs of his hands, and down his wrists. He climbed onto the U-truk and pushed the ignition bar. Rumbling and humming, the squat blue-green, all-terrain vehicle made its way out into the bright light. Roundacre looked around for Wilson and not seeing him, drew up against the boxes left behind. He thought of old-time bush pilots taking explorers into the wilds and dropping off their gear while circling the site. About as much contact as he had with his suppliers.

"Hey. Haven't got all day, you know."

It was strange to be talking to anybody at all, and not seeing Wilson helped to keep it a kind of normal strange. Roundacre started to load the boxes he knew contained his supplies and wondered whether this guy really expected him to load his gear as well. He never agreed to take care of anyone. Train, OKAY.

Sort of. Take care of? No way. What were they thinking of sending out a crip?

Something clicked behind him and Roundacre whirled around to watch Blake Wilson rotate a delicate block and boom that was part of his vehicle. In three twists, the boxes marked B. WILSON in space standard letters were on board.

"Is that home?" Wilson was pointing to a gleaming dome in the distance.

"No, that is."

On the other side of the dull gray U-shed was a single story, slightly larger version of the *Variable Building Needs* structure. It was no longer a mere U-shed with the addition of self-contained atmospheric controls, windows, and an Old Earth-house like interior. Roundacre thought it looked like a kid's playhouse set against the overhang of the canyon wall behind it.

"Cozy, isn't it?"

"It'll do," Roundacre said stiffly, "We shouldn't be here together long."

What he'd meant was that he'd train this guy fast and get out, but it sounded a little threatening even to him as he heard the words out loud. Oh well, he was better suited to living alone and had half a dozen psych-profiles to prove it.

Roundacre stared hard again at his living quarters. He went back in and touched the floor by his bed. Dry. Sitting heavily on the bed, he felt his legs. Dry and flaky as usual. He must have been dreaming hard. His stomach still felt queasy, though.

He'd been on the ocean a lot as a kid. His father had made him go out deep-sea fishing with him a lot. Rocking in the hot sun with the diesel fumes a foul cloud on deck made him so sick that at some point his father would finally would let him go below to cry quietly until he slept.

"I don't know why I bring him," he heard his father say to the other men. "He's such a loser. All he wants to do is mess around with computers."

His father had been a salesman who didn't believe in computers until he lost his job to someone who did. Bitter and bright,

135

Roundacre's father took his unemployment and bought a working share in a sport fishing boat. People still went out trying to boat the biggest marlin each season. The records kept getting smaller and smaller as the fish gave out, but made the price of blue-water fishing go up. Roundacre grew up knowing he was a traitor to his father. He was good at computers and hated the ocean.

Where had Wilson gone anyway? Roundacre had noticed early on when he was pissed with the guy, he thought of him as Wilson. He'd never called him Wilson to his face. Why was his room empty and why hadn't he heard him leave? Blake could take care of himself, there was no doubt of that after six weeks, but the rule was, nobody on deck unless there was back up.

Roundacre stepped into the air-lock and pulled on his SPBA. Wilson's was missing. He had almost forgotten the water in his room until he saw what looked like a dried puddle near the outside door. Impossible, he thought.

The wind outside the base camp had picked up. Roundacre remembered from last year that the wind stayed relentless for another couple months. No way to tell where Wilson had headed. There weren't that many choices, but it was still irritating not to know where he was or how long he'd been gone.

Roundacre shrugged on a pack that held emergency gear. It seemed ironic to be carrying such a small amount of water when he'd splashed through a roomful of it just minutes ago. That was a dream, he reminded himself. Seemed real there for a minute though. How many miles of beach had he walked in his life not to recognize walking through ankle-deep water? That would have to keep. Finding Blake Wilson was his first priority.

Superiors had always liked how he handled priorities. And as a bonus, it was one of the things that made living alone satisfying to him. He didn't need anyone reminding him about routine chores or second-guessing his decisions. Actually, Wilson around wasn't too different from living alone. The man kept to himself after their workday ended.

Wilson had been on time for their training sessions. He had been well prepared to learn the details of this particular site, even finding a way to respectfully brief Roundacre on recent developments that hadn't been organized for transmission to outposts as yet.

Mining technology was going to change dramatically when gas hydrates were understood well enough, but for now the standard blast, crush and load of the coal mines of Old Earth were the norm no matter how far out in the galaxy ores existed.

Roundacre tried to raise Wilson on the radio built into the SPBA. Static bristled at every frequency. Standing where he could see the dome of the work site, He noticed a glow of light. If he'd been anywhere else, he would have thought fire, but fire also was an anomaly on this island surrounded by deep space.

Pulling out small high-powered binoculars, Roundacre scanned the area near the dome. Wilson's ridiculous cowboy hat was there. Wilson was not. Roundacre swore. He started running to the U-shed.

Reaching the doors of the shed, he thought about getting a weapon from the gun locker. He wondered if he still could remember the combination. Fore and ring finger, thumb and pinky. He wondered if the security device would notice his hands were shaking. What was going on anyway?

Roundacre strapped on a Field Alternating Device. First developed for crowd control, FADs were issued to civilians instead of weapons in remote sites. He had to discard the small hammer he usually carried in his belt. He actually couldn't remember ever wearing a FAD except for training exercises. When he asked the grizzled weapons instructor what they were for, he was mining engineer, for crying out loud, not a chaos cowboy, the bos'n said, "Peace of mind, son, peace of mind."

Roundacre did not notice any appreciable sense of peace of mind descending on him. The U-truk started right up. He sat in the shed and quickly decided that he should drive right up to the dome. Calling for help would be a joke. The nearest help was the supply craft. Their schedule was tight and emergencies usually had to involve acts of God to get them to change course. Slowly Roundacre headed out the door he'd come in.

Taking the most direct route, he could see tracks in the dust of the vehicle Wilson used to call his 'Mustang.' Roundacre thought it was supposed to be a joke about an antique sports car, but Wilson also said things to it like "whoa" and Roundacre was almost sure the joke had something to do with horses. It was confusing. He never felt like he could ask. Too private. Too likely to be connected to the strange injuries that embarrassed Roundacre even to think about, let alone look at directly.

It was a good thing Wilson was as absorbed in learning the site as he was. He and Roundacre had looked at chart after chart, assay after assay and made field runs to the areas which seemed most promising. They had made a good team. A transition team, Roundacre reminded himself.

Wilson's tracks were deeper than tracks from previous days. Roundacre tried to think if he had noticed anything missing from their quarters. Whatever Wilson had been carrying had been heavy. Heavy enough to flatten out the tracks of his 'Mustang.'

The closer he got to the dome, the stronger the glow was from inside. Nothing seemed out of place at the entrance. He palmed in his code and the double doors opened to a scene of chaos. Wilson was sprawled in the middle of the floor, unconscious. His vehicle was overturned beside him. Roundacre had never seen him outside of the vehicle. Seeing Wilson and his vehicle separately was almost as shocking as seeing Wilson's crumpled hatless body.

The glow had retreated to a far corner.

Roundacre knelt next to Wilson, afraid to touch him. When he called for help they would ask about Wilson's vital signs; that much he remembered from an Emergency Procedures course required of all mining engineers. He gingerly reached for Wilson's thin wrist. It was cool to the touch. Wilson's pulse was ragged, hard to count. He didn't seem to be bleeding. His breathing was very slow.

Roundacre had never dealt with anyone unconscious in real life. It was clear to him that all the simulations he'd trained in were just that. Adrenaline racing, he started the call to Emergency Systems to start the report on Wilson's condition. A landing craft from one of the trading ships might be deployed if the emergency assessment was severe enough. It might take days for the craft to arrive, but if they were lucky someone would be close to them en route to another supply delivery site. Meanwhile, they could advise him and monitor Wilson from any distance. As Roundacre went to take the emergency monitoring gear from the U-truk, he noticed the glow moving slowly down the far wall of the dome.

He'd check that out as soon as Wilson was connected to Emergency Systems. Where to place the monitors was clear in Roundacre's mind, but the body Wilson presented did not look like the holographic simulations set up in Emergency Procedures Training five years ago.

For one thing, his throat was covered with those scars. Roundacre tried to set the contact point gently on a less scarred area. Lifting and turning Wilson's head slightly to attach two contacts at his temples, Roundacre thought he heard a faint sound. He could see the mechanical voice had been set in surgically. Roundacre heard another soft whir.

Placing contacts at Wilson's wrists, Roundacre thought he heard the noise again. He looked at Wilson's face. It was an unfamiliar mask. Roundacre lifted one eyelid. Only the whites were visible. The whirring noise deepened. He started the call to Emergency Systems; the sooner someone else was monitoring this guy the better.

Waiting for the connection, Roundacre shifted Wilson's hips enough to rest a scanning device across the thin abdomen. It was then that Roundacre saw the glow. It was creeping across the floor toward them.

"We read you, MS489."

The computer generated female voice, screened from tens of thousands to hold the right amount of sincere concern and clinical authority, assured Roundacre she was standing by. He was oblivious to this assurance.

The whirring glow had reached Wilson's side opposite Roundacre. Paralyzed with horror, Roundacre watched the glow seep over Wilson's throat and disappear into the metal opening in his trachea.

"We read you, MS489, please respond."

"We read you, MS489, please respond."

"We read you, MS489, please respond."

In a stupor, Roundacre pressed the reply button. It was coded for emergencies when speech might be impossible. He signaled for Triage Monitoring and connected Wilson to the system. He thought it would take longer, but within seconds the same precise, unaccented voice allowed that in regard to all systems scanned, "Blake Wilson, male, 35, Rh O/neg, was in excellent health. Did he, Martin Roundacre, want a written confirmation of his appreciated random test of the emergency system and would he fill out the accompanying form indicating his satisfaction with the response time, clarity of instructions and any other comments that would let them improve their service?"

Roundacre swore with great precision.

"You and I are gonna talk, buddy."

The adrenaline that had surged through Roundacre had subsided enough to let him consider the possibility that he wasn't going to pop this sucker a good one just because. That he hadn't been so close to peeing his pants since his father's drunken friends gaffed a dying six foot hammerhead on board and laughed while he tried to dodge its spasming walls of teeth. That if this bastard Blake Wilson really were in excellent health, he, Roundacre, was the oft-invoked queen of Old France.

Roundacre shook Wilson's shoulder roughly.

"What's going on, you little toad?

Wilson's eyes opened.

"What did you call me?"

"Don't mess with me, Wilson. Whatever this stunt was about, your ass is out of here. You can try and tell me what happened, but I don't need this mess and one thing's sure, you're no replacement for anything but a slot in PsychRehab."

Roundacre stopped for a breath. Wilson had closed his eyes. He was dragging himself toward his vehicle. Stolidly, Roundacre watched as he righted it, moved himself to the footrests which could lift his crouched and twisted body to the seat. Wilson reconnected himself to sensors pulled loose when he fell.

When he fell? Roundacre had never seen Wilson come anywhere near a fall in all the terrain they had explored together. "How'd you end up on the ground?"

Wilson said he didn't know or at least that's what Roundacre thought he heard as Wilson passed him heading for the entryway. He retrieved his gray felt Stetson and using a sensor-activated clamp, set it squarely on his head. What a ridiculous combination. Roundacre hated it. Realized he might hate Wilson as well. He wondered how many times he had wanted to laugh out loud and hadn't. And he didn't want to now. He really wanted to throttle the creep.

Wilson's soft voice suggested they go back to their quarters and talk. Roundacre wanted to have a tantrum. Instead he said, "Yes, that would be a good idea."

Looking around the dome before he left, Roundacre wondered whether he should check all the equipment. He told Wilson to go on ahead. Roundacre activated the systems check in the computer. Usually he had the printouts sent to their two desks in the quarters, but today he wanted to see all reports first.

Disbelievingly, Roundacre read three preliminary reports specifying water damage to three remote units. Further reports verified water damage to five testing lines, eleven cameras and an unspecified amount of stored data. Roundacre felt his knees shaking. There was no water on this damned planet. There never was and never would be. "No water, you hear me damnit, no water," he said raggedly to the blinking console.

Roundacre gunned the U-truk. Bouncing back to the cliff face, he tried to figure out what he wanted to know most, know first. It all kept running around in his head. Wilson had to be at the bottom of this somehow. He should have known. Anyone could tell the guy was a loser. Roundacre left the U-truk parked where he pulled up. He narrowly missed taking out the entrance to their quarters.

Slapping the entrance sensor got him a forty-five second recording about the sensitivity of identification devices and how the lightest touch was sufficient to activate the identification program. It was all he could do not to punch its lights out. Roundacre gritted his teeth and placed a hand that shook ever so slightly from sheer rage over the plate.

"Thank you," the sister to the Emergency Systems voice murmured. Roundacre ground his teeth. He realized the minute he took off his SPBA he was in no shape to talk to Wilson.

Roundacre was going to lock up both SPBA and tell Wilson to begin his separation reports and that they would meet later. That seemed manageable. Entering their communal area, Roundacre saw Wilson had cleared his personal gear from table-tops and bookcases. Good. His door was closed.

Water was trickling out from under the door.

Not OKAY. Not OKAY. Not OKAY.

Roundacre's brain fled down this loop for a full 15 seconds before he yelled and ran for the door. Jerking it open, Roundacre saw a huddled figure shaking with sobs. What the hell. The floor was dusty. Every wheel tread since the guy arrived showed.

"Uh, s-sorry," Roundacre stammered to cover the sick feeling he had seeing the tear-stained face of a man he thought had been dying the same morning. Why didn't Wilson turn his face away? Why did he have to show this side of himself? He really hated Wilson for being all weak and showing it.

"I'll be in the Site Analysis Office when you pull yourself together. There's a lot I need to know." Roundacre sounded grim.

Wilson nodded, tears streaming down his cheeks onto his smudged and disheveled shirt. Jeez. He looked awful. Closing the door behind him, Roundacre looked down at his feet. No water. Of course there was no water.

In the Site Analysis Office, he printed out two copies of the water damage reports. One set he tossed onto Wilson's neatly organized desk. The other set he carried over to his desk spreading them out under a 1:10 scale topo of the sites described in the printouts.

Water damage. If he hadn't decided Wilson was a bull-goose loony, he'd drive out to the sites now and see what water damage looked like on a planetoid registered waterless. That would be something worth seeing, he thought bad-temperedly.

Most of the damage was underground. But how could data be contaminated without destroying the sensory units. It didn't make any sense.

Sometime later, Wilson wheeled in. His hat was in place. He'd changed clothes and looked the subdued and competent engineer Roundacre recognized with relief. He also looked exhausted, which was surprising since he had just been checked out by a triage scan and found to be in excellent health. Go figure.

"Where do you want me to start?" Wilson's voice was almost too quiet.

"Is the beginning too hard, or don't we have enough time?" Roundacre's sarcasm was barely contained. It was his father's voice, he knew. Probably sneering his lip the same way, too. He didn't care.

"No, the beginning's a good place. It won't take long. No graphs." Wilson's voice had gotten stronger.

"Do you remember what made you decide to be an engineer, Martin? I do. They said they'd kill me if I didn't. Oh, they didn't come and actually say that. It was more like 'the apparatus required for your mobility has been developed through the Space Mining budgets for non-human reclamation of materials.'

"That is the closest I ever came to being called officially non-human out loud. And the implication was that without my cooperation, without my becoming a superb engineer, I would then be available for the benign neglect of the state.

"I took the hint. All testing showed I would excel in math and engineering. I did. I also had seizures that fouled up computers in two states. No one snapped to the connection until I seized while presenting a paper to the combined department heads of three universities on an electronic hookup put together just for that conference. It took three months to get all the systems back online. Nobody knew how to connect the damage to me, but all further conferences were in person. I wasn't allowed to fly on commercial flights. My research had to be done by an assistant who actually keyed in the material. It hardly seemed possible, but I was more of a freak than ever.

"That's when I started wearing cowboy hats. Gray felt in the winter, straw in the summer. I was an outlaw and figured I might as well look the part. I know it's ridiculous, like seeing a ten-gallon hat on a quart bottle of gin, but I had to take some ground for myself.

"Besides, in the time it took people to check out the hat, they've also had time to organize what they feel about a body like mine. Generally, people are polite. Kids want to be, but their parents tell them bullshit like don't stare. If my body isn't worth staring at, will you please tell me what is? Anyway, the ones who ask, I get to tell that I wasn't born like this.

"Hard to believe, isn't it Martin? Well, I was bent. Remember what that is? Decompression chambers? Or lack of them? I was a hot-shot kid hired by a big international wire-line testing crew off the Gulf Coast. It was more money than anybody I knew was making for seasonal work. I dove twice a week.

"They lied about having a working decompression chamber. Oh, it sat on deck all right. But when I needed it, it might as well have been an outhouse. They flew me off, but time poured through every one of my muscles and cells saying you've been very, very stupid. Gases in the blood are unforgiving about time.

"When I regained consciousness, I felt like a flounder finding both eyes on one side of my body. I wanted to die. The people at Rehab had been briefed on how I was to be reclaimed. Nice choice of words, I thought. That meant I couldn't authorize a

No-Code. Every time my lungs filled or my kidneys failed, I was hauled back to live another day.

"I really am working on being grateful," Wilson added sarcastically.

"And I could not figure why they were so determined to pull me through. When I asked the doctors, they pawed through my charts blathering something about all human life being valuable. I knew better. I asked every nurse what was going on and it wasn't until I was about to leave to start up my studies when one said, 'you really don't what they've done to you, do you?'

"If I could have shaken her, I would have. ' Just tell me what's going on, will you?' Her eyes filled with tears and she kissed the top of my head.

"Martin, I seriously wanted to kill her. I am not a murderer only because I couldn't move. The next day I was using the vehicle you see me in now to finish the curriculum for a math/ engineering major at the same university you attended. I didn't know that then. Alumni were the least of my problems.

"Since these fields were my strong ones, and should have been the strong ones of all my classmates, I could never understand why they begrudged me the grades and honors I got. I didn't want them. I would've given every part of my academic life up in a heartbeat to dive again. Still would. There are stranger looking things than me in the ocean.

"You know, one time off a remote Caribbean reef, I was diving with fish that had never been hunted. Big angelfish came up to me and peered right into my mask. They acted like St. Bernard puppies. I wasn't deep enough to have been euphoric, but suddenly I knew I could breathe water. I took my mask off and for a few seconds, I'm sure I did and then I was spit out again into my air-breathing mind and coughing body.

"So what does this have to do with this morning?" Roundacre was tired of the preamble.

"You ever hear about the Navy dolphin projects, Martin? Where they trained dolphins to take mines out to designated vessels, then set off the charge? I have been trying to find out for the past year whether I am some kind of trained dolphin."

Roundacre looked at him stubbornly. "What has that got to do with this morning?"

"When I was getting Rehab treatments, I got a lot of pain-killers. I thought I was probably addicted to at least the morphine derivative, and maybe the anti-depressants, too, but one morning I woke up pain free and not dying for anything stronger than fresh orange juice. I also had this speaking device. Martin, there was nothing wrong with my speech when I regained consciousness. I didn't need a mechanical larynx."

"I don't understand. You didn't know they were going to do the surgery?" Roundacre asked reluctantly.

"Martin, I didn't even think they knew who I was half the time. I was in a tiny locked back ward. When I first noticed that, I thought I was in a psych unit. When I asked the nurses, they said my rehab required special monitoring. I appeared to be the only rehab patient they had. Then I thought I was so screwed-up looking they were protecting other people from me. That's when the psych-medico came in and set me up with anti-depressants, as I clearly did not find that a happy thought. You realize I couldn't refuse meds or even hide them. I was just starting to get the little movement I have in my hands at that point.

"So, I spent a lot of time exploring the mental reefs of this drug-induced ocean. I noticed I kept circling this flooded city. When I got closer, I could see bodies and overturned buildings. It hadn't been flooded for very long. There was no coral started, very little silt and fragile stuff like paper was still wadded together.

"I thought it was just a recurring dream kind of thing until I woke up before I was supposed to one night and realized I was hooked to a machine I'd never seen before. There were standard sensors for monitoring a sleeping patient and then there was this collar around my throat. The collar felt like the working side of a bristle brush against my throat. When I squirmed, it felt like little worms hanging on from the inside.

"I don't know how I did it, but going crazy seems right. I screamed and wrenched my body in some wild contortion that snapped the collar. The pain was unbelievable; even after all the pain I'd been in for months.

"I guess I still thought someone would come and comfort me. They'd tell me there'd been a terrible mistake. But when I looked from face to face standing around my bed, all I saw was stark terror. Finally, someone gave me a shot in a bit of bony hip sticking out of my tangled sheets. I had a new voice when I woke up.

"The dream came back that night. Only this time, I recognized the city."

"What do you mean you recognized the city?" Roundacre was leaning towards Wilson to ask.

"It was the R&R hangout for the rig bums. I recognized one of the bodies floating out a doorway. We weren't friends, but we dove together a lot. Because I recognized him, I exploded awake from the nightmare. I was still sure it was a nightmare, but then I saw the glowing thing go back into the hole in my throat. At least that's where I thought it had to go when it disappeared. That and a kind of fullness in my throat that didn't make sense. I could not figure out what was going on. I knew gut deep something was really wrong.

"I'd had that feeling diving and sure enough, when I'd turn a corner, there'd be a couple sharks or a mess of fire coral. And I didn't believe in ghosties.

"When they changed the nursing shift, I pretended to be asleep. Whatever they had done had knocked out the pain all right, but I still was given a strong sleeping medication every night. I was so scared, it only put me under for a couple hours. I had hoped to overhear something that would give me a clue, but all I noticed was this glowing thing would creep back into my throat around three or four in the morning after I had been dreaming. Evidently, it didn't need the machine any more. It did need me. I never felt it come or go. I guess that was the whole point of the new metal voice. I hadn't connected to the dreams at all.

"I was still trying to figure this all out when the Feds turned up looking concerned about my being willing to go into mining school after my Rehab. ' You bet I said yessir Mr. Frog, how high do you want this mining student to jump?' I didn't anticipate having a full-time attendant of their choice who medicated me daily.

"Between the strain of being in a tough academic program and re-entering the world as a capable, independent, totally weird looking person, I didn't notice I couldn't remember much of my earlier life or my dreams. I thought it was natural. Now I know nothing in my life has been natural since I got bent. So, I don't know why I remembered this dream. Same old, same old. City underwater like a movie set. What blew it out of same old, same old was the baby caught halfway out a window, just flopping around, waving little baby waves to all the other dead people.

"And since I'm in the world now, not the loneliest rehab unit of all time, I overhear conversations like a normal person. Anyway, the next day after the baby dream, I hear this conversation in the cafeteria about a remote village in Greece where the ocean flooded the city in the night and no one had been saved. No one even knew it was coming.

"I went to a media screen at the other end of the room and there was the city I had dreamed about the night before. The announcer could hardly talk. He kept saying there was no warning.

"There couldn't have been any warning. All of a sudden I got it, there couldn't have been any warning. There's no seismology for dreams, is there, Martin?"

"What are you talking about?" Roundacre was getting mad again.

"Martin, I think I've been part of an experiment in distant meteorological warfare. Remember the classified stuff they were working on after second Gulf War in the '90's? World press screamed about criminal use of biological and chemical agents and got a ban through the UN. But and this is a big but, few people knew about secret work in Micronesia using dreams to control weather. Nothing was written to interfere with the research using human dreams to produce devastating weather anywhere the dreamer could imagine. The researchers thought they were getting close to finding a genetic variable that had produced the so-called rainmakers in every recorded culture.

"You're really crazy, you know that, Wilson, really crazy."

"Not me, Martin. These yo-yos finally managed to construct the dreaming component separate from a human dreamer. Or if you like, they isolated the part that dreams us. I personally, don't like any of it because I'm the best guinea pig they ever had. When this dreaming part is sent out of my body, it's luminous and sounds like riffles on water. It comes home after running amok to recharge.

"You are so crazy, Wilson. Where do you get all this crap?"

"Am I? Watch."

Roundacre looked out one of the hardened glass ports they called windows. The cliff face behind their quarters was turning bright orange in the late light. The wind was unabated. It blew spray from an impossible waterfall over the compound. Rivulets of dirty water covered the port as he watched.

"What the hell are you doing?"

Roundacre could hardly get his breath. When he looked back at the port, the mud was set hard and fragments were being blown off in the usual gusts. "What are you, some kind of monster?" Roundacre was yelling now.

"Me, Martin? I'm the monster?" Wilson shouted back at him. "They told my parents I was dead. Told me they gave them a huge settlement and I don't even know where they live because anything I remember from that time, the docs reclaimed. That means they took my memories and skewed them just enough so I wouldn't know where to start. And what do I do? Find them and show up like this? Doing this?"

Silence reverberated around them like heat waves. Finally Wilson started again, "I'm not here to replace you, Martin." Wilson's voice was set as quiet as the first day they had met on the landing strip.

"What are you talking about, you're not here to replace me?" Roundacre had seen Wilson's orders as they'd been cut and he was a replacement, period. He'd show Wilson the damned orders if he didn't believe it.

"The implant got out of hand the last couple of times they tried to use me. It isn't as exact a science, as they wanted to believe. I think my knowing the little I did started confusing whatever directs the dream. The wrong places got flooded twice. The last time it was the Director's hometown. He wasn't there, unfortunately.

"I was assigned to the most distant mining site possible. As far away as they could get me from any accidental triggering information. They were afraid to kill me any closer to home because the implant is clearly not stable any more.

"I'll die here. I'm too fragile to work full time. They knew that. I'm sure I was loaded with steroids the last few weeks of travel here, so you wouldn't get suspicious. They hoped the implant, that glowing thing, wouldn't be able to function here. You'd send back the sad news of my death and my nonexistent file would be closed.

"Pretty neat, huh? You'd get to watch me die and I don't think right now, you'd mind that much, and after a full, detailed report to all parties demonstrating a need to know; go on with your uneventful life. I envy you.

"I tried to kill myself this morning, but the implant blew out of me like an explosion. I don't think it is sentient, but it does know what it likes. Alive is what it likes. Got any ideas? I'm about out."

Wilson's head slumped forward on his skinny chest. His hands twisted in his lap like a hand-wringing screen-saver. Roundacre watched him and then looked out the window again.

"Can I get you anything?"

"No."

Roundacre decided he was blown. Too much information in too short a time. "Look, I'm going to go back to the dome. I'll do the end of the day test runs. Uh, you take it easy, okay?"

The ridiculous hat bobbed a few times.

Roundacre jounced just faster than was comfortable back to the dome trying to remember what he'd thought of first this morning. Water in his room. Why? When the implant made water events happen, the result was disaster, often catastrophic ruin. Whatever had filled up his room hadn't left a disaster.

Did it have to leave Wilson's body to organize dream space? What was it trying to do? Get Roundacre's attention because Wilson was trying to kill himself? Could the water effect be modulated somehow? Wilson's despair had set off local phenomenon, non-disastrous, and so had his anger.

And why hadn't he, Martin Roundacre, the stupifyingly sane, called the Psychline to get Wilson sedated after listening to this whole line of bull? Didn't he really think Wilson was crazy? Guess not.

All those reports of water damage, what about them?

He was getting mixed up just thinking of the questions. Roundacre opened the airlock entrance exactly as he had almost five hours earlier. Everything looked the same in the work area. That is, the way it had looked to him when he lived here alone. Roundacre walked through the different assaying stations and stopped in front of one that appeared to be malfunctioning. He pushed the re-set button reading a waiting printout while the machine booted up again. The report meticulously described an aquifer.

On this planet.

The malfunction was due to inadequate data the machine was trying to use. Most water data had been pulled from its system to save space.

Roundacre walked to a viewing port and looked out at the tiny barren planet. He wondered how long it would take for the implant to create enough water to stimulate an atmosphere. Early soil samples had been remarkably similar to terran soils. It was one of the oldest jokes among mining engineers that on these ore-rich planets, all you'd need for a real garden was to add water. Ha-ha.

Martin sat in the darkened dome for a long time thinking. If he allied himself to Wilson, it looked like he wouldn't ever get to retire on Earth and have a garden. But sending someone to his site and expecting him to let him die was a bad misreading of his psych-profile. He'd come to like Wilson. This story of his was screwy, but so was a roomful of water that went away, reports with aquifers on PL18-629, and that damned waterfall out back. Wilson really loved reefs. Maybe he was going to dream an ocean here. Couldn't hurt anybody.

He'd talk with Wilson tonight. Somehow if the implant could take a man's dreaming and send water, well, maybe if Wilson had a better dream and a friend besides. Martin stopped pacing.

Wilson was all right. No way was he was going to call in a report of a set-up death. And he sure wasn't about to wear that damned hat himself.

Roundacre punched in the number for their quarters. Fidgeting, he waited for Wilson to answer.

"Do you read me, Blake?"

"Roger, Martin."

"I've been trying to sort this out, Blake. How long do you think it would take to create an atmosphere here?"

"You mean, use the dreaming?"

"I mean I like to garden the way you like to dive. Living well and all that. You help me cover the changes on the reports they want I help you build a reef. What do you say?

So, the report Martin Roundacre filed on the death of Blake Wilson made its way through security channels and because it was marked *read and destroy all linked files*, within two days all traces of Blake Wilson disappeared.

He was in fact, alive and well on the small planet they decided to name Rubicon.

Martin Roundacre developed an earth-side reputation for being mildly eccentric as he became more passionately involved in his hobbies, breeding salt-water fish and collecting antique strains of open-pollinated seeds. Shipment after shipment of seeds arrived every two years. Reef fish, corals and kelps filled the rest of his elective supply quota. Unmanned ships, landing blindly but precisely, were oblivious to the new palm-lined beach with row after row of heartbreak blue waves hissing quietly ashore. Out on the farthest reef, two snorkel tubes dipped and swayed.

Aloha Oe.

Barbara Riley

Barbara Riley is an author and editor living in Santa Fe, NM. Her dark fantasy novel, *Elements of M'nee* has been accepted for publication by Antelope Press (Dillon, MT) and will be available online as well as soft bound in July 2002. Her children's book, *Grow! Grow! Grow!*, illustrated by artist Janet Guggenheim is being released by Azro Press (Santa Fe, NM) in September 2002.

Deviled Eggs

August 21, 1999. Black slime, red haze, and bubbling beads of sweat the size of Lake Erie pouring from their skin — just a typical first day in Hell for Edward and Simon. Unfortunately, they weren't dead.

"Where are we?"

"Where *are* we? God almighty, Simon, it ain't Disneyland. Something happened. We're...we're in *Hell!*"

"Hell! What? How... *why...?*"

Edward frowned at the hot ebony muck sucking at his feet. "I really wish I had that string of answers," he muttered as he hopped from foot to foot only to have the blistering goo string from his heels like licorice taffy then recoil with the boing of an axle spring. "I didn't even know we were dead."

Simon howled. Being in Hell was bad enough; remembering that death was required to get there seemed a whole lot worse. Slowly, his lips disappeared between his teeth.

Edward caught Simon's nervous transformation into Larry-Lip-Biter and clapped a sweaty hand on his friend's shoulder. "Simon, oh virgin one, double Ph.D. computer czar at twenty-two, Mr. Sunday dinner with Mom *every single week*, listen to me. What have you ever done in your life that would cause you to end up down here? Now, come on, get a grip. We're not dead. I can't explain it, but I *know* it. We just have to figure out how we got here and how to undo it." He lifted his hand from Simon's shoulder to rub the burning balls that used to be his sky-blue eyes. "Think, Simon, *think!*"

Simon popped his bloodless lips back out and spun a slow circle. There wasn't much to look at, just steam and flames, hard angles, and red. Red — everything except the sizzling glob beneath their feet was some shade of red. The devil's welcome cavern was irritatingly stereotypical. "I think I know. It was the computer, Edward; we were accessing that new Web site. Remember?"

Crisping up like a luau pig made remembering a definite chore, and Edward's brows knit into a swayback willy worm as he tried to focus on Simon's words. "The Web site?"

"Yes. I remember. We were in my office when you spotted that new Web site: 'Hell 101 — The Devilishly Fun Adventure For The Brilliant Of Mind'. Oh my God!" Simon slapped his palm to his temple. "We thought it was a new brain teaser game by those bozos at Games Bedazzle."

Slowly, the twisted reality set in and Simon's hand slunk lamely down the side of his head like an overcooked noodle. "Oh man," he concluded miserably, "it wasn't a Games Bedazzle site."

"Simon, give me a break. You can't mean…are you…are you implying the devil has his own Web site?"

"Well, it's no harder to believe than the fact that we're standing here heating up like Roman candles, is it? I can't figure the how of it, though," Simon continued glumly as he swayed his head, trying to arrange the puzzle pieces. "All I know is that we opened the site and started answering those questions on the screen. Now that I think about it, they *were* strangely technical for game questions."

Edward's head snapped up. "Damn, if you're not right. And when the questions were done we clicked on the warp speed icon to play the advanced game, and…"

"And the modem started to whine…" Simon put in.

"And the mouse got hot…" Edward added.

"And…"

Both men froze with the knowledge that what followed the latest 'and' was glaringly apparent.

"Jesus, Simon, what the hell are we saying? We just analyzed ourselves to the conclusion that we got sucked through a modem down to Hell!"

"Well, like I said, what is so unbelievable?" Simon reasoned, his 206 IQ finally booting his emotions back to their snug little cubbyhole behind his intellect. "After all, we are nothing but energy when all is said and done. And don't look at me like I should know all the answers. If I knew how to transport human beings through modems, don't you think I'd have chosen a better vacation spot than Hades? I feel like a blister about to pop."

"Okay, alright," Edward appeased, flinching as the wind suddenly bit his face with the brutal finesse of a whip tail, "let's say we've figured it out; now let's figure out how to get the hell *out* of Hell."

"Leave, gentlemen? No, no, no. I assure you your accommodations are quite permanent."

Bless the black slime beneath their feet. Without it, Edward and Simon would have flattened each other trying to escape their first sight of Diablo himself.

He arrived in a hurricane gust of blazing horns and hooves with an unnaturally fluffy tail swirling at his backside. But his face appeared quite human, and he was as gleeful as a New Year's Eve drunk. Just like his environment, Satan was red – all of him, even his eyes. If it weren't for the strange pink glow hovering about him, it would have been impossible to make him out against the equally crimson mist.

"Aren't they magnificent, Hittles?" the devil gushed, thrusting his rock-hard cherry-colored chest forward with pride. He had done it. He had finally gotten some prized eggheads in Hell. Now it had class. No longer would it be just the waste treatment plant of eternity.

"Yes, my liege, you have done it indeed."

Edward and Simon squinted in the direction of the seemingly disembodied voice, finally zeroing in on a human form sporting a blazing red jumpsuit with scores of medals twinkling from his chest.

"Hitler!" Edward hissed.

"Ah, they know you, Hittles," the devil sighed happily. "I told you eggheads were just what we needed."

"Don't call me an egghead."

Edward reeled with disbelief. They were toe to toe with the Prince of Darkness, and Simon was testy about a little name-calling?

"God, Simon," Edward whispered, "watch your mouth."

"*ARRRGGHHHH*! You'll not speak that name again! Never! *Never*!"

The devil's bellow nearly fried their brains. Both friends rocked from the volume, then sucked in their breath as the king of demons mutated over and over before their eyes. He morphed into everything from the human/goat form they had been addressing to nothing but blood red lightening bolts connected by threads of black. The scores of split-second transformations left Simon and Edward with eyes the size of cue balls. But they got the message. Mentioning God in Satan's presence was a definite no-no.

A second later, he vanished in a puff of fluffy pink. Hittles remained.

"Get the point?" the devil's right-hand man asked cordially.

"Uh, how...what..."

Hittles smiled and waved off Simon's stuttering. "Oh, that. The master is wonderful, isn't he? The form you saw was for your benefit. It was what you expected, so he gave it to you. He's very pleased you have joined us, you know. He's been so dejected lately with the steady stream of dimwits populating Hell – myself excepted, of course. Hell has always been dreaded by the holy and embraced by the wicked, but for way too long now, it has, so sadly, deteriorated."

Simon and Edward shared the same silent dubious question: '*It was possible to deteriorate Hell?*'

Hittles swung his arm in a wide arc. "Look for yourselves," he continued as his hand passed through the hot red nothingness that engulfed them. Instantly an opening appeared.

The portal allowed Simon and Edward to gaze into the never-ending fields of Hell. Everywhere they looked willowy human forms were moving about and carrying on as if they were still alive. But their actions were just so...*stupid*.

Judges in judicial robes pounded benches with their gavels; politicians wrestled over podiums, and paparazzi blinded themselves over and over with camera flashes. From criminals to HMO directors to trophy hunters, land developers, and tobacco execs, it was a veritable cornucopia of society's Wrong-Way Willies.

The repetition was awful – thousands of mercilessly wet human souls repeating, repeating, repeating, their indignities of life. Eternal damnation was a macabre merry-go-round of bad life choices mired in a pool of boiling salty yuk.

Simon squeezed his eyes shut. Edward stared. Hittles pressed on.

"As you can see, there is little enough sport for the master in this sorrowful lot. Hell needed an infusion, some thinkers, some *class*. And," he paused to close the window and spread his arms triumphantly, "here you are! Demons alive! You're just what my poor dejected king needed to perk him right up."

"Well, but of course," Edward vowed sarcastically, "we can't have a depressed devil, now can we? Why, let's just pluck 'em out and give the sad old guy our brains on a silver platter. What do you say, Simon?"

Edward was tempted to finish with the flip of a Heil Hitler salute, but Simon's roll of the eyes and a glance at the dead fuhrer stopped his hand from raising more than an inch. In the end, he turned it into a crotch scratch just to be safe.

The medals swung heavily on Hittle's chest as he shrugged off the sniping.

"Well, whatever."

He turned to leave, wishing he could go poof like the master, but alas, in spite the God-like pedestal he had put himself on, he had been but mortal after all. He would never get to poof out.

"But we are not eggheads."

Simon's low utterance made Hittles turn back, and his ballooning smile sent the square hair on his upper lip straight up into his nostrils. "Yes you are, and we know it. Brainy eggs, just what the master wished for. Only *you* answered all of the questions right. Well, you're the devil's eggs now. Hey, I guess that makes you deviled eggs!"

Misery slobbered all over the eggheads as Hittles split a gut at his own joke, turned on his heel, and disappeared into the mist.

"Never did like Mondays," Edward deadpanned in an effort to force a calm he didn't feel.

Simon's own nerves were sizzling like a slab of Sunday morning bacon. "Yup."

Each fell into uneasy silence. Edward stared blankly at his steaming shoes, vaguely wondering how long it would take them to disintegrate while Simon worked his lips past his teeth all over again.

"Pssssst."

Simon looked up. "What was that? Did you say 'pssssst'?"

"Simon, don't lose it on me now. No one's in this particular Hellhole but us."

"Pssssst."

Both men heard it this time and strained to scan the haze.

"Pssssst."

"Alright already," Edward shouted to no one, "we're listening! But if all you can say is 'pssssst', then don't bother saying it again!"

"Well, you don't have to be so ornery, you know."

Both men spun at the sound of the female voice but didn't see anyone who could have produced it.

"Who are you?" Simon whispered as his eyes, and those of his friend, bugged futilely in all directions.

"That's better. Finding yourself in a bit of a pickle is no reason to be rude. I'm here to help you. My name is Rosie, and you can quit looking for me. I'm not there."

Edward spit with disgust. "Oh great – the perfect cap on this winner of a day, a floating voice from Hell that's not even here."

"My, you're grumpy when you're overheated, aren't you, Edward?"

"Grumpy? I'm a lit match! Hell, yes, I'm grumpy. Who *are* you?"

"I told you. Rosie. You can't see me because I'm talking to you in your minds. I'm not a 'voice from Hell'; I'm an angel."

"An angel...how are you going to help us, Rosie?"

Simon's soft question was drowned by Edward's much louder one. "Are we dead?"

"Yes, Edward, you're as dead as a doornail, shucked of life like a cleaned ear of corn, pitted, spitted, and ready to roast; you're..."

"I get it already," Edward snapped.

"We really are dead?" Simon was suddenly greatly disappointed.

"Nope."

Edward's last functioning nerve sparked like a downed live wire. "Nope? What do you mean 'nope'? You just ever-so-colorfully outlined our complete deadness, Miss Self-Proclaimed Angel."

"Just a little bit of heavenly wit, Edward," Rosie replied with a tinkle of laughter.

"Well, aren't you funny. I can see you're going to be a big help. Besides, who ever heard of an angel in Hell?"

"Edward, ever heard of a little thing called faith?"

"I've heard of it, Miss Voice-Only Rosie," he grumped with lemon ball sourness, "I just don't know if you're worthy of it."

"Well, my friend, it's your choice. A simple leap of faith, or, you-know-who's newest plaything."

Simon jumped into the fray. "How do we get out of here, Rosie? We'll do whatever you say."

"Excellent! Now go home."

"What!" The bellow was a perfect duet.

Rosie was nonplussed. "I said 'go home'."

"Listen Miss Annoying Angel," Edward snapped, "are you new at this? Now, are you going to help us or what!"

Rosie's strum-of-a-harp sigh dashed a little more salt onto Edward's bleeding patience. "I don't mean to be confusing, really I don't," the angel voice continued sincerely. "But, I'm only allowed to give you the nudge you need to rectify the wrong being done to you. I can't really interfere."

"Rosie..." Edward drawled her name in exasperation.

"I'm sorry, Edward," Rosie lamented, genuinely frustrated with her guidelines. "I don't make the rules you know. And I just can't do much. But all you really need to do is remember why you are where you are. I wish I could do more, but I have to go now. Goodbye. Oh, and Edward? One more thing. Your foot's on fire."

Edward's chin dove to his chest, but even though they may have felt ignited, there were no flames shooting from his toes. He was about to let their haloed comedian have it when they heard her melodic laughter fade into nothingness.

"Well, ha ha ha," he sniped.

Simon was concentrating. "What did she mean 'remember why we are here'?"

"Stop it, Simon. I'm telling you she was no angel, just a trick of old Beelzebub. And I haven't got a friggin' clue why we are here. I only know that pretty soon our feet will not be the only things in flames. That big red guy ain't Santa, and I don't really wish to provide the chestnuts to roast on his open fire."

"*Egghead.*"

"Great, now you're calling me one."

"Not you, *us*! We're here because the devil thinks we're *eggheads.* That's what Rosie was trying to tell us – to use the brains God gave us! Now listen, we know we are not dead. We also know there's a way out of here if we use our brains. And we got here..."

"Through a modem!" Edward shouted, jumping on Simon's speeding train of thought. "If we came by modem, we can return the same way!"

"Right! All we have to do is find Old Red Eye's computer and reverse the transmission."

"But how? I can't see anything in this bloody wasteland!" Edward swiped the sweat from the back of his neck with both hands. "Judas Priest, if it gets any hotter, we'll be cinders before we get our snowball's chance of finding the damn thing."

"I know. I can barely function. But we have to try before Satan decides to scramble our 'eggs' for a few demonic jollies."

"Well, *I* sure as hell don't know what to do next!" Edward shouted, throwing up his arms frustration.

"Holy Moses! Edward, look behind you."

Edward's sweeping arms had opened two wispy windows just like Hittles had done. The first window opened on some kind of flat maze – like a big game board with hapless souls as the game pieces. Through the second chasm they saw a museum-like room filled with gilded pictures of the devil in various pursuits and pleasures, his very own egomaniacal satanic Hall Of Fame.

"Whoa! Simon, this could be it. See if we can open some more. Maybe we'll find the computer. Hurry!"

Edward swished his arms past the portals he'd opened and they closed right on cue. Moving a couple of feet in another direction, he swung again and another steaming ball of mist cracked an eye revealing a raging red river filled with writhing, bleating souls. High-ranking Hellsters fished for the poor sods with giant hooks baited with fluffy little clouds. Shaking his head, Edward swept the window closed and opened another as Simon tried his own hand at the magic.

In short order, four arms were spinning like the plastic wings of a couple of pink flamingo lawn ornaments. Desperately they flung this way and that – opening, closing, opening, closing, trying not to gape at every bizarre or wicked scene they produced. It was Simon who happened upon the devil himself pawing through a pile of computer books and Internet directories.

Gut punched and struck dumb, Simon poked Edward into turning his way. His mortification was instant. There was Mr. Red Stuff all decked out in a white shirt, coffee-stained red tie, black jeans, and golden wire glasses over those rotten apple eyeballs.

Edward's and Simon's eyes met and slowly scanned Simon's own attire as they exchanged the same sick realization. The devil was dressed just like Simon.

"Oh my God!" Simon wailed. "What does this mean? What is he planning?"

"This just can't be good, Simon; we've got to hurry. Keep looking!"

Simon sealed off the horrid scene then sidestepped to try another view.

Jackpot.

"Edward..."

Even with the taffy floor it took Edward only a heartbeat to get to Simon's window. "Damn, Simon," he whispered, "it looks like a thousand NASA mainframes."

"I've never seen anything like it." Simon's heart banged his ribs as he eyed the gargantuan boards. Millions of pulsating lights seemed to spread to infinity, and there, blinking boldly in front, was some kind of haunting count-down clock. "What the hell is that? Oh... my... God. Edward, it's counting down to 12:00 am, year 2000. *He's* responsible!"

Edward rolled his eyes. "Well, now, there's a surprise. I guess Bill Gates is off the hook. Now quit staring and come on! We've got to find a way to get to it."

"But, will we even know the language for this thing?"

"I don't know, Simon, but we'd better find out fast. Listen."

Simon cocked an ear to the sound of whipping wind.

He was coming.

Panic volleyed between them as they froze with shriveling fear and ignorant indecision. What to do next? They could see the computer, but there wasn't exactly a sidewalk leading to it. What good did it do to see it through those wispy windows when they didn't have an inkling of how to leave the hole they were in?

Two confused heads bobbed in all directions as if being manipulated by a drunken puppeteer. The wind grew louder and their sweat leaked harder.

"What do we do?" Simon hollered over the howling gusts.

"Why are you looking at me? You're the prized double-Ph.D. egghead. Do something!" Edward shouted right back.

"Dive," a sweet voice whispered.

"Rosie? Thank God!"

"Yes, Simon, do remember to thank God. Now *dive*."

The wind was peaking at a deafening keen.

"Knock, knock, my eggheads," the devil called out happily from just out of view.

Simon and Edward shared one bolstering look, lifted their arms and Superman'd their way into the computer portal.

With the suck of a hundred thousand Hoovers, they were pulled through the steamy hole then instantly found themselves belly-flopping very un-Superman-like landings.

Arms outstretched like fallen tree limbs, they cranked their necks in reverse to see if Satan the computer nerd had followed. But the misty hatch had closed on their heels; they couldn't see a thing. Unfortunately, they could hear.

"Where are they, Hittles?" The devil roared his disappointment. He wanted to play brain games, now!

Simon and Edward felt the roar as if they were inside of it.

"Rosie?" Simon whispered as softly as possible.

"No need to whisper, Simon, he can't hear you. His bellows do shame thunder, but fortunately, his hearing is not his strong suit."

"But I thought you couldn't help us anymore," Simon questioned as he picked himself up.

"I wouldn't be able to if you hadn't already figured it out for yourself. But listen, Mr. Short-Fuse Temper can look in a lot of places at once. Hurry up now."

With nerves packed as tight as fireworks, the kidnapped mortals launched themselves in opposite directions in search of a keyboard. Expertly, they fondled the towers of humming circuits buzzing with the devil's warped agenda, scouring wall after wall of ports, lights, screens, and buttons that seemed to have no rhyme or reason for their existence.

"I want them *now*, or souls will *paaaaayyyyyy!*"

Satan's reverberating ultimatum shot up the egghead's backbones with the velocity of a bottle rocket, exploding violently in their brains. It rocked both Simon and Edward off their feet.

"Son of a ...!" Edward rubbed a battered ear as he mustered the right stuff to wobble himself upright. "Well, thank you very much, Lucifer, you stinkin' goat. I'm pretty sure my eardrums are now located right behind my eyeballs. Man, would I love to ram a couple of tons of fertilizer down this guy's set of pipes!"

"Happy Birthday To You, Happy Birthday To You, Happy Birthday My Dear Simon..."

Rosie's little ditty fell soothingly on the searchers' scorched ears leaving Edward in complete confusion and Simon slapping his forehead in delighted recognition.

"Rosie, you're the best! Edward, the keyboard is in a drawer! Mom always hid my birthday presents in the bureau drawers and I always found them. Look for a drawer!"

Adrenalin pumping, both men pawed and pulled at the underbelly of the microchip beast for that elusive little conglomeration of keys that would be their gateway out of Hell.

Eyes down, immersed in their quest, they examined themselves right into a head-to-head collision.

"Holy..." Edward's curse never got to taste air as both men froze in morbid realization. Their pantlegs were flapping.

Wind!

Satan!

"Boys, BOYS!" Rosie's little voice shrilled like the squall of a harried seagull. "Tick-tock, time's flying; don't freeze now unless you're interested in a new permanent zip code, like 66666!

Hurry! You can do it!" Rosie wasn't allowed to show them the answer, but surely a little cheerleading would be permissible.

She launched her own version of the 'hot/cold' game, singing out with glee when they proceeded in the right direction and wailing sadly if they strayed. They caught on immediately and molded their search to her musical ups and downs.

But the wind howled fiercer and louder until Rosie's vocalizations were drifting in and out like a low-wattage AM radio signal. Tears welled up in four wind-dried eyes as Simon and Edward put everything they had into just staying upright in the face of the powerful gale.

"I have them now!" the devil thundered, and Simon and Edward knew time was about to stand agonizingly still. Like a raindrop in Death Valley, their hope of success evaporated in a hiss of steam before it could fully materialize.

Ragged fear shooed both men under the nearest bank of circuits. Simon landed successfully, but Edward yelped and cursed as he cracked his head. The stabbing pain and the score of imaginary bluebirds twittering before his glazed eyes proved, however, to be worth the bother. There, peeking from the recessed, head-butted drawer, was the elusive keyboard.

Simon wasted no time in grabbing the bonanza and pulling it onto his lap. "Edward, this is it! Find a screen and tell me what's there," he ordered as he pounded the keys in rapid-fire succession with file-searching commands. He tried every scrap of computer lingo that had ever flitted through his mind, meshing the languages he knew with some that just seemed to pop into his brain from nowhere before sailing freely out of his fingertips.

With the scent of victory filling his nostrils, Edward blinked away the fluttering hallucination and crawled to the nearest screen. It was ablaze with data, and he started calling out information as fast as his pounding head would allow while Rosie chattered in the background. He couldn't believe his ears. Rosie's voice became *his* voice, then Simon's, then his again, and it was coming from a hundred different locations. She was sandbagging the devil and that flunky, Hitler! Edward's gut roiled with hope as he rattled off the scripts scrolling before his face.

"I've got 'em!" Hittles called out over and over, each time coming up with nothing for his enthusiasm. Rosie's ventriloquist act was running the old soul ragged.

Seconds later, Edward called out the formula Simon had been praying for.

"Oh God! Edward, I've *got* it! Come on, we have to do this together. Hurry!"

Fighting Old Harry's wind, Edward dropped to his hands and knees and scurried like a sand crab back to Simon's side. He was laying his hand on Simon's when he heard a squeak from Rosie and spotted two cloven hooves and a pair of shiny red boots coming to a halt directly in front of their knees.

"Going somewhere, my little eggheads?" the devil tsk-tsked with a swish of his fat tail. "You haven't disappointed me. You're as smart as I'd dreamed, but your little games are going to cost you a few unpleasant blisters nonetheless."

Slowly the devil and Hittles squatted to face the runaways.

For a heartbeat, the four adversaries stonily squared off, then a smile snaked its way across Simon's sorely-bitten lips.

Gripping Edward's hand tightly to his, he punched the 'enter' key. The crescendoing whine of the giant modem caught the devil by surprise and he snapped his bulbous red face toward the sound then back to see his truant eggheads beaming with a couple of really big fat cat happy faces.

"Ever played 'Simon Says'?" Simon inquired with saccharine politeness. "It's a real fun brain game."

Furious, the devil started to waver, his signature precursor to a maddened morph.

"You want to play with us, Satan, old boy?" Simon taunted as the welcome heat shot though his and Edward's hands. "Okay, let's play. 'Simon Says' *bite me!*"

Then, like they'd never been there, they were gone. Rosie's cheerful giggles and a nearly melted keyboard were all that remained. The deviled eggs had won.

With a plop, Edward and Simon found themselves back in Simon's office, salty and slimy, but gloriously alive. Scrambling to their feet, they whooped and hollered, and jitterbugged their elation, only to have their triumphant dance pale against a larger momentum.

The floor swayed and bucked, and they heard someone in another office yell "Quake!". But Edward and Simon knew it was only the pouting of one very nasty computer-egghead-want-a-be. It made them deliriously happy.

As fast as the rumbling and tumbling had started, it was over, and a sobered Simon dashed to his safe, whirled the combination, and snatched a blood red disk from inside.

"Just his color," Edward sneered.

Simon's fingers blurred as he maneuvered his way back to the 'Hell 101' site. Once there, he popped in the disk and sent a viral bug with the appetite of Godzilla coursing back to that behemoth hardware somewhere in the pit of Hell. Soon 'Hell 101' looked like nothing but a field of daisies dancing in the sun.

Satisfied, Simon rifled a drawer and produced a pair of scissors. "You know we can never tell anyone," he instructed as he snipped the tie from his neck. "We'd be carted away for sure. This is Silicon Valley. Science, not science fiction, and all that. Besides, we'll *eventually* find the logical explanation. Agreed?"

Edward pulled a second pair of scissors from the drawer and laid waste to the curtain beside him. "Right. But you know what else?"

"What?"

Simon finished mutilating his tie then began to clip the lettering from a manual on his desktop.

"I'm gonna' be a good boy every day of my life."

Edward's promise, delivered between deep dimples, made Simon's own lips curve.

Ten minutes of slicing and hacking produced a cardboard box brimming with ruined paraphernalia. Edward shouldered the spoils as the devil conquerors made their way through the corridors, past dozens of other work-addicted 'brainy eggs', and down the elevator to the basement.

In minutes they arrived at the old incinerator, grateful it had been kept alive to obliterate evolving secret technology inappropriate for shredding or recycling. Simon pried open the door, not even flinching as the leaping flames produced a meager heat unworthy of two souls who had felt the ultimate boil.

"Well done, my friends."

Simon and Edward looked up at the sound of Rosie's voice.

"You saved us, Rosie," Edward admitted humbly. "I doubted you, and you saved us anyway."

"Ah, pish, Edward, I only nudged. You and Simon saved yourselves."

"Thank you, dear Rosie."

"You're very welcome, Simon. Now come on, you two; angels don't cry, so don't go getting mushy on me. Have a wonderful life, my friends."

Neither Simon nor Edward answered, for the skip in their heartbeats told them she was gone.

Turning back to the task at hand, Edward lifted the remnants from his shoulder and tossed them into the jaws of the boiler. Deviled eggs would not be the main course on Satan's buffet this day, and the dreaded Y2K would be nothing but a passing blip of annoyance. With indescribable relief starting to sink in, the victors took one last cleansing look into the inferno before Simon slammed the door.

With the sealing thud of the handle lock, they left box, contents, nerves, and memory to the fire.

There was no backward glance as they walked away, comforted that soon there would be nothing left but charcoal gray ashes.

No longer would everything in the box be... devil red.

Tricia Spencer

Spencer loves her husband, her house full of animals, and the written word, expressed in a variety of genres. Other works include a completed historical romance, *Elysium*, a variety of short stories, and *Tips, The Server's Guide To Bringing Home The Bacon*, a nonfiction self-help book for the restaurant industry. *Tips* was the winner of the Best Nonfiction Book Award at the Southwest Writers Workshop International Competition. In addition to the honor bestowed by Crossquarter, "Deviled Eggs" has been recognized as a winner in the L. Ron Hubbard Writer's Of The Future Competition For Science Fiction. Tricia was the author of a Spirit Prayer Calendar for the new millennium in 2000, and has received national competition recognition for songwriting. And, of course, as with all writers whose heads brim with words, she has a variety of works in progress.

Father to the Man

It was truly an alien world. Harrison often thought this. In the morning, the small sun threw countless rays, bright yet weak, onto the planet's mottled surface of black rock and purple grass. The sky blended lavender with blue, and the air was cold — especially after dusk, when the temperature dropped below freezing. It was like this for much of the sun's cycle, which was almost twice as long as a standard Earth year.

A few hardy creatures flourished in one region of this world: bear-like carnivores with deep growls and three-inch fangs; heavy birds which could not fly but lived off their own fat while shielding their thick gray eggs; long, golden fish whose third eye acted as a periscope as they swam near the surfaces of the lakes, watching for flying insects to grab with their quicksilver tongues.

A lone outpost also stood in this place: a cavernous dome housing a plethora of rooms, laboratories, supplies and equipment. A tall man moved slowly from one room to another, safe in his domain, protected from the outside. It was his kingdom, his name was Dr. Reynolds Harrison, and this was Harrison's World. He'd been the first to locate it and, by dint of his political clout, also the first to be transported to it. The Government of Earth sent him there after constructing and furnishing the dome according to his specifications; and the officials were still grateful to him for his many years of service as an astro-locator and cybernetic specialist.

Harrison had of late been working on two very disparate projects: calculating the probable existence and distance of planets and moons that lay much farther out in this star system; and refitting and enhancing the computerized, lifelike dog and cat which roamed the dwelling. He knew that the data on the artificial animals was eagerly awaited back on Earth, where efforts to curb the pet population humanely had met with limited success.

But he'd been forced to put these projects on hold for now, as another matter occupied him — a matter of life and death involving his only child, Alexander Reynolds Harrison — "Rennie," to his father. The boy was eighteen now, chronologically an adult. But he didn't think or behave quite like others his age, since his life and experiences were confined to this home, this world. He'd been here ever since he could remember. Rennie knew only his father and had no clear memory of his mother. Harrison had been both parents to him.

Now the older man had to play the role of healer as well. Rennie was ill; his body hadn't functioned properly for several days, and his father worried as he wiped the boy's glistening forehead with a soft, moist cloth. *The fever must break soon,* Harrison told himself. *It must, or Rennie will die.*

"Papa's here," the scientist whispered, unashamed of talking to his adult son that way. "I'm right here. I won't leave my boy. Rennie, can you talk to me? Try to say something — please?"

The cracked lips moved, ever so slightly, and a sound came out that Harrison had longed to hear. "Papa…" the boy rasped, barely audible. "I hear you…but I can't see you."

Harrison sighed, with the deepest sense of relief he had ever felt, and bent down to kiss Rennie gently. "You're going to be fine, son, just fine." Harrison blinked back tears. "You'll see me again very soon. Why, you'll be up and about in a matter of days, doing all the things you used to do before."

"Mmm…" Rennie's response was almost inaudible, but his father took it as an agreement. He ran another full diagnostic scan on the boy and was pleased to see the readings confirm what he'd thought: the life functions were slowly moving away from the red danger zones, into the gray normal ones.

Harrison stood up, stretching his tight muscles. *Not as young as I used to be*, he remarked silently. *But Rennie makes up for it. He'll carry on where I have to leave off.*

He reached down again to smooth his son's hair. Rennie looked much like his father had at that age: clear green eyes; sandy blond hair that refused to be managed; a lithe body and a husky voice; a Roman nose and prominent chin. Harrison chuckled as he recalled old jokes his colleagues had made about the nose and chin. He figured they would probably say the same things if they ever met his son.

But Harrison knew that would never happen. Conditions on Earth weren't getting much better, which was why so many of its inhabitants had been trying to leave, to seek out other, better places to live. Besides, Harrison's World was Rennie's entire universe, and there was no logic and kindness in uprooting him.

Harrison looked up suddenly, startled by the sound of jagged tree bark striking the window, blown by cold winds. The trees were in their shedding stage, peeling off their outer, brittle dead skin to reveal the renewed layers beneath. The wind grew in force and began to howl. However, the outer structure of the dome was made of material that could withstand almost anything, and Harrison saw no reason to worry.

Still, he shivered. He looked down at Rennie and said softly, "I'll protect you, son. Nothing will ever be able to harm you. And you'll live a long, long time.

"I swear it."

Rennie continued to scoop the synthetic eggs and toast into his mouth almost as quickly as he could chew and swallow, between gulps of black coffee extract.

"Slow down, son," his father said.

"Mmm…can't help it…it's like I haven't eaten in years." Rennie finished the food, wiped his mouth, then looked up at Harrison. "I had the strangest dreams, Papa. They didn't make any sense. I kept seeing machines I couldn't recognize, weird patterns and shapes, colors that didn't belong together..."

"Fever dreams, Rennie. At least we know you haven't suffered any brain damage; that's the important thing. Do you want to rest?"

"Oh, God, no more rest for me," the boy said, taking his items to the Wash-All unit. "I think I'll get some study time in, then take care of the animals, make some observations —"

"All right," his father said, "I give up. Just don't wear yourself out — please?"

"Of course not, Papa," the boy replied, heading off to the library. Harrison knew it would be a while before he returned.

This left the scientist with time on his own hands which he wanted to spend productively. But it wouldn't be easy trying to concentrate on internal dynamic processes or gravity shifts when something much more urgent occupied his mind. He would have to tell Rennie soon or else all would be lost.

But how? he asked himself. *How do I interrupt his life, upset him, to tell him we don't have much time left together?*

Harrison sat down at the auxiliary computer console, staring at the waiting blue screen.

"Rennie, am I bothering you?"

"Hm? No, Papa, not at all. I was just looking through an old holo series."

Rennie was seated at the enormous glass table in the library, his index finger poised above a green button on a console, as a colorful holographic image hovered two feet in front of him. Most people on Earth still had photo albums, but Harrison had seen to it that his own world would be as modern as he could make it.

The images continued to change: Rennie at different stage of life — crawling, walking playing with the pets, celebrating a birthday. Harrison gestured at one particular holo. "Oh yes, I remember that trip," he remarked, gazing at the image of himself beside a very young, grinning Rennie. The boy was bundled in heavy clothing, and he held onto a fishing line that fed into a hole in the ice.

His father continued: "One of the few days during the year when we can go outside and touch the rest of the world. Soon you can do that again, son."

"Not by myself, Papa. I mean — I could, but I wouldn't want you to miss out."

Harrison took a deep breath to try to calm himself before he spoke again. "Turn off the machine, please. I need to talk to you. Come over here to the sofa."

The boy did as he'd been asked and sat down next to his father. Harrison fidgeted before he spoke: "Rennie...You're an intelligent, perceptive, careful person. You know how to take care of things around here. You could handle it yourself if the need arose."

The boy nodded, though he looked puzzled.

"Well, you're going to have that opportunity much sooner than you might have thought, because —"

Harrison broke off when their cybernetic cat, Furball, wandered into the room and jumped up to sit between them. "I just finished her modifications," Harrison said, "and the one on Dagmar, too. He'll be along shortly."

"Papa, you weren't finished yet," Rennie reminded him.

The scientist forced himself to go on: "Son...I'm not going to live to the end of the year. I've got perhaps a few months. The illness I have is terminal; there's no cure. I was probably carrying it before I left Earth."

"Wh — what?" Rennie's response came out in a frightened whisper. "You're going to *die*? Oh, Papa, why didn't you tell me this before? You hardly left us any time to prepare —"

"I only found it out recently, son, in the results of my last bio-check. The damn thing was just lying dormant, biding its time. Don't you think I would have told you sooner if I'd known? Rennie, I'm sorry."

The boy was sobbing, no longer listening to his father. Harrison tried to embrace him, but he shoved away and ran from the room.

I handled that so poorly, Harrison said to himself. *Dear God...I just can't imagine how I'm going to tell him the rest.*

Rennie sat on the kitchen floor, absently stroking the pet dog, Dagmar. The animal lay with his tongue out, panting and occasionally dripping saliva — one of Harrison's most recent additions, designed to make the creature seem as real as possible.

Rennie had stopped crying and was settling, at least temporarily, into numb resignation. He hadn't seen Harrison for several hours and so decided to seek him out, to apologize for having run away when his father needed him most. *It will be so hard when he's gone,* Rennie thought. *But while we still have some time together, I'm going to do everything I can for him.*

Rennie's brief search of the dome led him to Harrison's bedroom, where the older man lay deep in slumber, his face pale and worn. Rennie's eyes filled with fresh tears as he realized that this fatigue was probably borne of illness. He left a few minutes later, closing the door quietly.

Harrison's main lab/study area was down the hall, so Rennie headed there next. He knew the area well; nevertheless, he wanted to re-familiarize himself with it since he would have to continue where his father had left off on several projects.

As usual, several small machines were operating automatically, and Rennie ignored them. He gave a cursory examination to two of the files that Harrison had called up on the primary screen: Pet Analogs Furball and Dagmar. Rennie had to smile. He wondered, though, where File 1 could be and what its designation was. It didn't make sense that the first of the major files wasn't in a more prominent position on the display. Rennie also thought it odd that he couldn't remember having heard of the first file before. He'd always had permission to see and even to assist with his father's work, ever since he could remember.

Curiosity digging at him, Rennie sat down at the computer and attempted to locate the file. Standard methods failed, so after a few minutes he began using more creative techniques, including guesswork. Eventually, he set the computer to search by high-speed, random selection of codes, hoping the right one would turn up and enable him to gain access. Rennie wondered, in the meantime, why he felt so compelled to do this. *What could it possibly matter, anyway?* he asked himself. He stopped thinking about it when the lights and the beep indicated that he'd found the hidden file. Punching the buttons, Rennie delved into the program, only to find that it was at the end of its extensive data listings. He didn't feel like taking the time to go back, laboriously, though all of it to get to the beginning. But a quick check revealed that the computer would not let him close the file and re-open it at the start, either. *Strange,* he thought. *It's as if I'm supposed to work at it to get the information I want.*

Rennie began scrolling up slowly from the bottom of the text, ignoring Furball, who was brushing up against his ankles beneath the table. Much of the data consisted of figures and formulas, so Rennie yawned as he stared at the moving characters.

He straightened up when the tail-end notes appeared: fragmentary phrases, interesting yet cryptic: *memory implants holding...good responses to manufactured images...development, normal...appearance, normal...structure, normal...*

Rennie stopped scrolling and frowned. *What's Papa talking about?* he wondered. *If he built a new artificial life form, or he's working on the plans for one, why didn't he tell me?*

Shaking his head, the boy resumed his search and came across a series of familiar graphics: the holophoto images he'd been looking at much earlier, in the library. *Why were these duplicated for this file?* he asked himself. *And why does each one have a specific code number beside it?*

Something began gnawing at the pit of Rennie's stomach, an uneasy feeling. He tried to will away the feeling, but it settled inside him like a slow-burning coal. Running through the rest of the graphics seemed to take an eternity.

Finally he came upon another list hat described, in precise terms, several physical characteristics: eyes, hair, lips, teeth, nose, chin, brow, cheekbones, ears —

Rennie gasped and pushed himself away from the computer, knowing all too well who it was that possessed those features. It had been like looking in a mirror.

No no no no! the rational part of his mind screamed, while in his gut the truth made itself known, palpably, like a painful blow. But he forced himself to move forward and touch the controls again, compelled to see the rest of it, no matter what.

Gender — male, the screen said. *Physical appearance upon completion and incept date — eighteen standard Terran years. Fullest possible range of self-awareness, filial love impulses, and protective engrams...*

There was more of the same kind of data, but Rennie only skimmed the blurring words as he raced frantically to the beginning of File 1, which had been named what he had dared to hope it would not be: Project — Son Analog Rennie.

He felt himself coming to, his vision still blurry, as he raised himself to a kneeling position. Rennie didn't know how long he'd been unconscious. He knew only the memory of a wave of nausea which had felled him.

That thought triggered yet another emotion: intense anger. *It's not even real,* he thought, suppressing the impulse to laugh hysterically. *None of my feelings can ever be real, because I'm not real to begin with. Memory implants, false holograms of a childhood I never had, a baby I never was...*

Rennie caught sight then of Furball, who had been cowering in the corner. The boy took a writing stylus and hurled it, furiously, at the cat, which fled the room with a short, sharp cry. "I'm nothing more than *you* are!" Rennie said in a savage whisper. "I'm just another creation, a two-legged pet to keep the master company."

Rennie got slowly to his feet, taking several deep breaths to calm himself, and thought of the sleeping man down the hall. "He's not my father," the boy said bitterly, "I can't call him 'Papa' anymore, because it's just a filthy lie." Rennie bolted from the lab, ran to Harrison's chamber and kicked the side of the bed fiercely. "Get up, damn you!" Rennie shouted, even as his throat threatened to close up. "Get up and face me. *Now!*"

Startled, the scientist rubbed the film of sleep from his eyes and managed, slowly, to sit up. Rennie was standing before him, fists clenched, uncharacteristic fury on his face. "What — what is it, son?" Harrison asked, in a tone of bewilderment.

"Don't call me that!" Rennie shouted. "I'm not your son. "I'm *nobody's* son. All I am is another experiment, but you made me believe we're *family!*"

Harrison was sick and weak, but he stood up and took a step towards the boy.

"I don't want you near me," Rennie said, his voice about to break. "I don't want you to touch me. All I want is an explanation: why you made me, and why you made me so damned *well*. And I want to know why you didn't tell me before. You owe me, Harrison. You owe me at *least* that much."

Harrison took a deep, shuddering breath before he began. "Oh God, Rennie. Perhaps you're right. I should have told you sooner. I would have, after you got over the shock of learning about my illness. But the point is moot now, and there's more to it —"

"You're not giving me complete answers, Harrison."

"I know. It's very difficult. I was all alone here, in this dome, for many years. My wife and I weren't able to have children, and she died on Earth. I tried to adopt a child, but they said I was too old. I never stopped wanting a family, someone to love and care for and be with. I made the pets for a while, and their presence helped a little...but I was still lonely, Rennie. You can't know what that's like. You've never been alone."

"I haven't even *existed* for very long," Rennie retorted. "How can you expect any sympathy from me when I've never had the same experiences as you?"

Harrison sighed. "I don't expect sympathy. But I would ask that you try to understand how I feel about you, Rennie. We had a special bond, the two of us —"

"It wasn't *real!*" Rennie screamed, trembling with anger. "You programmed me, Harrison. You made sure I was everything you wanted in a son, the perfect boy for your artificial world. And it worked pretty goddamned well, I'll grant you that.

"But you made one mistake. You should have installed a program that would have blocked me, kept me from being so curious. That would have been the humane thing to do."

Harrison shook his head. "No, Rennie. I wanted you to be as complete as any human being, and even to find out your true identity, in time. You have all the drives of a human being, all the thoughts and emotions, the ideas and functions. Don't you think I've ever gotten angry, or cried? What you're feeling right now is what I've impressed upon you with my own engrams."

"There's a part of me within you, son — and that's *not* a dirty word. You *are* my won. You're an extension of me. But I made you sufficiently different so that you could be your own person, too —"

"*Stop it!*" Rennie ran to the other side of the room, picked up a porcelain statuette and hurled it against the opposite wall. The figure shattered into dozens of fragments on the floor. "Stop lying, Harrison, *please!* I can never be my own person, or your son, or a real human being, because I'm not alive. And feelings don't count if they're manufactured."

Rennie approached Harrison, with sweat trickling from his throbbing temples. "I could have thrown that right at your head, you bastard. That's what I *should* have done. So why didn't I? Did you see to it that I'd never kill you? Is that part of my programming too?" Rennie hesitated, thinking hard, then added: "Did you put in a safeguard against suicide as well? Maybe I'll try to find *that* out instead."

Harrison closed his eyes, briefly, then sat down on his bed. "Everything I tell you is the truth, Rennie. You can even look at the blueprints if you want proof. The fact is, you can do as you please with your life, just like anyone else. And if there's to be a death, or two deaths, in our home tonight…I can't stop it." Harrison folded his hands in his lap, gazing steadily at Rennie.

"I could kill you," the boy whispered, moving towards the scientist. "I could strangle you with my bare hands."

"Yes. You could."

Rennie's arms dropped to his sides, and he fell to the floor on his knees before Harrison, sobbing. The older man embraced him as well as he could, bending down to kiss the boy's head.

"Papa, how can you love me?" Rennie asked, clinging to him. "How?"

"You don't understand, but I'll try to explain it again. You see, it doesn't matter that you're not truly human, as you insist on calling it. I don't believe it makes any difference that you don't have real flesh and blood. I think of you as my son and of myself as your father, and the feelings we have for each other are real. In the end, that's all that matters."

Rennie closed his eyes tightly, tears squeezing out of them. "I want to understand, Papa. I want to believe. I do. But how can I say good-bye to you now? You're going to die, and I'll be all alone here. Oh God…I'd rather die along with you than live like that."

Harrison took Rennie's chin, gently, and tilted it up so they were nearly eye to eye. "There's no reason for you to do that, son, because you don't have to be alone. I'm not talking about the pets, either. I'm talking about someone else."

"I don't know what you mean?"

"Don't you? Did you miss all the implications of what I said about wanting someone to care for?"

Rennie rose slowly, then sat down next to his father. Lost in thought, the boy said nothing for several minutes — then finally spoke. "Yes…I see what you're saying. I understand. I think I know what to do." Rennie paused again, then added, "I'm sorry about…before."

Harrison put an arm around him. "So am I."

They sat there, quietly, for a long time.

Harrison lived for four more months, growing progressively weaker — though he never suffered much pain — until his tired heart could beat no longer. Rennie, who had cared for him faithfully, now took his body out onto the tundra, where he labored for several hours digging a hole in the cold, hard ground. When he finished patting down the dirt, later, Rennie took out a laser-stylus and wrote, on a permanent marker:

Reynolds Harrison, Beloved Father
Reynolds — meaning, to rule; counsel; judgment
Harrison — meaning, the ruler of an enclosure
He will live in the memory of his descendants
Forever

Rennie drove the marker into the ground and rubbed his sore hands together briskly, then turned and walked back to the dome.

In the evening, the planet's three moons cast a pale, eerie glow onto its surface. The large carnivores hibernated, while the birds tended their young beneath outcroppings of rock, and the sated fish moved languidly through the water.

Inside a huge dome, a tall man went from one room to another, secure within these walls, as a dog and cat followed him. He was Alexander Reynolds Harrison, his first name meant "defender of men," and he was twenty-one Earth-years old. He'd located a planet and two asteroids farther out in this star system and sent this data on Earth, along with more information on the artificial pets. The receivers thought they were still getting transmission from Reynolds Harrison.

At the moment, the tall man was concerned only with his child, Robert Alexander Harrison, whose first name meant "bright" or "fame." The three-year-old knew only one parent, Harrison, and had no memories of a mother.

Robert was "Bobby" to his father, who hovered over him anxiously, knowing he must monitor the child's vital signs closely during this crucial stage. Bobby had been semi-conscious for a day and a night, but Harrison believed that the crisis would soon be over and that the boy would be up, running and shrieking and playing.

Harrison wiped the boy's forehead with a soft cloth and smiled down at him. Someday, the father would die, as all things must, but his descendants would still be there, for this was Harrison's World.

This would always be Harrison's World.

The Way Home

This was not the first time he had brooded, alone, in darkness, and it would not be the last.

Why? he asked himself. *Why does it have to be me?*

The Box. That was what the crew called the ship's Control Center. It was hardly a bridge, with its compact, utilitarian design and minimal human activity. The computers did the bulk of the work, and if nothing was threatening the ship, few people needed to be in the *box.*

But I like it here, thought the Executive Officer, Marlana Rashid. She thrived on structure and discipline, so this was the perfect environment, and she'd been in it for several hours. Two others were present: a helm/navigation officer and a representative from the Sciences Division with an interest in comets. One was passing nearby, easily observed through any of three viewing screens.

"Helm," Rashid said, "ease us away from the comet. When it's out of range, resume our regular course. With the — the mission we've got," she added, "we have to use the utmost caution. Captain's orders."

The officer nodded and complied.

Rashid sighed. She'd nearly slipped and said "cargo" instead of "mission." It was difficult not to think in non-human terms sometimes, with all the high-tech, state-of-the-art monitors in the Cargo Bay keeping a mechanical vigil on the 150 colonists suspended there, somewhere between life and death, being transported to a new existence on another planet. The ship had recently come out of hyperspace — which had saved them considerable time — and was now proceeding at standard velocity to a planet in the Xi Bootis System, 22 light years from Earth. The planet had been approved several years earlier after a bio-sensor probe had *brought back evidence of inhabitability.*

The 75 officers and crew of the New World were charged with the colonists' welfare; it was their purpose to care for the settlers by preserving them in stasis; to bring them to their new home and help them establish a colony, then return to Earth — quite likely to gather another group, if all went well with this one. They had already tried seeding the moon and Mars, but people didn't react well to living in artificial environments and had insisted on going back to their crowded home. Closer, potentially habitable *systems, like Tau Ceti, had been ruled out for a number of reasons.*

No one has ever taken so many people as far from Earth as we have, Rashid mused. She suppressed a shiver just thinking about it; the prospect was both exhilarating and frightening. But she'd had such feelings before, having worked on colonizing missions for years. Only her superior, Captain Miles Vance, had more experience.

Mysterious Miles, she thought. *The enigma.* It was probably useless to wonder how he felt about this mission, but now that she was thinking about it, Rashid grew a bit restless and decided to pay him a visit on the pretense of making a report on the ship's status. He required such a report, verbal or written, every six hours. She turned command over to the woman from Sciences and left the Box.

Rashid stopped by her cabin, briefly, to touch up her appearance; she prided herself on looking neat and professional at all times. She tugged at the reddish-brown dutysuit covering her tall, athletic frame, then tucked a few loose strands of coarse black hair back into the simple barrette at the nape of her neck. A quick check of her light brown, unblemished face revealed a bit of puffiness beneath her dark eyes, but nothing worse. After a while, she would have a good, long sleep.

A few minutes later, Rashid was chiming for entry into Vance's cabin. The door opened, but Vance was nowhere to be seen. Rashid went inside and called out: "Captain?"

"I'll be out in a minute, Rashid," came the husky voice, from another chamber. "Sit down if you like."

"Thank you, sir," she said, taking a seat. *Probably shaving off the proverbial five o'clock shadow,* she thought. Like her, Vance looked proper every minute. But unlike her, his demeanor was reserved and very controlled, his movements smooth and deliberate. *We balance each other,* she mused. *We've made a good team—*

"Is there something you want to tell me, Commander?"

She jumped a little at the sound of his voice and got to her feet. He'd come up beside her so quietly, she hadn't even noticed. His large, open face was clean-shaven, though it looked reddish, like his eyes; and he had slicked back the thinning black hair just starting to gray at the temples.

"Everything has been fairly routine for the past six hours, sir," she reported. "I eased us away from a comet, then put us back on course before I left Control."

Vance nodded, his expression unreadable. "Good. I'll be going to Control shortly. And the colonists?"

"No change in status. The monitors have been double-checked for accuracy, per your orders."

"Excellent." The captain seemed to be looking right through Rashid, as if reflecting on some other matter. It seemed to her that he had grown increasingly concerned with the people and machines in the Cargo Bay recently — ever since they'd come out of hyperspace — almost as if he expected something to go wrong. He'd always been dedicated to those in his charge, but this time something was different.

Rashid was curious by nature, and decided on impulse to do a little digging. "Captain..." she began tentatively, "I share your sense of responsibility for the new colony. Everything that can be done for the settlers' welfare is being done. But if anything were to go wrong — "

"*That* will not happen, Commander," Vance told her in a firm, cold tone. He hadn't raised his voice, yet he'd startled her. His ice-blue eyes bore into hers.

The exec tried to regain her composure. "I — I simply meant that if…the unforeseen were to occur, however unlikely…well, sir, it wouldn't mean the end of the seeding program. It's been trial-and-error from the start, and even if the worst happened, we could try again…"

Rashid's voice trailed off as Vance's ruddy features darkened. "Do you think it's so easy?" he said, as if accusing her. "Do you think it's like growing a new garden in place of an old one, never mind the losses?"

"Captain, I didn't mean — "

"This is serious, Rashid. More serious than you apparently understand. This colony *must* survive. I will not allow anything to prevent that."

The tension was heavy as Rashid waited for him to finish.

"In fact, I will now require an update every *four* hours on ship's and colonists' status. Understood?"

Rashid's response came weakly: "Understood, sir."

After a moment, Vance's expression softened and he opened his mouth slightly, as if he wanted to tell her something — but he closed it again, abruptly, and she knew he was back in his uncompromising mode.

"Anything else, Captain?" Rashid inquired.

"No. That will be all."

She took that as a signal to leave, and did so quickly, sighing with both relief and frustration once she was back in the corridor. A flurry of mixed emotions passed through her: embarrassment, anger, bewilderment…

I hit a hell of a nerve — that's for sure, she thought, walking towards a ladder that would take her quickly back to the deck where her cabin was. *What's going on? He looks tired, but that doesn't explain his jumping down my throat.*

Rashid felt a twinge of guilt, as if she were being disloyal, but quickly dismissed the feeling. *He's keeping something from me,* she reasoned, climbing the ladder. *Something to do with the colonists.*

Rashid waited until she was locked away in her cabin before continuing the conversation with herself. She flopped onto her cot and laid her arm across her head. *I don't know if I can reach him anymore,* she realized suddenly, with a chill. *If he's cut me off…I'll have to find the answers on my own.*

She closed her eyes, knowing full well what could happen if she were caught investigating and it turned out to be nothing —

"No," she said aloud, determined to convince herself. "I'm not wrong."

Vance sat at the personal computer console in his cabin, staring at the symbols on the screen. The special code had been developed by a cryptologist back on Earth and was decipherable only to those very few, including Vance, who had been chosen to oversee this mission and who had the proper descrambling programs in place. No one else on board had any knowledge of it, not even his Executive Officer.

Vance shook his head, frowning. He considered Rashid a friend. Under normal circumstances he would have sought her out, confided in her. But not this time. Not yet.

Soon, he said to himself, nodding, as he scrolled slowly through the codes. *Soon she'll know. Everyone will.*

Until then, the *New World* would continue on course, and the precious contingent of people in the Cargo Bay would be kept alive and healthy — even if it cost Vance his friendships, his officers' loyalties, his crewmembers' lives. Only the mission mattered. It could not fail.

"God help us if it does," he whispered.

Rashid walked around in the storage area the next day, looking over the extensive supplies, limited weapons, sturdy building materials, food regenerators and water purifiers. Only the top officers, Quartermaster and Scientists were allowed here; the rows of the crew were kept away by a Security Team.

The precautions per se were not unexpected, but Rashid had wondered why the measures and restrictions on this mission seemed more severe than on others. It was just one more piece of a puzzle that she was now intent on solving.

She wasn't making much progress. The Security people on duty were respectful but reticent when she discreetly questioned them — not necessarily as though they had anything to hide, but rather as though they simply had little or no knowledge pertaining to Rashid's inquiries.

She located the Quartermaster himself for one last attempt. "Isn't it odd to have such a large amount of space allotted for supplies that might be superfluous after a while?" she asked him, in what she hoped was a tone of amusement. "The colony is sure to be thriving completely on its own within less than a year of settlement."

The Quartermaster, a shy man devoted solely to his work, merely shrugged before answering: "Probably true, Commander. But it never hurts to be on the safe side."

"Of course." Rashid nodded, then strode out before she lost her temper in front of him. Once outside, she hit the bulkhead with her fist. *What is this, a conspiracy?* she wondered. *Have they all been told to evade me?*

Tugging angrily at her uniform, which suddenly felt hot and uncomfortable, Rashid went on to her next destination.

"It's normal, Captain, I assure you," said the ship's doctor, Celia Sanchez — a middle-aged, friendly woman in a tan smock. She and Vance were in the Cargo Bay, hovering over a capsule that held one of the younger colonists, a preteen boy whose readings showed slight fluctuations.

"You've got to stabilize him," Vance insisted.

"His body should stabilize itself in a very short time," she replied. "It's just because we recently came out of hyperspace. The process can be unsettling, even for those of us who aren't conscious. I'd really prefer not to intervene unless it becomes absolutely necessary."

Vance remained adamant. "You'll intervene, or I'll get someone else to do it. I wont' tolerate any risks where these people are concerned."

"I would remind you, sir," the doctor told him firmly, "that I have the authority, as the senior medical officer, to say what's to be done with these people — "

"And I would remind *you* that I could have you relieved for defiance," Vance returned.

Sanchez glared at him for a few moments, then said, "I will monitor the boy very carefully, sir." She began working the rows of buttons on the side of the suspension unit.

"I'll be expecting a positive report from you on his condition," Vance said over his shoulder, as he left the Bay.

His head ached, but he wasn't about to go back in there now and ask for a pain-killer. He only wished he could make the doctor and everyone else understand: they couldn't afford to take any chances. *If only there were some way to let them know without revealing everything,* he thought. *If only I could tell Rashid...*

He wanted very much to consult with her. She had a sharp mind and plenty of valuable experience. *But how will she react when I finally tell her?* he wondered. *Maybe I should have disregarded my directives and shared it all with Rashid before we left Earth.*

That had all been rendered academic now, of course. The plans had been set in motion, and Vance knew he was caught up in them — no more and no less than anyone else.

He did not see his Exec, not did she see him, as the two crossed the corridor at opposite ends.

Several people greeted Rashid as she entered the Sciences Division. Two were on duty; the others, she suspected, were there because they loved the process of exploring and recording. Doctor Chen, a wiry, intense-looking man, motioned for her to sit down next to him at his work station.

"You look as pleased as I've ever seen you," said Rashid.

"This is the most satisfying opportunity I've had in years, Commander," Chen told her. "We're looking so much more now than we ever could have from a probe."

"There were several other planets considered for this mission, as I recall," Rashid said casually, hoping he would jump at the chance to tell her all he knew.

"Oh yes, but the Global Leadership, the Science League, and the Colony Project insisted on Xi Bootis B," Chen said. "The others were acceptable, but this one they considered ideal. To be honest, Commander, I thought it would have been wiser to seed several planets, so that if one colony failed, at least the others would be successful. But I'm a pragmatic scientist, and the ones who sent us were very emotional, now that I think back on it."

"Interesting." Rashid tried to sound non-committal. "When was the last time you heard from them?

"Right before we went into hyperspace. A standard inquiry as to our research status, very dry and terse. Just a formality."

"Is that all?"

"Yes, so far. We responded, and they should have sent us another message by now. But with the distance, not to mention all the different kinds of interference, I'm surprised anything gets through. I admire those wizards in Communications who sort it out for us."

Of course! Rashid thought. Communications. *Who better to keep a secret than the ones who control what the rest of us hear?* She chided herself for not having realized this, but spent several more minutes in Chen's company to make her visit appear routine.

She went back to her cabin, reevaluated her strategy and concluded that this business of sneaking around in person would have to stop. Computer searches were by nature much more subtle than footwork.

The prospect of subterfuge bothered Rashid nonetheless, even as she voice-activated her personal computer and gave it her executive access codes. *I have to play their game if I want to win,* the commander told herself. *Whoever they are.*

She ordered the computer to lock into Communications Banks to search for and relay all of the transmissions received from Earth from they time they had left orbit. Next, she deleted everything that seemed routine or irrelevant, and was left with several disturbing facts: no general transmissions had been received — or perhaps they had been interrupted or hidden — after the ship came out of hyperspace; many intership communiqués had been monitored on the sly; and trace evidence of one lengthy transmission from Earth had been recorded, but the substance of the message was unknown to anyone except the person for whom it had been specially scrambled and coded: Captain Vance.

Rashid closed her eyes for a moment. *It all comes back to him in the end,* she realized, with a troubling clarity. *He must have known I'd catch on eventually —*

"Oh, God," she said aloud, as the full force of the truth struck her. "He figured that by the time I found out, I wouldn't be able to do anything about it."

The commander shut off the computer and got to her feet, trying to keep her fury in check. Vance had to be confronted, rank and consequences be damned.

But before she was out the door, an urgent-sounding call came over the intercom: "Commander Rashid, this is Security. Come to the Cargo Bay immediately. The captain is — " The message crackled, then went dead. Rashid paused just long enough to send a discreet message of her own to the rest of Security, then bolted for the door.

A shocking scene greeted her inside the Cargo Bay. The other two Bay doors had been fired on and sealed. A guard stood with a weapon pointed at Vance, who had a gun pointing back at her in one hand and his other hand holding Doctor Sanchez by the throat. Her hands were tied behind her. Nearby, on the floor, was another guard, unmoving. Rashid knew he must have been the one who had summoned the commander before being knocked unconscious, or perhaps shot. To the side was the unit containing a boy whose suspension monitor had gone black, indicating his death.

"Seal that door, Rashid," snapped Vance. "I don't want anyone else coming in here."

"The situation is already out of hand, sir," she countered. "What difference would it make if — "

Vance fired at the door's locking mechanism, effectively locking them in — then switched to the most powerful stun setting and fired at the other guard, who had been momentarily distracted by the blast. The captain now had his gun trained solely on his own executive officer.

"Well what are you waiting for?" asked Rashid. "You've got two hostages left. Or is this some kind of selective insanity?"

"That's enough, Commander. You don't have any idea what this is about."

"No, I don't. Give me an idea, Miles. Make me understand." Rashid held her breath, waiting for a response.

"She let the boy die," Vance said a moment later, glancing at the doctor, whose face was slick with perspiration. "She should have done more to save him. I told her to get out and bring another medic in here, but she refused. I called Security to remove her, and she told them I was unfit for duty. I grabbed a gun from one of them — "

"You *are* unfit," Sanchez interrupted. "Sometimes people die in suspension, captain, you *know* that. I've told you — "

"Yes, he knows," said Rashid. "Captain, you're perfectly aware of the hazards of suspension, the variables, the unpredictability. The colonists knew it too, and they chose to risk themselves and their families. This won't be the last time that someone dies in deep sleep."

"Yes it will," Vance insisted. "And if that means that I have to hold a gun on the medical staff every minute of every day, that's what I'll do."

Rashid took a cautious step towards him. "Captain, do you hear yourself? What's happened to you? Let me help — "

"No, Rashid."

"Please — let me take over, just for a while. You're exhausted."

"Stop right there," he told her, his eyes narrowing. "Turn around, slowly."

She did as he said.

"Why did you come here unarmed?" he asked her, suddenly. "What have you done?"

At that moment a blinding flash came from one of the lighting panels directly over Vance's and Sanchez's heads, and a powerful beam from a guard's gun knocked both of them to the floor, unconscious.

"Good timing," Rashid said grimly. She paused a moment before looking around at the others and giving separate orders to each by turns. "As of now, I'm taking charge; log it in the records that the doctor and I have certified the captain unfit for duty. Take Sanchez to her quarters and have someone stay with her until she wakes up. She can resume her duties when she's able. Also, send a maintenance crew to make repairs to the Bay. As for Vance..." She hesitated briefly, then said, "Let him sleep it off in my quarters, and keep him guarded. Contact me when he wakes up; I'll be in his cabin."

The others hurried to obey her orders. She left quickly as soon as Maintenance repaired one of the Bay doors.

Once inside Vance's quarters, Rashid was struck by the full impact of what she had done. She sat down at the captain's personal computer and began the search.

Naturally, she was shut out from the usual access points: name, rank, serial number. Even her attempt at an emergency security override was thwarted. The captain may not have been totally stable, but he had been alert.

The computer continued to insist on a password before it would allow the user any access to the encoded messages and the descrambling program. The commander had no choice but to make a series of educated guesses. She started with obvious words and combinations: *Earth, colony, New World, ship, mission.* No success.

Then she mentally replayed some of the things which she had thought or said, or which had Vance had said to her recently — and input another flurry of phrases and terms: *mystery, secret, enigma, seeding, deep sleep, truth, garden* —

The computer beeped, indicating that she'd deciphered the second half of the code. *Garden* — that was one word.

"What's the other part of it?" Rashid wondered aloud. Seizing on another idea, she entered a series of absolutes, keeping in mind the captain's recent predilection for speaking and thinking in extremes: Never, always, yes, no, life, death, first, last —

The computer beeped again. She'd broken the code. But she felt no elation, only a chill as she accessed the descrambling program with the password: *Last Garden.*

The commander sat quietly while the information she had sought printed out on the screen, bit by bit. As painful as it was, she had no choice but to accept the truth. Rashid's reaction could easily have been one of outrage and grief. But the shock was so great that it almost numbed her. She did not know how much time was passing as she held herself tightly, eyes closed, hearing nothing except the sound of her own heart, until the door chime sounded. It was a security guard with the news that Vance was regaining consciousness.

Rashid's eyes were blank. "I'll be right there," she said, in a ragged voice. "I want two guards posted outside. I don't want anyone else inside with me."

The guard nodded, though she looked a bit puzzled, then turned away. Rashid walked slowly in the opposite direction, towards her quarters.

Vance was sitting up, rubbing his reddened eyes, when Rashid entered without warning, gun in hand.

"You won't need that," he told her. "I wouldn't attack you, and I've nowhere to go."

"You were ready to attack me a while ago. Would you have killed me? Or the others?"

Vance shook his head as if insulted. "For God's sake, Marlana. At most I would have knocked you out. And I didn't *want* to kill anybody."

Rashid sat down on her couch. "You can act indignant, Miles, but it just won't wash. You've contradicted yourself more than once. You kept the truth from us. You assaulted your own people, and now we can't trust you."

Vance got to his feet and took a shaky step towards her. "What do you want me to say? That I'm sorry for protecting the crew and the colonists at all costs? That I didn't reveal the true mission to everybody and have chaos and panic on my hands?" His voice grew louder, angrier. "What would you have done, Marlana? How would you tell your people that they're the last humans left, because all life on Earth has been destroyed by a rogue asteroid?"

Rashid, too, stood up, then said evenly, "I would have come clean from the start. They could have accepted it. After all…what other choice is there? Everything they once knew is dead or dying. There's nothing to go home to."

"Would have, could have, should have," Vance said flatly. "The three most useless phrases in our language." He paused a moment, then continued: "As you probably know, a small group of representatives from the Global Leadership, the Colony Project, and the Science League met behind closed doors when they discovered the trajectory of that asteroid — *twenty miles* in diameter — on the top-secret, long-range scan. One of the things they agreed on, besides saving this select group of people, was that I shouldn't say anything until we got to Xi Bootis. And I agreed that it was the right time, the right place."

"For me, too?" asked Rashid, bitterly. "Those people are all dead now, Miles; you never had to follow their orders. All this time, you've have had my support. But you had to go it alone, had to be a martyr. The savior of the human race."

"So your sensibilities are different from mine, Marlana. You can accuse me all you want, but it doesn't change a damn thing. We've got a colony to settle, and a new planet to call home."

"How can you be so casual about it?" Rashid nearly shouted. "You talk like it's some sort of holiday — "

"Don't say that. Don't even think it. This is the hardest thing I've ever done. You don't know what it was like…" His voice had begun to break, and he took a moment to compose himself. "You have no idea how many times I wanted to tell you."

The commander stood still, her gun dangling at her side.

Vance broke the silence: "How do you want us to start our lives on Xi Bootis, Marlana? With a new jail, and me as the first prisoner?"

Rashid looked away from him and headed slowly for the door. "I have to inform the others," she muttered, then walked out.

"*No!* No, it can't be true — it can't be!"

"Oh my God…we're the only ones left…"

"We should have been told."

"You're right," said Acting Captain Rashid. "I'm sorry." She was facing down an agitated group of officers and crewmembers, feeling vulnerable even though she was armed and flanked by some of the people that had sided with her. Once the news of Earth's destruction had been split by their different responses: some had broken down in tears or had fainted; others had become violent and had to be restrained or sedated; still others had resigned themselves to their fate and been sympathetic to Rashid when she explained the circumstances — although not all of them were willing to forgive their former Captain for his silence. Rashid was now in the position of having to defend him.

"We should kill that bastard Vance right now," snarled one of the young men. "He's responsible."

"For what?" Rashid asked him gently. "For the asteroid? For bringing you and the others to a safe haven?"

She could see that the man was fuming, but he said nothing further, so she added, "I agree that Vance is guilty of dishonesty. But he'll pay for it whether or not we condemn him."

To her surprise, no one in the group challenged her statements. She figured they had enough to deal with already, without adding to it by killing her or Vance. Even so, after the group dispersed, Rashid ordered her supporters to keep an eye on the more volatile members of the crew. She knew it would be some time before anyone could rest easy.

They would make planetfall soon.

Captain Rashid knew this without confirming it. She was pacing in the small space of the Control Center, unable to sit still though she knew it was distracting to the others in the Box. They were quiet, very deliberate in their movements, still subdued from the news Rashid had given them hours earlier. Most of the seasoned officers had taken the news extraordinarily well, all things considered. Vance was still under house arrest, in his own quarters; she'd had no contact with him since the day before. But the decision she would have to make weighed heavily on her now, with the planet called Xi Bootis B only a few hours away.

Just then, Doctor Sanchez came into Control. "How are they doing?" the captain asked her, referring to those among the crew and revived colonists who had broken down.

"Coming along. I can release some of them soon. As for the rest…well, Captain, I've never had to deal with trauma on this scale before, so I can't be certain about the long-term damage."

Rashid nodded. "I know you'll do everything possible for them, Doctor."

"Is there something I can do for you, Marlana?"

Rashid returned her gaze. "No, thanks." She paused, then asked, "How is Vance?"

"Very quiet. He hasn't tried anything."

"I see. Thank you, Doctor."

Sanchez nodded and left Control. Rashid remained lost in thought, staring out at the stars. The steady glow of the star system grew stronger as the ship drew closer to it, showing them the way home.

"Go ahead, son. It's all right."

"Mom, look over there!"

"Go back inside and get my kit."

"So this is home."

Rashid listened, a tiny smile on her face, as the colonists ventured outside, onto the planet that was home now not only for them, but for everyone from The New World. She watched them from atop a small hill. Already the colony leaders were organizing the work and the protocols that would be necessary for a new society to function. They had accepted Rashid's advice to proceed as planned long ago, as if they were simply a test group — not a group upon whom the future of the human race now depended.

She had also convinced the others that the ship should not be entirely dismantled, as there might come a time when some of the people would improve its capabilities and use it to settle on another world, further insuring the survival of humanity. Certainly, there was no guarantee that Xi Bootis wouldn't be in mortal danger itself someday, just as Earth had been.

Rashid was still lost in thought a moment later, when she heard several people approaching from behind. She turned to see two armed guards flanking her former captain, who wore magnetic cuffs around his wrists. She had left orders earlier that he was to be brought to her.

"Deactivate those cuffs," she told the guards, without looking at Vance.

The two men hesitated, then complied, and Rashid gave them a look that told them to hang back. She met Vance's eyes for the first time since the confrontation. He seemed docile and resigned, though she couldn't bring herself to trust him based solely on that appearance. Several moments passed before Rashid said, "Everything seems to be proceeding well."

Vance returned her gaze. "Everything, Marlana?"

"Some things take longer than others."

"I know," said Vance. "I...I have a lot of regrets."

"I'm trying to understand too, Miles."

He was silent for a time, then said, "You never did answer my question — about myself, as a prisoner."

She looked away from him, focusing on the activity below. "They could probably use some help," she said at length.

Vance nodded. "I imagine so."

He followed Rashid down the hill, the guards close behind them.

Overhead, a native bird circled, looking down at the groups of people as they worked together, building their world.

Ellen Straw

I began writing at age six. I've had short stories, non-fiction, and poetry published in many small press magazines and college journals, and have won a number of writing awards from various contests. I also self-published a book of my own short stories called *Creative Writhing*. The idea for "Father to the Man" came out of my interest in artificial intelligence, androids and robots, and our potential relationships with them. "The Way Home" is one of many stories I've set on a spaceship, which is a unique community because of its confining nature, and which allows me to explore the characters' limitations and possibilities.

I teach composition, creative writing, and literature at two community colleges in southern California.

Ezekiel's Wheel

My name is Malachi B. Levin. My mother would tell me, numerologically, it was the only name possible for me. She insisted I was the solitary origin of life (at least as far as she was concerned) and my name should be the number of creation. My name equals three, and, by extension, I carry the seed of genesis within. I was also the third child born into my family and my mother thought this made perfect rhythmic sense, thus proving her case. The B., my middle name, stands for Ben. Not as in Benjamin, but as in Hebrew for "son of." My father's first name is Levi. Levi ben Mordechai. His father was named Mordechai ben Levi. Names, numbers, generations. They all go round, just like wheels.

I am, by vocation, an eighth grade teacher of Social Studies. By avocation I am a wheelwright. My obsession. I must state here, it is not by compulsion that I build wheels; no one compels me. Quite the opposite, as my determination comes from within and not through any external force.

When I was quite the small boy, my father told me a story about a fellow named Honi. Honi the Circle Drawer. Honi could do nothing very well except one thing: he had the ability to draw a circle with such precision and care, so without flaw, and station himself within it with such perfection, it could create a conduit for the Most High. I do not remember when he first told me that story, but it was within my very early years. It set me drawing circles. I have been doing so ever since in ways few people could imagine; creating patterns of sublime elegance, supernal desire. I have had many years to practice, turning my wheels into creations of beauty and movement, of austere generous space born of matter here, but not there; all that is not, built of the little that is.

There are but few places in my home that are not full of wheels within wheels. Those that are not contain wheels incomplete of their associates; single wheels waiting for their satellites, their planets, their center of rotation. The only place empty of such creations is my workspace, and that glutted with parts and pieces yet to be placed, yet to be wheels; parts of wheels, spokes, rims, joints, axles, structures. Everything needs structure. Everything turns around something else.

Miniature dinosaur Ferris wheels. Creatures of metal and rubber, bearings and grease, precious metal and semi-precious stone. Merry-go-rounds of time and energy, whirly-gigs at every angle, within and without. Planetary models. Atomic schematics. Universes of wire and hub, center and centrifuge. Galaxies of creative rotation, systems of spin and myself as their sun.

Ezekiel 1 : "Now, as I looked at the living creatures, I saw a wheel upon the earth beside the living creatures. One for each of the four of them. As for the appearance of the wheels and their construction, their appearance was like the gleaming of a chrysolite, and the four had the same likeness being as it were a wheel within a wheel. The four wheels had rims and they had spokes, and their rims were full of eyes round about. And when the living creatures went, the wheels went beside them and when the living creatures went, the wheels went with them, for the living creature was in the wheel."

I use to have a book in which I recorded my plans, details and discoveries. Every time I really got going the book would disappear. Just as I was about to hit the right combination of wheels and stars, materials and colors, my plans would vanish. The Watchers knew. That was how I knew I was close, because only then do the Watchers see, looking out from rims only when a wheel is nearly right.

But now I have no plans. I have wheels and how can even the Zophim, the Watchers of Elohim, dain to remove them all?

No, they cannot. If they remove the wheels, how could they watch?

And so I keep building against the structure of the Universe, emulating its form. Wheels within wheels like planets going around in their orbits. The living creatures, the constellations of the zodiac, turning round in the heavens as planets in their orbits move with them, with each living creature in the wheel. The constellations wheel their orbits along, as do the planets. Eyes all around as stars in the sky, studding the celestial rim.

It is the way of creation; the structure of cause and effect is similar to Ezekiel's "wheels within wheels." Imagine a circle. Imagine another circle within that circle, but different planes and directions of rotation. Keep imagining on and on. It is a fractal structure and the genesis of creation, the very seed of destiny, the whole embedded in the part; the macrocosm within the microcosm.

That is my goal. Nothing short of Ezekiel's wheel. I shall station myself within it. And that is how I shall meet God.

•••

I work within a field of stars. Stars above and stars below. Shields of David cover the ceilings and walls, painted in color and gilt, one hue or metal interlacing with the other, suspended among and from wires, swaying and moving – many on wheels spinning in an orbit within the rooms of my home, against the depth of the dynamic heavens.

Pentagrams below, painted in my own deft hand upon the floor, engraved into the wood, etched into the tile.

And I, I am in the center. Man in the center, between Heaven and Earth. I shall change that.

•••

I follow the law, the four indispensable conditions set by Eliphas Levi, as closely as I can. To my own knowledge, this is my first infraction; that I communicate with you my work and intentions. I fancy Levi to be an ancestor, though I know his last name was really Constant. That too, I take as a sign.

I know what I do. I understand what I am doing. Who knows better than I about wheels?

I have faith in what I do. It will work, as long as I am persistent. As long as I keep my knowledge to myself.

I use my imagination, as it is how I am guided by the angels who, in turn, are guided by God. It is where my plans are kept, now that I have none, unknown in whole even to me, divulged, as needed, part by part. I have an intelligence tempered by the extreme discretion of unconsciousness. Still, I am watched, from the rims, by the eyes. From the within and without.

I have the will - an unchecked and uncheckable intrepidity. Surely, that is apparent. My will is strong. It has always been thus; as I know these wheels place me out of time. Causes and effects are not like points on a line of time with causes always in precedence. Causes and effects lie on circles of time, wheels of time. Look on a small piece of the circle. Who can tell whether it is the cause or effect? First or last? When a cause is in the future of its effect we have meaning, purpose and destiny. I have meaning and purpose. I have destiny.

And, I keep silent. I have told no one. I have no contacts save those who watch, and that is enough. No one knows what I do. I have no one to visit, no one to share this with. No Malchezedek has entered my door as long as I know no one has entered at all. I commit this infraction to the last rule only now that I am so close. If I succeed, who would understand? How will it be known the feat I have realized, what miracle can be done? If no one else knows, I shall ascend alone, to join those so few souls who have come to the Most High without benefit of death.

I have not allowed even myself the luxury of thinking about what I do, as the Watchers can see what is within as well as without. Yet now I think of what I've done, what I am doing, even sometimes aloud. Let them hear. I know there are those who will understand that I say, what I think. The good and the bad will hear. Perhaps this shall bring about the battles of which I have read so much. Who will gain the art even as the artisan is no more? Who will fight to create or destroy the knowledge of the way to Heaven? Surely, if they do not know now, they will when I arrive.

•••

It is a monstrous affair, the work of the ages for which I have had to rebuild my workspace, creating space below and above, removing part of the Earth below my floor, venturing into the sky, having removed part of roof, replaced with a large domed skylight painted black against the Watchers. This is the road to creation and is surrounded by its lesser siblings throughout the space of my home; centered in my workroom, but extending into time and space, captive neither dimensionally nor temporally. Bound only by its own being, its limit in function alone.

The center is composed of Shields of David, five in all, spinning, each around its own center, all circling the space within. Gleaming of gold and silver, chrysolite and beryl. They spin in solitaire and in unison. They spin within the larger circle, against the rotation of the sun; the finite banished by the infinite.

Around the center circle rotates a wheel not unlike the smaller within. It is larger by π to thirteen decimal places, and each star is composed of blades of steel, double sided rays of direction, elemental destiny in motion, shining of the sun as it follows it in rotation. Sprit directed toward its ultimate destination.

And so I have built them, and I believe the one in the center is the conduit. I have just now realized this - just now - in the brief moment before I reach for the wheel. I have awaited, patient yet anxious, the appropriate day, the perfect time, the precise midpoint between the autumnal equinox and the year's longest night. I have waited until all is complete but the motion of the wheel, the cycle around the center. If they are to destroy it now, let them come. I can reach out and spin, even as the Earth begins to quake, as the rains begin to fall. What is to stop me?

What is left but to spin and step in? I have yet to place the ladder that will give me access to the center. I can barely conceive of a more fitting way to enter Heaven than the means by which the angels visited Earth in the dream of Joseph. In Hebrew school, my Rabbi once asked me why it was that Joseph saw the angels coming down the ladder then up? Do not people go up a ladder first? Joseph may make his dream anew after I am done here today.

Placing the ladder, I must be careful to position it just beyond the rotation of the outer circle, not wanting it to hit the ladder, not wanting it to hit me. Damage to myself is the least of my concerns; if I damage the wheel, I doubt I'll have time to repair it before they come.

Moving the outer wheel by hand, checking the boundary of rotation, I set the ladder. I have given it enough extra room to compensate for sway (precisely thirteen inches to satisfy my penchant for the symbolic), though the gyroscopic effect should keep the whole system axially steady. I have tested this over and over again on other wheels and I am confident it will work. This added distance makes it harder for me to start the wheel, which I shall also do by hand. Still, I must be ready for anything, be it the movement of the foundation upon which I stand or the hand of the Watchers upon the Earth.

I will have to step off the top of the ladder at the right time, as the inside and outside rotate to leave me an opening. Inside, waits the Most High.

I climb the ladder and stand, unsteadily, at the top platform, reaching out for the inside. Overreaching, I take hold of one of the shields and push out and down. Through a mechanism of my own design it begins to spin, each star around itself, each around its center, all around the core, turning on two axes composed of the most delicate apparatus. Shining and sparkling around the workroom, off the other wheels, exposed walls, upon the night of the ceiling becoming clear autumn sky in an time lapse movie. Brilliant in composition, impossible to tell what is what.

I reach above my head and out again, moving to begin the outer wheel and, immediately as it turns, it seems everything explodes. I real backward from the shock of the blast and brilliance. At first I think it is the Watchers, but I, and the Ezekiel's wheel, are intact. But the center has moved. I do not know where it has gone - perhaps receded, perhaps vanished. That startling sound must have been the air rushing in to fill the void, now shining with an effulgent gold behind a luster of lambent blue. Though, it is so bright, I cannot vouch for how it truly looks. The blue I see may be damage to my eyes. I had not thought of this, the necessity of protection from the radiance of Heaven. But, for how long shall I need it?

Every ten seconds, the outer and inner synchronize, leaving me space to enter. But I can no longer look at the wheel and cannot know when to enter by my own reckoning. I can feel the movement of the outer wheel in the currant of air against my face. I dare not take the time to descend the ladder and look for sunglasses and I'm not sure they would be of sufficient strength to shield my eyes of the glory of God.

I have built this vehicle of my own volition but not my own design, having been led step by step along processes beyond my apprehension. I shall now have to trust those same guides will allow me to enter. For what other reason should it have been built and no others know of it? So, within the flash and din, I listen for the signal the time is right. I shall enter Heaven by my wheel, or I shall enter Heaven by my death, but surely I shall enter.

A count starts in my mind and I follow it from ten. At zero, I take my final leap of faith and leave the solid for the space of the wheel. I step off.

At once, having stepped into the air, I am rushed by a whirling of wind. My eyes still useless, I know nothing of what is about, I keep them closed so I may, I hope, see Heaven, look upon the face of God. I am alive. I have touched neither ground nor any other surface, though how I would tell one from the other I do not know.

Bound. I am now bound by arms, or so it feels, and one around my neck. I cannot breath, though I try. I cannot move, though I try. And still the air rushes against me, chilling. I feel as though I have been grabbed and gagged, but rushed forward toward a destination. Perhaps captive, perhaps assisted by this living creature, the creature of the wheel that I knew not was created by me when I fashioned the wheel, or came to abide within it upon its completion.

Still, I am captive, though the wind has stopped and, while still I am chilled, I can breath. The arms have come loose and I feel ground beneath my feet. What is left but to open my eyes? Though scarcely should I believe them even if they do allow me to see. And so I stand, eyes open, soul agape. I flinch.

Oh, the Fire. Oh, The Glory!

Oh, my God!

Adam Byrn Tritt

Adam Byrn Tritt was born on August 11, 1964 in Brookline, Massachusetts. Adam, who has degrees in Psychology, Education and English as well as a Ph.D. in Religion and was awarded an honorary D.D. for his work in religious tolerance, is an English teacher by vocation and award winning poet by avocation. Adam is the author of *Tellstones: Runic Divination in the Welsh Tradition*, the only book extant on the subject. Adam lives with his wife Lee, daughter Sef, son Alek and some ridiculously large alligators very near the Everglades of south Florida — all under a very big tree.

The Summer Season

It was a sweltering day at the front. I'd drawn office duty again, and was slowly being bored to death.

The job, after all, amounted to guarding a telephone on a desk in a little gray room, and holding the keys for the storage rooms, just in case someone felt the sudden need for their instruments or props or costume, or to rehearse. Yeah, someone Higher Up really apparently thought this might happen. But then, brass down through history has always had such delusions. I wrote it off to the destructive effects of sniffing carbonless triplicate forms for too many years, and did my task like a good soldier.

The radio was out for repairs, and the mail had only kept me amused for the first hour, even though I'd tried my best to string it out. After that, an hour polishing my trumpet, the good one that I keep in my locker, was about all I could take. The thing's usually spotless anyway, which shows you how desperate I was for distraction.

Besides which, there was nothing resembling air conditioning, that also apparently being out for repairs. The gunmetal-gray fan sat on its stand in front of the window, washing warm, humid air around the office. About as pleasant as being hit with a mildewed sponge, repeatedly, but the alternative was slow death by self-basting.

My stomach was growling, and heading over to the canteen for a sandwich and maybe a beer or three was sounding better every time the fan turned its face toward me. *Who's to notice?* asked a little voice. *Nothing has happened all morning, so what makes you think anything will happen during lunchtime? Nobody will ever know you were gone.*

Being a staunch soldier, trained in all sorts of privation in the name of Music, I was halfway out the door when the phone rang.

"See?" I berated the voice. "That's a great way to get drummed out of the business entirely. If I had a good lawyer and lots o' Irish luck."

I snatched the phone on the second ring. "Fourth MOC, Sergeant Tortuga," I said, with the right combination of boredom and superciliousness to assure them I hadn't been asleep or heading out for a beer or anything.

The voice on the other end was a Lieutenant Somethingorother, a butterbar at Command I'd met once and disliked from about grenade-toss distance downwind. Luckily, he was too much of a martinet to notice anything but a direct affront. The news he brought made me like him even less, though he apparently took my stricken tone as one of utmost respect, and warmed to me enough to flesh out the orders a little, for which I will someday thank him, right after I reshape his face.

Seems there was a war next door, and we were invited. Months behind, we were finally mobilized.

To the front. In fact, the looey said, maybe just a *little* tiny bit beyond it.

I made a few frantic calls up, through, across and under the chain of command, logged it, and went and had those beers anyway. And logged that, too; what, they were going to *fire* me, especially for keeping accurate records?

•••

Next thing I knew, I found myself minutes away from jumping out of a perfectly good airplane, surrounded by the rest of the 4th. Some looked hung-over, some tired, a couple scared, and many eager. Half of them were discussing the drop, and what the hell were we doing there. The usual.

The office was a suddenly pleasant memory. The beer, meanwhile, was still unpleasantly hanging on.

"Awright, you clowns, listen up." The inspiringly stentorian tones of Captain Rossini. He never needed the P.A.

"We're just about over the drop zone, so get ready. Remember, we hit as close to the brush as we can, and head for cover. After we regroup, we hit the objective, and dig in. The 11th Heavy Mobile Orchestra Division will be two hours behind us from helicopter, and we have to assists in covering equipment delivery when the planes skid it in."

Groans all around. Bringing the big pieces into a fire zone never went over well. Whenever we could get away with it, which was usually never, we'd just swoop in on a pre-staged area, fully rigged by our attached platoon of Union specialists, and take control of the area.

Besides, we had never gone behind the lines before. That was the next gem Rossini dropped on the faithful.

"For those of you who haven't heard the chatter, the Fourth Medium Opera is taking an advance position with this drop. Since the Big Boys at HQ made this decision based on the company's past performances, you've got nobody to blame but yourselves for the good reviews."

The little red light came on. As this is usually followed shortly by the little green light, which we had all come to know and love in our airborne green-room, we started checking pockets and accessories.

"Button up and get ready," Rossini added needlessly. "This has got to go like clockwork, so make sure you've got everything. If anyone leaves their costume or their only tube of pancake on the plane like last time, there'll be hell to pay. So look alert!"

Then we got the green-light go, and I was in the air, starting to get sentimental again about overheated offices.

•••

As senior noncom, I was in charge of a platoon, a mongrel group of different specialties but all pretty nice folks, and competent enough to be in a war.

My team regrouped, and we were about to start casting around when I found myself getting a snappy salute from a strong-faced woman in tigerstripe. "Corporal Mowbray, 2nd RDO, ready for your orders, Sergeant."

I was very happy that the Screaming Meemees were waiting for us. These rapid-deployment types were nothing to mess with, even back then, and the 2nd Chamber Ensemble was somewhere near the top of the list, or beyond. This team was Airborne all the way, the "Hell on Strings" shoulder-patch logo impressive even in battlefield black-and-green: the classic Electric Chicken clutching a viola de gamba in each talon, surrounded by lightning bolts.

Speaking as a hard-liner, it was a great day when the military started sending women into front-line action. I mean, cripes, the 29th Heavy Opera Company was doing Wagner the tour that change went through, and seeing those guys in Valkyrie costumes had taken almost as many casualties among our own troops as from the enemy.

And women have proven that they can stand up in combat as good as the boys, sometimes even better. I saw one, couldn't have been over five foot tall in bunny boots, haul a sousaphone five miles in a single day, through some of the heaviest jungle around. And another one, Suzette was her name: when a Recon from the 12th Medium Jazz collapsed into tears after finding his sax's pads rotting at a pre-field inspection,, Suzette repadded the whole thing with some old web and a tube of tire sealant.

Hell, troupers like that just don't grow on trees.

I quizzed Mowbray about storage points for the equipment skids as they came down. Her people hadn't been there long, but they'd done a thorough job of placing small marker flags as reference points. By the time I'd double-checked it all, just to be on the safe side, a runner told us that air was on the way in.

The 11 H-MOD was right on schedule. They came screaming in, low and hard. As the Sikorsky people-movers hovered overhead, dozens of troops rappelling down, the planes came charging through the alley they formed. With a plane about a half-meter off the ground, the weighted drogue chutes went out, yanking a sledge out of the plane's belly and into the dust. These people just couldn't stand being out of the spotlight sometimes.

We'd charge out while a sledge was still bouncing and skidding, lever wheels under the corners when the whole thing came to a stop, and race off into the bushes with the kiddy-car in tow by a half-dozen troops. As they hit the ground, the team from the 11th dove in, so we kept the place clear in good order. When the heavy artillery hit the ground, a big battle-grade slab of green particular Obendorfer grand, we were done.

Wrestling those last few sledges into place under a camo canopy, I saw the commander of this expedition. I was always impressed when any of the brass chose to lead from the front, instead of some comfy office in Washington or Nashville, but I was downright awed by seeing the Old Man himself.

Major Harrison Capizzio. The man who had single-handedly done more for modern music than Patton himself. He just stood, watching us finish that task with our vaunted efficiency. He must have read the reviews: he didn't look surprised that we were such a solid outfit.

I shook some of the dust off, made sure my fly wasn't open, all that important stuff as I walked over to check in with him.

There I was, a couple years in the field, supposed to be a battle-weary hard-liner, and I must've been grinning like the greenest stateside recruit. He must've been used to it, though, because he just gave this half-smile as I ripped off the snappiest salute I've ever managed before or since.

He braced me for my team's accomplishments so far this mission, and nodded along, checking the necessaries off mentally. I must've said all the right things: he turned to his aide and told him to spread word that we were tight to schedule and to continue as briefed.

Well, by then I was getting sweaty. I mean, I wasn't deserving to hand Capizzio his baton, so I made to dismiss myself, seeing as he had the big picture on his mind. I figured I'd get the usual officer-style nod, but he turned me a solid responding salute, eye-to-eye.

I left at speed, afraid everyone would see me blushing.

My team and Mowbray's had polished up our preparations very nicely, making sure everything was stashed but findable, so most everyone had fallen into their ways of keeping the jitters away without losing that fine edge you get from the adrenaline. Some were swapping food rations, others telling backstage stories, off in the bush a couple of violins were quietly tuning up more from habit than immediate necessity.

Off in the staging area, other teams got their step under way, lots of quiet bustling in the near-dark as we prepared to open up at dawn with the everything we had, and then some. It was getting pretty clear to us about then that we were sitting in the middle of the next big move for the Good Guys.

Me, I took some of my platoon and an assortment from the props crew and cast, and we set out to make sure of our perimeter after I signed it into the duty log. For stiffs like me, it's the easy part, and I had found it to be a lot less nerve-wracking than the jitters I get preparing for an assault. A trot through the bush, around the edges, was always a nice way to relax and burn up some energy.

We never made it. We walked flat-footed into an ambush.

One minute, we were coming around a clump of trees. The next minute, the bush parted, and there it was: a *Noh* play. "We're dead," someone whispered hoarsely.

They'd seen us coming. A few airy notes from a shakuhachi, an opening chord on the koto, and the minimal battle-zone lights came up with us in the middle of things—and in deep, let me tell you. The Japanese traditional instruments are some of the most subtle and deadly ever created by any race on the face of the Earth. If I had held any hope by then of living to see the next day, it died when the first white-faced actor swept out of the wings: the guy had the regal bearing of a pro, and costume to match.

Inside of two minutes, our patrol was dropping like flies: I knew the play was excellent, and I don't even speak Japanese. We didn't have a chance, trapped without our costumes and only a few of the primary actors, and not an instrument among us.

Then, suddenly, one of the enemy dropped a line. It was obvious; the whole cast, musicians and all, stopped dead, as if the guy had just farted in the hot tub. I heard a samisen hit the ground, a hollow *boing* and a catgut *snap* that said it all.

Discretion being the better part of valor, we ran like rabbits as the enemy began to berate our savior.

Beating through the bush, we had only a vague idea exactly where our staging area was, since we had been walking the far fringes on a line-of-sight rectangle. It wasn't helping maters any that the technicians were working mostly with infrared viewers and almost no light.

But we had to get back, we just had to. The whole operation was ready to go, and now it looked like we had lost the element of surprise.

I darn near did myself serious damage, charging face-first into that Obendorfer. I was catching my breath with a few bruised ribs before somebody at the area thought to play sentry. At that moment, I was so happy we'd found 'em at all that I forgot about raising hell for that kind of sloppiness.

Between gasps, and with lots of gesticulation limited by my sore chest, I made myself well-enough understood that a couple of the onlookers half-carried me to the command area. Someone ran ahead to let the Major know there was trouble.

By the time I got there, all the brass was standing around looking blearily depressed. I took only a few words filling them in on what had gone down, during which we moved into the command tent. The looks didn't lighten up any as I told them of the soldiers I had seen fall in the terrible onslaught of that finely honed Oriental artform.

Major Capizzio took the news with a look of grim determination.

There was a silence after I finished my report. Then, the Major opened a flat case on his field desk. "Men," he said, pulling out his matte-green cymbals, "Let's do it."

I got in charge of a squad of assorted extras and most of the critics and reviewers attached to the operation, and we fanned out to keep an eye on the perimeter, while everyone else pitched in with the techs and the gaffers, and made sure the whole stage was perfectly assembled, and every instrument and costume and prop was right where it should be, ready to go like clockwork on a moment's notice.

When the first rays of false dawn rose on the horizon, every last member of the operation was in position, alert and just waiting for the word. Major Capizzio watched the east as if it were his own personal Conductor, then, as if on cue, he raised his baton, slowly, grandly, and the whole world held its breath. The Major's cymbals, dark in the reddish half-light, sat in front of him; that great man was going to be part of the assault.

The baton came down.

•••

From there, it was all downhill. The enemy troupe had been so rattled by the backwash of their blown ambush that they hadn't gotten together a search for us until too late. We not only caught that group out in the open, but we took out an airstrike and about half a division of armored percussion they'd called in as backup.

The staging proved to be the turning point of the entire conflict, and we wrapped up the season within two months. The final engagements met with rave reviews, from both sides.

And that was the war. Some of the best moments of my life, as well as some of my best clips. The encore shows were murder, though.

Wolfgang "Greg" Zeuner

Wolfgang "Greg" Zeuner passes his days as a data analyst ("spreadsheet jockey") in order to fund his two serious callings in life: Irish music, and writing. "Since I can't carry a tune in a bushel, I have to settle for being an avid listener. Meanwhile, though I haven't sold any of my writing, I've written over a million words, making every mistake imaginable—and then some—so I like to help steer other readers around these obstacles." Greg has completed more than 30 stories, hundreds of articles on a wide variety of topics, and is working on no fewer than seven novels, none anywhere near completion. He lives in Minneapolis with his cat, "the only person who really understands my need to be ignored."

Superiority

What am I doing here?

The reason I became a history professor is because I was so shy. When I'm not in my classroom, I'm still as shy as a kid walking into the first day of kindergarten. So how come they've got me here in front of this huge crowd of students? There must be half the university packed on the grass of the quadrangle.

"Professor Langley, the ViewScan is hooked up."

It was Jon Strin, the president of the Class of 2059, my brightest student, beaming with anticipation. He adjusted his transparent burnoose, the garb which seniors have adopted this year. "We're ready for you to speak."

Me? I felt like a boa constrictor was holding my body in a death grip. "I can't," I muttered. "I'm not prepared for all this."

He started at me. "But professor, all you have to do is spell out that great idea you flashed in your letter to the Univnet."

I turned away and my head dropped. "I didn't expect all this, Jon."

Jon grasped my arm. "Just explain your ideas, like in class. Privilege means privation. It means cruel injustice to the majority of the people. This will cause a revolution. That's what we students are all programmed up to hear about."

I stared at the gold bolo tie around my neck, the costume identifying professors, and fingered the strings. "I'm no speechmaker. I've got to leave."

He wasn't going to convince me, and the restless crowd grew noisier.

Then Sen Torin took my arm and began gently persuading me. She's a History major and has been especially attentive to me after class. I've been attracted by her sweet compassionate manner. She asked how I could possibly disappoint all those earnest students out there, plus the thousands who'll be watching on the Net. In her own charming way she soothed the butterflies in my stomach and led me out onto the makeshift platform.

I had difficulty getting started, but amazed myself once I felt the fervor reaching out to me from my audience. I pointed out the grinding consequences of our society, where one percent of us, the Superiors, were lording it over the rest of the people. Employers are accepting only Superiors for middle and upper range jobs. Business and industry are wholly run by Superiors. Even government at all levels is controlled by "Supes," as we are called.

Not that this wasn't inevitable. Once society developed the means to escalate intelligence and memory via DNA injections into the brain, more and more babies developed into Superior Beings. And as they matured, they naturally commanded the top roles in every area. Now, for example, one can't qualify for college unless one is a Supe.

I was being transformed by my thesis into a polished orator. "The problem," I underscored, "was that this has resulted in our society being segregated not just by intelligence, but by income." Since the intelligence escalation procedure cost $475,000, only the wealthy could afford to have their children treated. And only each succeeding generation of Supes can afford to have *their* children enhanced.

I paused for effect. "You might think it's ironic that I focus on this basic inequality, this horrendous injustice, with an audience who are all Superiors—I, a Superior myself. After all, we are the top of the heap, enjoying all the advantages."

The audience was riveted on me, awaiting the climax.

I spoke in measured, conservative tones. "But I specialize in history, which not only looks back but attempts to peer forward from the shoulders of the past. And what I see is the inevitability of a disaster."

All those faces staring up at me, and I almost lost my thread. After a long pause, I picked up the last word. "Disaster, yes, a disaster facing all of us."

I pointed out that twenty-five years ago, the world had succeeded in the virtual elimination of unemployment and poverty even though 80 percent of the world's assets were controlled by 20 percent of the people. Five years later, the Supes controlled five percent of the world's assets. In another five years, Supes had achieved 25 percent, which doubled in the succeeding five years. My voice pitched to a climax, "Today, ninety-five percent of the wealth is controlled by the five percent of the people who are Superiors."

A gasp of surprise went up from the crowd. "This hasn't been made public, but the trend to a historian is unmistakable. Despite clever planning by Superiors at top levels, hunger and other aspects of poverty are reappearing. Most alarming is the rapid growth of unemployment throughout the world, for there simply aren't enough jobs for people with *average* skills. Inevitable result: revolution. Not today. But inevitable."

I didn't need to say another word. I was speaking to Superiors, who saw things as clearly as I did.

"Justice," welled up from the crowd in booming tones. "Justice for all." They ride the crest themselves, but like students in most generations, they are mesmerized by a cause.

I glanced behind me and was startled to see myself projected on a 20 x 30 foot screen. I slipped away before I could be mobbed.

When I walked into the History office the next day, Aly Yoris greeted me by saying, "Professor, the three ViewScans have been trying to reach you all morning."

Aly has been our administrative assistant for the past fifteen years, extremely intelligent for a Normal, and very likeable. "I know," I said. "I refuse to answer my Viewnet."

Aly smoothed her shining black hair. "You surprise me, Professor Benya. First you get up and speak before half the college. And even though you're a Superior yourself, you speak against the wisdom of the Superiors."

I smiled at her formality after we've worked together so many years. "Well, Aly," I said, "there comes a time when one must stand up for the truth."

I hadn't noticed before that she had piercing blue eyes. "But don't you realize," she said, "that the wave of publicity will fan the feelings of resentment against Superiors, and will bring the day of revolt closer?"

"Mine was just a clarion call. The Superiors in government are too intelligent to let things get out of hand."

Aly wasn't just persistent. She was perceptive. "Doesn't history prove that nobody likes to give up power?"

We had been ignoring the knocks on the door, which now became insistent. "I'm sure that's the ViewScan camerapeople," said Aly.

I sneaked out the back way.

When Dr. Thor, the president of the university, suggested that I accept the invitation to be interviewed, I assumed it was an order.

So there I was, squirming in a chair at the wn5p.j studio, answering questions in front of four cameras.

At the beginning I was able to sketch out my hypothesis smoothly and logically. But then the interviewer (a Superior of course) tried to put words in my mouth to portray me as a revolutionary, out to stir up trouble in a world where wars no longer broke out and where all problems are solved through negotiation.

"I'm simply pointing up the problem," I said. "We are shutting our eyes to all that unemployment today. Millions of people have nothing to do but watch ViewScan or clutter up the streets."

The interviewer, famous Rab Rahn, smiled indulgently. "They're all taken care of, Professor. You said they were starving, but every one gets the monthly Ease Allotment—the generous government stipend."

"Sure," I said. "And they get so bored that many spend it all on drink, drugs and gambling, then starve till the next stipend."

Rab Rahn insisted that people who didn't have to work are happier. The interview went downhill from then on. I took the aircar home wondering if I had opened a Pandora's box.

Early the next morning I was called down to see the university president. Elton Thor told me gently but firmly that I was on extended leave with pay, to concentrate on research.

So much for expressing the hard truth.

As I scrunched through the dried autumn leaves on the way to my History office, I was hailed by a cheery voice. Sen Torin, my graduate student, congratulated me on my speech and interview before noticing my depressed demeanor. Hearing of my enforced leave, she grew furious and wanted to organize a student demonstration. I managed to talk her out of it.

She put an arm around my shoulder and looked into my eyes with a soft tenderness. "I'm sorry you're feeling low," she said. "If we go back to your apartment, I can make you feel a lot better."

Her closeness and subtle perfume sent a crackle of excitement through my body. Here was this blond beauty with appetizing curves propositioning me—a forty-eight-year-old recluse.

I demurred. I thanked her warmly, but said I would rather be alone at this time.

She stared directly into my eyes. "Professor," she said. "I know this may seem sudden, but I've had a crush on you for two years—ever since I took your first course. So it's not that I just want to sleep with you." She tightened her grip on my arm. "I love you."

Now I was nonplussed and speechless. I managed to stammer my leavetaking, sounding like a pitiful fool, and rushed off home.

To ease my jangled nerves, I switched on the ViewScan. Another surprise. All the stations were filled with experts— history experts, economic experts, every kind of expert—all debunking my hypothesis. And they attacked me viciously as a verbal terrorist, tearing at the fabric of society and fomenting violence.

This savage campaign went on for weeks, and I wondered why the Superiors running the government weren't concentrating on solving the problem we all face.

Instead, they were concentrating on me as the problem.

I was beginning to fall into a depression. My friends among the other professors were shunning me as if I had caught the plague. I felt isolated.

Sen Torin kept calling, but I was too embarrassed to speak with her. The poor kid thinks she's in love with me. What could I say?

The only person I could speak with was Aly Yoris at the History office. She reported on my ViewNet that the student movement which I had ignited was spreading like wildfire to other campuses, even though it was played down in the ViewScans.

She told me that monster demonstrations had already taken place, even though the student leaders were frustrated in being unable to get me to speak. "You're now a famous man, Professor Benya," she said as she signed off her Net.

I languished. Finally I had to get out of my place for some air. As I put on my coat I prayed that all the ViewScan people were no longer camped on my doorstep. Luckily, they had given up.

It was bitter cold but I didn't care. My life had become bitter and the fresh air was a welcome change. My feet automatically took me toward the university, and that was a mistake. Soon I was recognized, and found myself surrounded by excited students hurling all sorts of questions at me. I hurried along silently, hoping they would give up and leave me be, but the crowd only grew larger and I grew more desperate.

Aly rescued me. As she came out of the History office, she saw my predicament and managed to shepherd me back to our sanctuary. There I sank into a chair with a gasp of relief, and soon found that I was unburdening myself to Aly.

I was surprised at this, for I had always been close-mouthed. But Aly was such a sympathetic listener, warm and understanding. As we talked, I began to realize that this was more than the two-dimensional administrative assistant I had spent so many years with.

"I feel for you, Professor," she said. "Without intending to, you have placed a bomb under your secluded lifestyle. You are now a world-famous personality. And with riots sparking among the unemployed, the media is blaming you for upsetting the peace. They need someone to blame, and you are elected."

I groaned, knowing she was right. "What can I do now?"

Aly gave a thin smile. "You know the answer to that, Professor. Two choices. You can become the leader of the movement which you inadvertently created. Or you can keep hiding until this all blows over."

That woman is so smart she should be a Supe. I gave her a friendly peck on the cheek for the first time, and sneaked back to my refuge. I can always hide in my apartment, working on my research.

I was wrong. I felt a big hole in my life. It wasn't only that I couldn't teach. I began to realize that I missed the company of people. Man is a social animal and I always thought I was an exception. Until now.

As I walked through the snowflakes to the History office, I wondered why I was headed there. All I needed for my research was on the Web. It came to me that I had the desire to spend some time with Aly. After all these years? Ah, but the world changes, as every History professor knows.

"Haven't seen you for months, Professor," greeted Aly. "And I've missed you."

She had never said that before, and certainly not in that tone of voice. I began to have the feeling that we had somehow grown close.

"I've missed you too," I said, and I reached out for her hand.

She stepped closer and took mine. "Your face looks so worn, Professor." Her voice was sweet caring.

"Would you do me a favor, Aly? Please call me Endar. It's time we were on a first-name basis."

She searched my eyes as we held hands, and I could see she liked what she saw. "I need a friend," I said. "I'm sorry it has taken me this long to realize that I have a true friend right here."

Before she could respond, the ViewNet buzzed. The face of the assistant to the university President appeared on the screen. I was being summoned to the head office again.

"Sounds ominous," I said, putting on my coat.

"What's the benefit of worrying ahead of time?" said Aly, and again I marveled that I hadn't appreciated the depth of intelligence of this woman I had known over so many years.

Elton Thor greeted me with unexpected familiarity as I walked into his office, putting his arm around my shoulder and leading me to a chair.

"Professor Benya," he said expansively, pacing back and forth in front of me, "you've been with us for a long, long time. The university has been proud of the papers you've published, and the students have flocked to your classes."

I felt I was being bound and trussed before the altar like Abraham's son Isaac. And I was right.

"Professor, your recent theory has its brilliant aspects. However, once you expanded it beyond academia, it is causing serious unrest... among students, among the general population. I'm sure you recognize that."

Yes, he's placing me on the altar now and preparing to light the firewood. But I don't expect God to send down an angel to rescue me.

He stopped pacing and grasped my arm as if to bond us. "That is why I must ask you to make a sacrifice. You have become a serious embarrassment to the university. It is vital that you sever relations. You have tenure, Professor, so I must ask you to resign. It pains me, but you must do it for the good of the university we both love."

I didn't answer. I stood up and walked out in a daze. Resign? From the only job I had known all these years?

And under fire? What other university would hire me? I was too young to retire. And for simply revealing the truth? For the first time in my life, I felt a growing anger welling inside me.

Resign? Never. And they couldn't force me.

I found myself walking into the History office. But before I had a chance to unburden myself to Aly, she greeted me with unbridled excitement, her arms waving.

"Endar," she declared, "you can't imagine what just came over the ViewScan news. You know Professors Zondik and Orban. They've just published their massive research study into superiors. It seems that they couldn't find a single Supe above the age of 51. Most have died around 50."

Wow! There have been rumors that stepping up intelligence was limiting longevity, but people refused to believe it. I immediately accessed the Net to read the full research report. The data was incontestable. And our two professors were the leaders in their field.

I didn't even stop to think of the impact on me at forty-eight-and-a-half. I was a history professor, and my mind was frantically groping for the implications of this discovery on the massive changes we night expect in the structure of society.

I squirreled myself in my apartment to keep the ViewScan people at bay, ordering my meals in as before. The world was reacting in line with my new historical predictions. Nobody was paying attention to my "revolutionary" theory of Supe control anymore. CEOs of the largest corporations were rapidly taking early retirement, as was Elton Thor, the president of our university. The President of the United States suddenly appeared on the ViewScan to announce that, at the age of 49, he felt compelled to resign and spend the rest of his life at his favorite recreation, fishing.

The treatment of new infants fell to almost zero. Parents felt it was unfair to doom their children to an early death.

Sen Torin's lovely face appeared on mv ViewNet and pleaded with me to take the call. I finally relented.

"Endar," she said, "you know that I love you deeply. Why can't we marry and, for the little time you have left, enjoy the ecstasy of our love together?"

This was the time for frankness. "Sen," I said, "you must face reality. Your idea of fun is the huge Dance Metropole with music blaring the eardrums. Your idea of excitement is the weekend excursion to the 4th Dimension Playcity near the Moon Dome. You should enjoy the many years ahead to the fullest instead of being stuck with an aging man doomed to die.

"And there's the most important thing, Sen," I added. "I don't love you."

As her tearful face faded from the ViewNet, there came a pounding on my door. I paid no attention till I heard the insistent voice of Aly. "You must let me in, Endar."

Of course. My mind had been so occupied with the incredible societal changes that I had even been out of contact with Aly. My only real friend.

She never looked more attractive as she came close to me and, for the first time, placed her arms around my neck, her deep blue eyes locked onto mine. "Endar," she said, "we have very little time left together. I have loved you for many years. What are you going to do about it right now?"

The rest is history.

Sam Zitter

I am not a novice writer. My novel was a finalist in the Writers Foundation Best Novel Competition. My film script won the $3,000 First Prize in the New Century Writers Competition. I've had six paid works published, including in the first U.S. edition of Strand Magazine, the famous British publication where Rudyard Kipling got his start. I actually started writing fairy tales at the age of nine, and am an omniverous reader of whatever is in print. The idea for this story came to me as I read news articles about the future possibility of escalating intelligence via DNA injections, and I extrapolated what impact that would have on our culture.

The Judges

Henry "Bud" Ensley

Born and raised in Toledo, Ohio, I started to read about age 10, and it was SF. After a tour of duty in the Air Force, I now live in Minnesota with a wife, three cats, a hedgehog, and sometimes a box turtle — who generally lives at the high school but comes to visit on holidays.

I'm still reading SF. I have three book cases of SF and a whole public library just miles away with more SF. Over the years I have expanded my reading into other genres. I even let my wife have a few mystery books on the shelves.

I have also learned that one of the places not to visit is any of the local book stores — costs way toooo much to visit.

Two of the series I like are "Harry Potter" — it is a great grown-up type of book — and "Wheel of Time"; I'm waiting for the next book in each series.

Sometimes I have been known to go to work, just to get money for more books.

Therese Francis

I think the first science fiction I read was *The Wonderful Trip to the Mushroom Planet* by Eleanor Cameron, but I didn't really start reading voraciously until one fateful summer when I found out that I was allergic to poison ivy *and* calamine lotion. Unable to do much since any sweat resulted in intense hours of itching, my mother handed me *The Beast Master*. "You'll like this; it's got horses and Indians." She was right, and *Lord of Thunder, Storm Over Warlock*, and what was then available in the Witch World series quickly followed. Thirty years later (I started reading in my late teens) I'm reading, writing, and now publishing science fiction!

Judith Hamlin

I was just old enough to be fascinated by sex, when I saw one of my father's magazines that had a bug-eyed monster on the front menacing a scantily clad woman whose dimensions made Marilyn Monroe seem straight by comparison. I read the entire magazine, *IF*, but found no story that related to the cover. I was seriously disappointed, but by then hooked. That was almost 50 years ago and I still find science fiction/fantasy my genre of choice. One of my dreams of retirement is to read all those books I have not had time to in the last several years. My cats even agree that when they are napping I may attempt this.

Anthony Ravenscroft

I have been editing professionally since 1984, and still find it both entertaining and rewarding. I was thrilled to move to New Mexico in 2000 to join the staff of Crossquarter, a company I think of as a neonate; it's far younger than its years would indicate, so there's a surprising amount of energy as we learn its strengths. My expertise in e-books is largely unheralded, since nobody really knows what they are yet, so there's not really any market. Aside from editing, I spend my little spare time learning how to use computers for music production, but since it still feels weird being over 40 and making dance music for teenagers, I won't mention my stage name until I'm a glowing success. I insist that writers of speculative fiction need to attend fan-run science fiction conventions; I recommend DemiCon (Des Moines), OryCon (Portland), CONvergence (Minneapolis), and BuboniCon (Albuquerque), all for different reasons.

Gretchen Riddle

I discovered Sci Fi when I was six years old — *Stowaway to the Mushroom Planet*, by Eleanor Cameron — and was instantly hooked. Later I moved on to Andre Norton, Bradbury, Jack Williamson, Heinlein, Clark, Tolkien and as many others as I could find. Forty-two years later, science fiction and fantasy is still my favorite genre. I read enough to cheer up the clerks at Uncle Hugo's when I show up for a 'fix'. (Uncle Hugo's is one of the perks in Minnesota for putting up with the weather.)

Science fiction/fantasy — now there's a recreational drug more folks should get into!